A NEXT GENERATION SHORT

CONTROL

J.M. WALKER

IBSN: 978-1-989782-01-9

FAMILY TREE

Angel and Genevieve "Jay" Rodriguez
(Grit, King's Harlots #1/Grim, King's Harlots #3)
Angelica "Gigi"
Ryder
Meadow

Asher and Meeka Donovan
(Stain, King's Harlots #2)
Aiden
Ashton

Coby and Brogan Porter
(Rude, King's Harlots #4/For You, King's Harlots #7)
Zachary "Zach"

Dale and Maxine "Max" Michaels
(Numb, King's Harlots #5)
Piper

Vincent "Stone" and Creena Stone
(Rust, King's Harlots #6)
Luna
Vincent Junior

Greyson and Eve Mercer
(Greyson, Hell's Harlem #1)
Jaron

Tray and Zillah Lister
(Tray, Hell's Harlem #2)
Beatrix "Bee"

John and Beatrix "Trixie" Butcher
(Hell's Harlem Series)
Cyrus
Samson "Sammy"

PROLOGUE

ZACH

DARKNESS SURROUNDED ME. IT *swallowed me whole, enveloping me in a blanket of bliss as I curled into myself on the hard cement beneath me.*

My stomach twisted and churned, the agony of having no food in my belly making it hard to concentrate on anything but the hunger ripping through me. I could try sleeping. Maybe that would make the pain go away. But slumber was lacking no matter how long I kept my eyes closed.

Footsteps sounded above me. They became closer and closer. With each step, my heart thumped, pounding against my rib cage. My skin broke out in a cold sweat. Fear rippled down my spine like icy fingers danced along my small, frail body.

Please, God. Make her stay away. Make her forget I even exist.

But my prayers went unanswered. No one heard them. It was like as soon as I sent up my prayer, the steps only became louder and faster.

I tried moving away from the sound but the chain around my ankle prevented me from going very far.

"Come out, come out wherever you are," she sang.

Pretending to be asleep did nothing. I would only get whipped awake. So instead, I brought my knees up to my chest, curled my arms around them, and waited for whatever punishment I would get.

"You've been a bad boy, haven't you, Zachary?" Her voice was louder as she stood on the other side of the closed door. The locks released, revealing the person who invaded my nightmares.

"Aww, my little toy. Why are you so scared? I'm only doing this to make you stronger. You know that."

A whimper escaped me, even though I didn't want it to. I couldn't control it. This woman terrified me.

"I have some food for you, but I need something first." Her bright blue eyes flicked to mine. "You want food, don't you?"

I nodded. I would give anything for even a piece of moldy bread.

"I'll unchain you and you can come with me. Same thing as last week. Understand?"

"Please," I croaked through my parched, cracked lips. "Not again."

"I know you'll do anything for this food. Can you smell it?" She smirked. "So good. I made it myself."

I swallowed hard, knowing the food was laced with something. I may have been just a boy, but I knew when food tasted funny. But at that point, I didn't care. She could kill me. As long as I had a full belly, I would die happy.

My stepmother came farther into the small room and unlocked the chain from around my ankle. "Come with me, Toy, and I'll give you your food after you give me what I need."

I spent the next couple of hours doing everything she asked of me, just so I could have a slice of moldy cheese on stale bread. She had promised me a full meal but lied. That sandwich gave me the strength to survive through another night of hell. I didn't know how long it would be until I got my next one, so I savored it.

I savored every damn crumb.

ONE

ZACH

I WOKE IN A COLD sweat. My sheets were stuck to me, my hair matted to my forehead. I hadn't had a nightmare in months. I didn't like them. The way they made me feel. The terror they forced through the marrow of my bones. The vulnerability. But the lack of control was even worse. I needed to get it together for fear I would lose myself completely. The demons of my past threatened to take over my life. I worked out. A lot. It was the only way I could mute the noise in my head. But sometimes, even putting myself through that rigorous activity didn't help.

The dreams were few and far between now but when I had them, they stuck with me for a while. My parents had tried getting me to speak to someone, but I refused.

There was only one person I could talk to and even then, she didn't know everything.

Sitting up in bed, I pinched the bridge of my nose and waited for the remnants of the nightmare to fade away. It did but not enough. That quiet little voice was still there.

Nagging. Nudging. Poking at me. Reminding me that it had control over my life. As much as I didn't care to admit it.

A soft knock on the door interrupted my thoughts. "Come in."

My mother peeked her head into the room. "You okay?" she asked, her eyes holding wrinkles at the corners from years of happiness with my father.

I glanced at the clock. It was almost five in the morning. "What are you doing up?" I asked her instead of answering her question.

She smiled softly, her dark eyes shining with a hint of sadness I saw every so often. She didn't think I noticed but I did, and it always made me sick to my stomach whenever she was hurting.

"I could ask the same about you." She sighed. "Your dad couldn't sleep." Which meant she took care of him in any way possible.

Sex.

I wasn't oblivious to their ways. Although they were my parents, they were open enough to tell me how they took care of each other. Especially after I accidentally found the shackles beneath their bed.

"Anything I can do to help?" I asked even though I already knew the answer.

"No." She opened the door fully but still remained in the hall. "Want to talk about it?"

I nodded. She had been the only woman I talked to lately. The only woman I actually trusted enough to tell my problems to. Or that was what I tried telling myself anyway. There *was* someone else. But I wasn't good enough for her and she had a father. A large fucking father.

My mother left the room and closed the door softly behind her.

Brogan and Coby Porter adopted me when I was ten. They took me from a horrible situation that no child should ever go through and welcomed me into their home with open arms. They gave me love, support, and never-ending encouragement no matter how difficult I had been. But it still wasn't enough. I wasn't sure why. I never felt this way when I was a kid but now that I was getting older, there was something missing from my life. That nagging little voice inside of me told me what it was, but I always chose to ignore it. There was no point. *She* deserved better and whenever she got too close, I pushed her away. It was the only way I could protect myself from getting hurt.

I quickly threw on pajama pants and a hoodie and made my way out into the kitchen. No matter what time of night it was, if Dad or I had a nightmare, Mom was always there to talk us through it.

She handed me a mug of hot chocolate with three marshmallows swimming in the steaming liquid. I smiled softly. It was always the same ever since I was a little boy.

"Here."

I sat at the table when Brogan placed a mug in front of me. "What is it?"

She smiled softy. "Hot chocolate with three marshmallows. My brother used to make this for me when I was your age."

I looked up at her. "Did you have nightmares?"

"Yeah, sweetheart. I did." Brogan sat beside me and cupped my hand that was resting on my lap. "I'm here, Zach. For however long you need, I'm always here. Both of us are."

Ever since then, I had looked forward to the hot chocolate. It had been a special bonding time for Mom and me. A part of me wondered if Dad knew that, so he would let her take care of me before asking me about the nightmares later on.

"Was it the same nightmare as last time?" Mom asked, sitting across the table from me with her own mug. Even though she was now older, the only wrinkles that sat on her face, were at the corners of her eyes. She always said they were her love lines because the love she had for my father and me, made her smile.

"Kind of. It's been awhile but this one was intense." I stared down at the marshmallows in the hot chocolate. "I almost forgot what they could be like."

"Your father goes through the same thing." Her gaze hardened. "If I could murder the woman who destroyed you, I would." She shrugged. "But I have to behave. I am a mother now after all." It had been something she said often. She wasn't lying when she said she would kill her. Mom was part of a female motorcycle club that could give most men a run for their money. She had a past. A history. They never talked about the woman who hurt my dad, but everything told me that she was no longer breathing.

"Why are you looking at me like that?" she asked, her cheeks reddening.

"Just thinking how amazing you are."

She laughed. "You are so much like your father, it's unreal."

I smiled, taking a sip of the hot chocolate. Even though we weren't blood related, I had taken on a lot of my adoptive father's traits. He protected my mother. His wife. His best friend. And I only hoped I could be half the man he was.

"Have you considered seeing Dr. Santos like we talked about?" Mom asked, pulling the elastic free from her dark curly hair and putting it back into a messy bun on top of her head.

"No." I hated talking. It opened up too many old wounds that I just didn't want to think about.

"I know it's hard, but you really should." She raised her hand. "Before you argue with me, just give it some thought. Please."

"So this is what you do when I don't find you in bed beside me."

Both of us laughed as my dad joined us at the table.

"You good, Son?" he asked me, cupping my shoulder.

"Nightmare," was all I said.

He grunted, kissed Mom on the temple, and sat down beside her. "Sucks. Doesn't it?"

"Yeah." But at least he had someone who could take care of him after. Mom helped me through it as well, but it wasn't the same. I needed someone I could spend the rest of the night holding, talking to, just being beside. It didn't have to end in sex. I just needed something other than hot chocolate.

While they talked quietly amongst themselves, I continued drinking from my mug, distracting myself.

Once I finished the hot chocolate, I brought the mug to the kitchen. When I returned to the dining room, I wrapped my arms around my mother's shoulders. "Thank you for the hot chocolate, Mama." I kissed her cheek.

She patted my hand. "Anything for you, sweet boy. Try and get some sleep."

"You heading to the city today?" Dad asked me, rising to his feet.

"I am." My dad owned half the high-rises and hotels in the city that was a couple of hours away, thanks to my grandfather before him. Since retiring officially from the navy a few years ago, this business was all Dad had. And it left a cozy cushion for his family which was why I followed in his footsteps.

"You *are* allowed a day off," Dad chided. "You've been going strong for the past few months. People are going to begin to think your boss is running you ragged."

I chuckled, clapping him on the shoulder. "The business is all I have right now. Until I get a family of my own, I need this." I was working toward taking over the business so he could retire officially and spend time with his wife. But it was taking a little longer seeing as Dad didn't want to retire just yet. Instead, I was learning as much as I could from him.

"I understand." He looked down at his wife. "It was all I had before you." He cupped her cheek, brushing his thumb over her mouth.

She smiled up at him.

Looking away, I cleared my throat and excused myself.

I loved them. They took me from hell and brought me into their home. I hadn't always been easy to get along with. I knew that. But sometimes their love was overwhelming. Was I jealous? Maybe. I didn't know anymore. I dated a few times, but it never resulted in anything more than that. No pussy was going to tame this beast inside of me. Or that was the rumor that went around anyway. Truth was, I hadn't had sex in over a year. The rumors still went around that told a different story, but I never corrected them. What was the point? I was wild in my high school days and people assumed it followed me into my twenties. It didn't. Sex was an out for some but for me, it wasn't enough. This need for more was only getting worse and I knew I needed to do something about it before it consumed me completely.

TWO

Luna

I COULDN'T SLEEP. IT was past five in the morning and I had been laying there like a damn lump for the past couple of hours. The house I lived in with my three best friends was eerily quiet and it made me uncomfortable. Our house was never this quiet. No matter what time of the day it was, someone was usually always up. Whether it be a random stray that one of my best friends brought home or just someone who spent the night after drinking too much, there was always noise. But tonight, the loudest sound going on, was inside my brain. I hated nights like this.

Rolling over onto my stomach, I reached for my phone and texted the only other person I knew who could possibly be up at this hour.

Me: You awake?

Zach: Yeah.

My stomach twisted that he had responded so quickly.

Me: Nightmare?

A couple of minutes went by and I still hadn't gotten a reply. Everyone knew that Zach Porter had a shitty childhood but none of us was aware how far it went or what exactly had happened. He was always quiet and withdrawn. He threw himself into his work and stuck mostly to himself even though we had all grown up together thanks to all of our parents being friends. But for whatever reason, I had been the only person he actually opened up to. Even though I had known him since I was a little girl, I had a feeling that I still didn't know him completely.

My phone chimed, making me jump.

Zach: How did you know?

Me: That's usually why you're awake at this hour.

A video call came through, revealing Zach's handsome face. My heart skipped a beat. My skin became flushed. Good thing it was dark in my room, so he couldn't see the damn blush in my cheeks that he always caused. It was no secret that I had a crush on the guy. I just wasn't sure if he knew it or not.

"You are the only guy I would even consider video chatting with while I'm in my pajamas." I laughed, not looking him directly in the eyes. The dark, almost black orbs sucked me in every time. I could spend hours getting lost in them.

"You're beautiful, Moonbeam." Zach smirked, that tiny dimple in his right cheek, popping at the movement. "You have nothing to be embarrassed over."

My cheeks warmed at the childhood nickname he had given me after finding out my name meant *moon* in Italian. My stepmom loved it. My dad, not so much.

"Why did you call?" I asked Zach, turning on the lamp and leaning against the headboard.

"You know I hate texting."

"But you always text me," I pointed out.

"That's because I want to make you happy."

My heart stuttered. "Well...uh...thank you."

"So..." He waggled his eyebrows. "What are you wearing?"

I giggled, shaking my head.

"I love your laugh," he murmured, his deep voice hitting every nerve inside of me.

I smiled softly. Our flirting back and forth had always been fun, fresh, light. Nothing more. But as the years went on, my feelings for him grew. I wasn't sure how he felt though. He probably still looked at me like I was the little girl in pigtails who had a crush on the older boy.

Even from the other end of the phone, he was the most beautiful man I had ever seen. With dark eyes, black hair, and that sexy as hell dimple, I was lost to him.

"So, remember when I was a kid and fell off the swing?" I asked. Although the conversation was random, I knew Zach needed distracting from whatever nightmare he had. "You kissed the booboo on my forehead even though I didn't have one." It was one of my favorite memories and also when my crush for him started brewing.

"I remember," he said, his voice deepening. He pushed his dark bangs off of his forehead, his bicep twitching at the movement. "You remember the first time you wore those teeny tiny shorts in front of us boys? I thought your dad was going to have a coronary."

I laughed. "My dad always looks like he's going to have a coronary."

Zach chuckled. "Well, you are beautiful and..." He cleared his throat. "Anyway...why can't you sleep?"

"I...I'm not sure. Just feeling antsy I guess." I wasn't sure what my deal was. I was still young but at a time in my life where I should already be making plans for the future. Instead, I felt...stuck. Like my feet were planted in quicksand and the only thing I could do was sink into the murky depths beneath me.

"Luna?"

"I don't know." I shrugged. "Tell me your plans for today." I needed to change the subject off of me or else we would go down a road that I wasn't sure either of us was ready for. Maybe he would tell me about his job. When it came to his work, he could talk for hours and I would always willingly listen.

"I have to head into the city. I have a few meetings and then dinner plans with a prestigious restaurant owner." Zach grunted. "The guy only wants to meet me, so he can get a free room for his mistress whenever she's in town."

"Well, at least you get free food."

"True. That's only if he pays. They never usually do." He paused. "Come with me."

My eyes widened. "What?"

"Come to dinner with me. He'll probably have a date with him anyway. You won't have to say anything. You can just be there."

"So, I'd be like the hot piece of candy on your arm?" I asked, raising an eyebrow.

"Well, I wouldn't go that far."

"Hey," I cried, laughter bubbling out of me.

Zach laughed along with me. "You know what I mean. Like you said, it'll be a free meal and maybe I won't be so nervous if you're with me."

"You get nervous?" Zach was slowly trying to take over his father's company, so he could retire completely. He had already left the navy and now he just needed to tie up loose ends with his business. I knew he had nothing to worry about when he was leaving everything to Zach. But I still never imagined a guy like him would get nervous.

"I do, Moonbeam. So, what do you say?"

"I…" I inhaled a sharp breath. "Okay. I'll come with you."

"Great." Zach's smile widened. "Thank you."

"You're welcome. Now I have to figure out what to wear." I tapped my chin. "I have a red dress that—"

"No," Zach snapped.

"Excuse me?" My heart thumped.

"I mean." Zach coughed. "Don't wear red," he said gently.

"Why not?" I loved the color red.

"Because the guy's a dick and I don't want him eye-fucking you because when you wear red, you look hot as hell," Zach said all in one breath.

"Oh. Is that all?" I muttered.

"Listen." Zach shifted, placing the phone down in front of him. "I want you comfortable but don't go out of your way to impress him."

"What if…what if I want to impress you?" I asked, not sure where this newfound bravery was coming from.

"You don't need to wear a pretty dress to impress me, Moonbeam."

"So, you're saying that I could wear a paper bag and you'd be impressed?" This conversation was beginning to become…weird.

"Something like that." Zach winked.

"Why, Zachary? Are you flirting with me?" I waggled my eyebrows.

He grinned, rubbing his jaw. "Maybe I am."

"Luna? You awake?" Angelica Rodriguez called out from the other side of the door.

"I am," I yelled back.

"I'll let you go, Moonbeam," Zach said. "I'll see you tonight. Be ready for seven."

"Okay." We said our goodbyes as the door opened. "What's up, Gigi?" I asked, using the nickname I had given her as a child when I couldn't say her full name. Gigi stuck, and everyone started calling her it.

"Meadow's making breakfast. She tried out this new recipe for some pastries."

"She couldn't sleep either?" I asked, sliding off the bed. Meadow was Gigi's younger sister and working her way to owning her own bakery. She never admitted to that of course but we all knew it was what she wanted to do.

"No." Gigi sighed, pulling an elastic from her wrist and putting her long auburn hair back into a ponytail. "Neither could I, so I figured we'd at least start the day off right with good food."

"I like that idea."

"Were you on the phone with Zach?" she asked, leaning against the doorframe.

"Yeah." I rummaged through my dresser, pulling out a pair of gray shorts and a white t-shirt.

"Everything okay?"

I met her gaze in the mirror. "Of course." I wasn't sure if they knew that Zach got nightmares every now and again, so I kept that piece of information to myself.

She shook her head. "I don't get you two. Clearly there is something there, but you are too stubborn to do anything about it."

"Well…" Were we too stubborn? Sure, Zach and I flirted, but it never amounted to anything more than that. Besides, as much as I liked him, he slept with a lot of women. And I couldn't compete with that.

"But I get it."

My head snapped up. I slowly turned toward her. "You do?"

She nodded. "Our fathers are over-protective. I'm not sure if that's the issue here but I do know that it could cause a problem."

"My dad hasn't really said anything." Not that I ever dated anyway but he never laid down the law when I became old enough *to* date.

"Well, that's good at least. My dad ignores the fact that I have a boyfriend." She laughed lightly. "Anyway, I'll let you get dressed." Before I could respond, she left my room and shut the door quietly behind her.

Her boyfriend.

My stomach twisted.

Matt Hillman was a douche, but Gigi was happy, so we all put up with him. The guy didn't deserve her and treated her like an object rather than the wonderful person that she was.

I quickly got dressed and left the room. As soon as I stepped out into the hall, I was greeted with the scent of something sweet mixed with bacon, eggs, and coffee.

My stomach rumbled.

"There she is." Ashton and Aiden Donovan greeted me at the same time. The twins came toward me.

"Hi, guys." I gave them each a hug. "What are you doing here so early?"

"We were on the way to the center when Meadow texted that she was cooking breakfast." Ashton hooked an arm around my shoulders. "You know we could never turn down her food."

"It also gives us an excuse to delay our arrival a little bit," Aiden said, wrapping an arm around me from the other side. "I love the center, but our father likes to work us to the bone."

I laughed. "He's trying to make you hard workers for when you take over his company."

Ashton grunted. Both of them were built like their dad, Asher, but had the bright blue eyes of their mother. Even though they complained, I knew they loved working for their father and doing the work they did to help fix up and expand the center. The Dove Project had been a part of our lives ever since we were kids. Now that the guys were older, they helped with the construction on it. The center, as most of us called it, was a safe place for human trafficking victims. It offered shelter, food, clothing, therapy, schooling, and even jobs. It was something our mothers had started before us kids were born and it still left me in awe at how big it had become over the years.

"It's the summer. We shouldn't be working so damn much." Ashton released me and sat at the dining room table.

"I love working," Gigi added. She had just opened up her dance studio the year before but also worked at The Dove Project. She was a new teacher, so business was slow at the moment until her name got out there more.

"Of course you do." Aiden sat beside her at the table. "You actually have a business."

She scoffed. "Yeah and I have only a handful of clients. I need to get some more fliers printed."

"Meadow, are you done with the food yet, woman? I'm fucking starving." Ashton leaned back in the chair, stretching his arms up and over his head. "I'm withering away."

"Do you kiss your mama with that filthy mouth?" she called from the kitchen.

"No, but I'd sure as hell kiss you with it," he threw back at her.

"Ha!" she scoffed. "You wouldn't even know what do with me if I was laying naked before you with my legs spread open. I bet you wouldn't know where a woman's clit was even with a neon sign pointing directly at it."

"What?" Ashton's face turned bright red. "Fucking women."

Laughter sounded around the room.

I joined them at the table when Meadow started bringing plates out.

"Did you need any help?" I asked her, moving to rise from my chair when she lifted her hand to stop me.

"No thank you." She smiled her widest smile. Her full red lips pulling thin.

"Why do I feel like you messed with these?" I asked her, glancing at the plates of pastries on the table before us.

She laughed, placing the last plate on the table and tugged her shirt down. She only ever did that when she was nervous. "One of the plates has special cookies that I made. I don't suggest eating them if you have things to do today or need to drive somewhere."

Ashton leaned forward and popped a cookie into his mouth. "Looks like I'm sleeping on your couch again."

"You are helping me today. I'm not making up excuses for you again." Aiden shook his head and picked up a croissant before breaking off the end and shoving it into his mouth.

"I have to work today, so no special cookies for me," Gigi said, pouting.

"I'll just stick with eggs and bacon," I muttered.

"Try a cookie, Luna," Ashton said, waggling his eyebrows. "We could have some fun."

I grimaced. "No. Thank you."

"Have you talked to Zach today?" Meadow handed me a plate of food.

"I did," I said, picking up a piece of bacon off the plate in front of me. "He couldn't sleep either."

"Must be something in the water," Aiden mumbled.

Ashton grunted.

"Is he coming to the party tonight?" Gigi asked, shoving a forkful of eggs into her mouth.

"I believe so. He has a dinner meeting at seven first that he invited me to. It's with a possible client." The parties that Gigi threw were once every couple of months. Since all of us worked hard, it was her way of making it so we could relax, forget about our day jobs and just unwind. I knew that once we got older and started getting married, having kids and so on, the parties would be few and far between. So she threw them now while she could.

"Which reminds me, I'm going to need help in deciding what to wear," I told Meadow and Gigi.

Silence fell around the table. You would think I just told them that I was pregnant.

Ashton broke the silence by letting out a cheer. "I knew it. That's fifty bucks, brother."

Aiden rolled his eyes. "It wasn't a bet, asshole."

"Doesn't matter." Ashton punched him in the shoulder. "You still owe me."

"We never shook on it." Aiden leaned back in his chair. "Doesn't count."

"Wait." I looked between them both. "You guys had a bet going about me?"

"No. My brother did," Aiden said, nodding toward Ashton.

"Placing a bet on your friends is a little immature, don't you think?" Meadow asked, raising a dark eyebrow.

Ashton glanced between her and the rest of us. "Nope." He glared at his brother. "Fifty. In my hand. Now."

"No." Aiden sat forward. "He made the bet. Not me. Like I said, we never shook on it."

"What was the bet?" Gigi asked, rising from the table and gathering up the empty plate.

"That Luna and Zach would be the first ones to go on a date out of all of us." Ashton held out his hand and tapped his palm. "I don't see any money."

Aiden rolled his eyes.

"It's not really a date. I'm going with Zach out of support." Although as I said the words, it didn't stop the nervous flutter from racing through me.

Ashton tapped his palm again.

Aiden slapped some bills in his twin's hand. "Happy?"

"You guys need to get lives," I laughed, shaking my head.

"Alright, kids." Meadow placed another plate of pastries on the table. "Eat up so I have an excuse to make more stuff."

"How the hell did you have time to make all of this?" Ashton asked, grabbing a croissant off the plate.

Meadow laughed. "I don't sleep."

While they continued chatting amongst themselves, my thoughts traveled to what could possibly happen tonight and that only sent my nerves into overdrive.

This was a bad idea. A really bad idea. I had a half an hour before Zach was picking me up and I still wasn't ready. My nerves were shot, my skin was clammy, and I had nothing to wear. Absolutely nothing.

A soft knock sounded on the door.

"Need help still?" Meadow asked, peeking her head into the room.

"Yes." I rushed to her, pulling her into my bedroom.

Gigi laughed, joining us and went right to my closet. "Still can't find something to wear?"

"No." I sighed. "I have nothing, and I don't have time to go shopping. Why did I agree to this?"

"Because he asked you and you said yes," Meadow said. "Because you want to jump his bones and ride him like a pogo stick. Because—"

I clapped a hand over her mouth. "We get the idea."

"Maybe this is a step in the right direction finally," Gigi said, searching through my closet.

"We're friends. Besides, he doesn't think of me that way." Not that I ever asked him though.

"Right," both of them said slowly.

"What?" I frowned. "What?" I repeated.

"You really don't see it, do you?" Gigi stared at me.

"See what?" I looked between the both of them. "What am I not seeing?"

"He likes you, Luna," Gigi told me. "And you're the only one of us that he actually talks to. Sure, we've all known him our whole lives, but I've never carried a full conversation with him."

I stared at her. "Yes, you have."

Gigi shook her head. "Have you?" she asked Meadow.

"Not really." Meadow joined her sister at the closet. "He does ask me how my baking is going, and he's always been nice. We don't know him how you know him though."

"I didn't know that." I thought back to all of the conversations we've had over the years. How he would always ask me how my day was or how he would tell me the last book he read or movie he watched.

"And I know there are rumors going around that he's slept with half the city, but I don't think that's true." Meadow pulled a dress out from the closet, frowned and put it back. "I know he was wild in high school. That's what the twins say anyway. But I don't think he's like that anymore, no matter what the rumors are."

"I…" Could the rumors be lies? It wasn't like I had ever asked him about his sexual exploits. It wasn't any of my business anyway and I didn't even want to know. "Really? How come?"

Meadow shrugged. "I just don't." She pulled out a green dress. "What about this?" She grimaced. "Never mind."

The dress had been shoved into the back of my closet for a reason. It was old and an ugly shade of green.

"You don't see what we see," Meadow continued. "The way he looks at you, thinking we're not watching. Or that he's being discreet. Or the way you look at him. God, you two are in love and you don't even know it yet."

"Uh…" I wasn't sure what to say to that.

"What about this?" Gigi pulled out a red dress this time.

"I can't wear that one." I grabbed it from her and hung it back up.

"Why not?" Meadow pulled it back out of the closet. "It's perfect."

"Yeah, it is." I snatched it out of her hand and hung it up again. "But apparently the guy we're having dinner with is a pervert or something and…"

"Zach doesn't want another man lusting after you?" Meadow raised an eyebrow. "But you really don't see it."

I huffed, pulling another dress out of the closet. "I have no idea what you girls are talking about. Zach and I are just friends. We are not in love and whatever you think you're seeing, there's nothing there." But even though I said those words, I had always hoped for something more. He had been the only guy I ever felt comfortable with. I could be myself around him and he never judged or made fun of me for my quirks.

"Come on, Luna. You can't honestly believe that," Meadow said.

"Leave it alone," Gigi told her sister. "She'll see it eventually."

"I feel like we've overused that word," I mumbled.

"Fine." Meadow reached into the closet. "What about this?"

I looked between the dress in my hand and the one she was holding. I ran my fingers down the black fabric. I stewed over their words. Could Zach be wanting more from me? Could he be feeling something different? Could he finally see whatever it was that they saw? I shook my head, chewing my bottom lip. I wasn't sure, but I was willing to find out.

I took the dress from Meadow, pressed it up to my body and moved to the floor-length mirror. "It's perfect."

THREE

ZACH

ALL BREATH LET MY lungs as Luna approached me. The sound that escaped my chest was a half groan, half growl. Fuck me, she looked good enough to eat. I shook myself. I couldn't have these thoughts about her. But I did. On one hand, I was thankful that things between us were finally moving in a different direction other than just being friends. And on the other, I was terrified.

My stomach clenched, forcing that fear to the back of my mind.

There were only a few years between us but these feelings, this want, this *need*, it was new. I always thought she was beautiful. Being half-Italian made her skin glow with a delicious tan. I still shouldn't have these thoughts about her. Besides the fact that her father was a scary fucker, she deserved better. So much better than my broken, moody soul.

The inner turmoil trembling through me, tugged and pulled, damn near splitting me apart.

"She deserves better."

My stomach clenched.

Luna's chocolate brown eyes caught mine, a slow smile spreading on her beautiful face. Her dark hair fell down around her shoulders in waves. The black dress that hugged every inch of her curvy frame, sat snug against her body. It fell just below her knees. It left little to the imagination but was still sexy as hell just the same. It accentuated her figure in ways I had only fantasized about. My dick twitched, pushing against the fly of my pants. Even *he* was happy to see her.

Confusion coursed through me as this newfound awareness slid through me. I hadn't reacted this way to a female in a long time. Too damn long if you asked me.

"How do I look?" Luna asked, twirling around.

I forced back the urge to bite my knuckles. The fabric of her dress hugged her hips and sat snug against her ass. Her body would fit perfectly in my hands.

"Good," was all I said instead.

"Really?" Her face fell. "Just good?"

No, Moonbeam. I want to reach beneath your dress, swipe my tongue between those full thighs and show you exactly how beautiful I think you look.

"Yes," I croaked. Fuck, this was going to be a long night.

"Oh. Okay. Well you look handsome." She walked past me and that was when I caught it. A sweet sugary scent wafted into my nose.

A growl escaped me then.

She paused, looking up at me, her brows furrowing in the middle. "Zach?"

I had to rein it in for fear that I would do things to her before she was ready for them. My gaze dropped to her full red mouth. She hardly ever wore makeup but tonight, her lashes were long and thick, and her lips were painted a deep crimson. The color heightened the red in her cheeks while her dark lashes made the slight caramel in her eyes, pop.

"I'm having a hard time, Moonbeam," I said, wrapping my hand around her forearm. Brushing my thumb back and forth, I reveled in the way her skin erupted into tiny goosebumps. "A really hard fucking time."

"W-What do you mean?" she asked, her voice shaking.

I leaned down to her ear, placing my hand on hers that was on the door handle. "Something...I don't know what but this...fuck." Taking a chance, I licked along the shell of her ear. An electric current shot between us at the soft contact. It was so small, but it was definitely there. "I've known you for years but I've never...this..." I couldn't form a coherent thought where she was concerned. Something switched between us recently. I wasn't sure why or how, but I *did* know that I wanted to explore it more with her.

"Zach," she whispered.

My hold on her arm tightened. I was losing control. She was making me forget everything I had come to know and just feel. Just be. But I couldn't. Not with her. Maybe never with her. It was too dangerous. I could never be enough for her.

I pulled back before I did something both of us would regret.

She watched me, her dark eyes billowing with lust that I felt all the way down to the marrow of my bones.

"Get in the car, Moonbeam," I grumbled, heading around to the driver's side. Before I got in the car, I adjusted myself and took a deep breath. This was a bad idea. A very bad idea. I was playing with fire where Luna was concerned, and I knew that it was only a matter of time before both of us got burned by the raging inferno growing between us.

(Luna)

Zach was looking at me differently tonight. He had been looking at me differently for a while actually, but I only just noticed how much when he licked along the shell of my ear. My skin tingled. I could still feel him. His desperate grip on my arm. Hear the growl of his deep voice. See the lust in his dark eyes.

Maybe the girls were right. Something was definitely growing between Zach and me. But even if that were the case, I could still feel him holding me at a safe distance. We may have been close, and I was the only one out of our friends he actually made a point to talk to, but he was still pushing me away.

My chest tightened at that thought.

His hands white knuckled the steering wheel. That sexy muscle in his jaw ticked. He looked good even though he was pissed about something. He wore a black tailored suit that was made for his big, strong body. A red tie sat against the white dress shirt covering his torso. The jacket to his suit hung in the back.

"Why aren't you wearing your jacket?" I asked, figuring that was a safe question.

"Because it's proper etiquette. Also, driving with a suit jacket on, is uncomfortable as hell."

"Oh." I ran my hands down my thighs. "Dresses aren't overly comfortable at times either."

He only grunted.

I looked out the window. We were still in our city, if you could even call it that. It had grown quite a bit since our parents were kids, but it was small compared to most.

"I hate these dinners," Zach confessed, tugging on his red tie.

"Why do you do them then?" I asked, thankful that he had broken the silence.

"So, my father doesn't have to and if I want to take over the business, this is my job. Although I could just hire people to do it for me..." His dark eyes flicked to mine. "I like being in control too much to let someone else do it."

I shivered at the innuendo. "Well..." The questions were on the tip of my tongue, but I wasn't sure if I wanted the answers or not. So of course, I asked anyway, "What's going on? With us?"

Zach looked back out onto the road. "I don't know, Moonbeam. I really don't know."

I cleared my throat, running my hands up and down my thighs. "Well...let's enjoy dinner, have a drink or two and go from there. I'll sit quietly while you do your business stuff and be the eye candy on your arm. Okay?"

Zach blew out a slow breath and scratched the dark scruff on his jaw. "Alright, Moonbeam. That sounds perfect if you ask me."

We pulled into the parking lot of an Italian restaurant. I had never been there before because it was expensive, but I had always wondered what the food tasted like.

"Wow." I sat forward, taking in the smaller building that had a noticeable chandelier hanging from the ceiling inside the restaurant. "I've driven by this place but I've never eaten here."

"I only come here when I want to impress my clients or if they choose to eat here. The client I'm meeting tonight picked this place. I can't really argue with him since I'm trying to buy one of his buildings."

"Really?" My head whipped around. "You want to buy his building?"

"Well, I want to buy several of them actually. They're in the perfect spot in downtown New York. They overlook Central Park and would be perfect for a hotel. I want to gut them and put up one big building."

"Are they apartment buildings?" I asked, worried that people would be losing their homes.

"No, Luna. They're businesses and before you say that I'm trying to take jobs from people, I'm really not. They've already been notified that the buildings will be sold. That was on the owner's part. I just got notice that he was selling them in the first place."

"Oh. Okay."

Zach gave me a small smile. "You were worried that I was taking someone's job from them. Weren't you?"

"Well…I was actually worried that you were taking someone's home. But I also know how hard it is nowadays to get a decent job." I shrugged. "I didn't think you were like that, but I've never seen you in business mode, so I wasn't sure."

He smirked. "My grandfather was the ruthless one when it came to shutting businesses down, so he could buy the buildings. My father taught me different. I learned from him to search out places that are already listed and put in an offer that way. I also gave each of the employees a job opportunity."

My heart warmed. "You're a good guy, Zachary."

His grin grew. "Let's get this dinner over with."

(Zach)

Luna was absolutely breathtaking. She would pass a glance at me every so often when she thought I wasn't looking. But I was. I was always looking at her because I couldn't help it. I looked at her because seeing her was something that helped me through my day. Even when we were kids. There had always been something about her that calmed me.

When we walked into the tiny restaurant, I could feel all eyes on us. The men watched her, wishing it was them she was latching onto. The women looked as well but I didn't give a shit. I only had eyes for Luna. I just wished I would have made a move years ago.

"People are staring," Luna murmured, pulling me from my guilt-ridden thoughts and curled her hand tighter around my bicep.

"Let them stare, Moonbeam." I kissed her temple. "You're beautiful. The men are jealous."

"So are the women," she countered.

The lust billowing between us was like a bomb and I couldn't wait to watch it fucking explode.

She stared up at me, something flashing behind her dark eyes.

A throat cleared.

Both of us turned, finding a tall man standing at a table. "Mr. Porter." He held out his hand. "It's been awhile."

"Luna, this is Chase Black. Chase, Luna Stone." I returned the handshake. My stomach twisted at the way he was looking at her. His cold calculating eyes raked over her, no doubt imagining her naked and writhing beneath him.

She shivered, tightening her hold on my arm.

"It's a pleasure meeting you, Miss Stone." Chase offered his hand again.

She took it.

He caught my eye, winked, and placed a peck on the back of her hand.

Luna stiffened, snatching her hand back.

Chase chuckled, sitting. "I wasn't aware that we could bring a date or else I would have brought one myself."

"I assumed you would be bringing a date. But that's beside the point. *I* brought a date, so you would keep this professional," I threw back at him, knowing that if Luna wasn't there, he would have threatened me already. It was why I was sent to meet with him instead of my father. Because my dad would have killed him already.

"How are your parents?" Chase asked, ignoring my statement. "I'm actually surprised it's you here and not your dad. Although, if he brought your mom—"

"Careful," I bit out.

Chase's grin grew. "Anyway, let's get down to business because like you, I have better things to do." His gaze flicked to Luna's before giving me a small smirk.

Luna shifted beside me.

I reached under the table and grabbed her hand. She stopped moving, finally relaxing beside me which then caused me to do the same.

I still had to play it cool. Especially where her father was involved. I was man enough to admit it, Vincent Stone Senior scared the shit out of me.

"My father said you were looking at selling the building near Central Park." I took a sip of my water. "You already told the residents, so I don't have to do your dirty work." I sat back, placing the glass on the table. "I've also been told that your own father is adamant on you not selling the building. Or any of the buildings for that matter."

Chase's jaw clenched. He sat back in his chair, running his fingers along the dark scruff on his jaw. It was funny in a way. Although we looked nothing alike, we were similar in the way we worked. But I would never throw anyone under the bus to get to the top. Not unless it came to bulldozing through someone like him. Then, I would have no issues doing it.

"My father left me in charge of the company after he became sick." Chase sat forward, his dark brows narrowing in the center. "So, I highly suggest leaving him the fuck out of it."

I bit back a chuckle, knowing I had struck a nerve. I didn't give a shit. I didn't like him. I didn't like his father. I also didn't like how both of them tried to undermine my own father by bribing the owner of a hotel to sell the building to them and not my dad. It was a ruthless business, but these people didn't have to resort to that shit.

The waiter took that moment to come over. "Good evening. I'm Jacob," the young man smiled. "I'll be taking care of you this evening. Can I start you off with some drinks?"

"I'll have a glass of your best red," Chase said, not taking his gaze off of mine.

"What would you like, Luna?" I asked her, brushing my thumb over her pulse point.

Her breath caught. "I'm fine with just water," she said. "Thank you."

The waiter nodded, looking my way. "And you, Sir?"

"Water is fine as well." I would have a drink later. I was already on the verge of saying whatever was on my mind. Alcohol would only make it worse. I didn't need that to happen. I had to close this deal.

The waiter nodded again and headed to the bar to put the order in.

"Alright, Zach." Chase crossed his arms over his chest. "Care to tell me what that shit was about? If your father were here, he wouldn't resort to pissing me off."

I shrugged. "My father isn't here, now is he? Just like yours isn't either. We're doing this our way. Without them. So, are you wanting to sell the building or not?"

(Luna)

Watching Zach in action was hot as hell. His demeanor was something I had never seen before. I knew that he was a powerful businessman due to his dad teaching him everything he knew but that was it. I had never seen his performance.

Zach's jaw was set, his hand never left mine and his words flowed. By the time he was finished, Chase had buckled and sold the building to him.

"You're a stubborn fucker," Chase mumbled, throwing his napkin on top of his plate.

Zach shrugged. "I come by it honestly." He gave my hand a squeeze.

Chase chuckled, running a hand through his dark hair that was short on the sides and a little longer on top. "Only one man has ever made me cave that quickly and he's dead."

I shivered at the thought.

Zach rolled his eyes. "He's referring to his grandfather," he told me. "So dramatic, Chase."

Chase's laugh deepened. "It worked." He nodded my way. "It made her squirm."

"It seems that Zach made you squirm as well," I threw back at him. "Or else you wouldn't have signed over the building to him in less than ten minutes. Next time, I should keep time. See if Zach can crack you sooner."

Chase's mouth fell.

Zach only grinned.

"Well this has been fun." Chase stood, stuck his hand out and waited.

Zach rose to his feet, returning the handshake. "Until next time."

Chase grunted and left the restaurant.

"He didn't even offer to pay," I said, watching him leave before turning back to Zach.

"I'm not surprised." Zach finished off his water when the waiter returned.

He smiled down at us. "Would you like dessert?"

FOUR

Luna

"**THANK YOU FOR DINNER,**" I told Zach as he put the car into park. I realized then that he didn't park directly in front of the house I shared with the girls. Probably a good idea with the peering eyes that lived with me.

"You're welcome." He turned toward me. "Thank you for coming with me and keeping me sane. And calm."

"I didn't really do anything," I told him. It wasn't like I did a whole lot of talking.

"You did." He cupped my hand that was on my knee. "You did more than you could ever know."

My gaze flicked to his. An unknown energy passed between us. "Zach?"

He pulled my hand to his mouth, placing a soft peck on the back of it. "Luna, I don't know what's going on and I'm probably going to go to hell for this but fuck it."

Before I could ask what he meant, he pulled me against him and crushed his mouth to mine.

I gasped, which gave him the incentive to push his tongue between my lips. A moan escaped me. I had been kissed before but not like this. It was like Zach was trying to reach inside me and find out all of my dark and dirty secrets. Secrets that were only meant for him to know.

His hands roamed down my back, a path of goosebumps following with them.

Snaking my arms around his thick neck, I deepened the kiss, taking his tongue farther into my mouth.

A soft growl escaped from somewhere deep inside his chest.

"Zach," I whispered against his lips.

He broke the kiss, leaned back, and rubbed his nape. "Shit, Luna. I'm...fuck, I'm sorry."

"Don't be." My heart pounded hard behind the walls of my ribcage. "I just...I wasn't expecting that."

"Neither was I." He cleared his throat, dropping his hands in his lap. "I *am* sorry."

"Don't be sorry. I'm not complaining," I confessed.

His dark eyes twinkled.

"But...I should go." As much as I didn't want to, I also didn't want to make out with him in his car.

"That's a good idea." He glanced in the back seat. "Especially before I do something we'll regret."

I laughed lightly. "I don't think either of us would regret that."

A slow grin spread on his face. "True." He brought my hand back up to his mouth. "Chat later?"

"Yes," I breathed. "Definitely later."

"Have a good evening, Moonbeam."

I leaned toward him and placed a soft peck on his cheek. "Thank you, Zach." Before I changed my mind, I quickly left the vehicle and headed home.

(Zach)

My lips still tingled from the kiss Luna and I had shared. It had been the first time I had felt her lips on mine and I wanted more. Fuck, did I ever want more. But I knew she was a virgin. I also knew that she didn't date. Hell, I wasn't sure if she ever even had a boyfriend. The idea that she was completely innocent stirred something feral inside of me. I wanted to show her, to teach her. I wanted to use her body to make both of us feel good.

Once Luna left the vehicle, I waited, watching her walk up the sidewalk to her house. I hadn't parked in front of her place, knowing there would be people watching. It was hard to keep anything private amongst our group of friends.

I slowly drove toward Luna's house and once I saw her slip through the doors, I was about to drive away when a tap on the window stopped me.

Ashton stood on the other side, motioning for me to roll down the window.

I did and put the car into park. "Hey, Ashton. What's up?"

"You're not coming to the party?" he asked, leaning his arm on the hood of my car.

"Party? I didn't know there was one." I wasn't overly surprised that Luna never mentioned it. She was usually holed up in her room whenever her roommates had people over.

"Yeah, this one was last minute. Not a lot of people. More like a get-together, I guess. Gigi said we've all been working hard and just wanted to have some friends over." He shrugged. "I just go with the flow and besides, the girls have some hot friends."

I chuckled, shutting the car off. "I was going to go home but I can stay."

"Good." He pulled away from the car and leaned against the hood. "How was your date?"

"It wasn't a date," I told him, really wishing people would mind their own business.

"It wasn't?" Ashton raised an eyebrow. "Did you pick her up? Was there dinner? Did you drive her home and kiss her goodnight?"

"I have no idea what you're talking about," I told him. I loved the guy like a brother but right now, he was starting to piss me off.

"Right," he said slowly. "The girls talk. You should know that. They helped Luna get ready."

"It still wasn't a date," I said, even though I knew it actually was. But whatever was going on between Luna and I, I wanted to keep it to myself for now.

"Alright." He clapped my shoulder. "Then if it wasn't a date, you wouldn't mind if I set you up with someone."

I stopped walking. "Are you fucking kidding me right now?" Even if there wasn't anything going on with Luna, I still wouldn't agree to Ashton setting me with God only knew who. "Not interested." I shrugged him off.

"Why not? You're single, are you not?"

"Still not interested." My friends had been trying to set me up for a while. At first, I didn't want a relationship. It had never been my thing. Only because I had never found that one person I wanted to spend time with. I tried convincing myself that there was a person out there for me when really, she had been in front of me the whole damn time.

Luna got beneath my skin and that kiss sealed the deal. She would be mine.

"She's a good girl, Zach," Ashton continued. "She's not one of these girls that you keep diving between."

"I don't do that shit anymore," I mumbled, not that he would believe me anyway.

"Right," he repeated.

My blood burned through me, my hands clenching into fists. I loved him but right now, I really wanted to smash my fist into his face.

I shoved my hands in my pockets. "If she's so great, why don't you date her then?"

"Because." He didn't say anymore on the subject, but I knew. Ashton and his twin brother had been sharing another one of our friends. But I wasn't sure if that had been a one-time thing or not. "Besides, she would be perfect for you," he added. "She's taking over her daddy's business when he retires."

"Why, Ashton?" I stopped at the base of the steps leading to the house that Luna shared with a couple of our friends. "I never pegged you for a gossip."

Ashton rolled his eyes. "I'm not gossiping. I'm stating facts. Listen, one date. That's all I'm asking."

The answer was still no but I *was* curious. "Why?"

"I'm being nice, alright?" He shrugged. "Even if you end up just being friends, you can never have too many of those you know."

"How do you know her?"

"She volunteers at The Dove Project every now and again," Ashton explained. "We told her about you and she's happy to go on a date."

"You told her about me?" Fuck, I did not need this right now. If she volunteered at the center, Luna must have known her.

"It's just one date, Zach." Ashton clapped my shoulder. "It's not like there's anyone else you're interested in, is there?"

"No one I can have anyway," I muttered.

"Exactly. See? What are friends for?" Ashton winked.

Aiden took that moment to join us. "What's my brother going on about now?" The twins weren't identical, but you could still tell they were brothers by their blond hair and big builds. With their matching piercing blue eyes, they both looked at me like I was a lost little puppy.

"He's trying to set me up on a date," I told Aiden.

"Ah." Aiden smiled. "Yes. Clara's looking forward to meeting you."

I sighed. "I'm not going on a date. With anyone."

"Listen." Aiden placed both his hands on my shoulders and turned me toward him. "I know you like Luna. You don't have to confirm either way but I'm not stupid. I also know that her father is the reason you haven't made a move. I'm sure there's something else holding you back as well but I know that Stone is a big reason. I get it. But I also know that you want something. Anything. Maybe trying something that's not within our circle would be better for you."

My stomach clenched. "I hate that you can read me so well." But there was no way I could do that to Luna. I could be an asshole but dating someone else after kissing her would surely prove to her father that I was not good enough for her. I didn't need that.

"Call it a special talent." Aiden gave my shoulders a squeeze before he let me go. "One date, Zach."

"The answer is no. I'm not dating another woman when I went out on a date with the actual woman that I want tonight. It's not happening." My mouth snapped shut. I never expected to admit that Luna and I went out on a date. At least not to my friends.

Ashton's brows narrowed.

Aiden smirked. "Well it's about time that you admit there's something there."

"I…" I shook my head. "I didn't admit to anything."

"You admitted that tonight was a date. Good." Aiden released me and crossed his arms over his chest.

"You are confusing as hell," I mumbled.

Aiden chuckled but still, Ashton never said anything. Was he hoping that I would agree to the date? Either way, it didn't matter what he was hoping for.

Luna was *mine*.

FIVE

Luna

LATER THAT EVENING, I was carrying a tray of drinks out to the back deck. Our parents had joined us early on and would leave before the night was over, allowing us 'kids' some time to ourselves. Much to our fathers' dismay of course. They liked to stay behind and throw their weight around, thinking the guys would leave because of the big bad daddies. But it never worked.

"Hey, *piccola*."

I spun at the sound of my own father's voice, my smile widening when my gaze landed on his face. "Hi, Daddy".

"How's my girl doing?" He wrapped me in a hug, placing a soft kiss on my head.

"Good. Trying to be social even though I'd rather be reading right now." I caught sight of two other girls I had come to know through Gigi. They were giggling and talking amongst themselves. They pointed our way every so often. My father had that effect on women. He was tatted up and big. Girls liked that thing it seemed.

I only laughed, shaking my head.

"What is it?" he asked, looking around us. "Something wrong?"

"No." I patted his arm gently. "You worry way too much. All of you do."

"It's our job," he grumbled. "Gigi sure knows how to throw a party. I don't even know half these people. I'm not sure I like that fact."

"This isn't a party." There were a few other people that we had come to know from living in the same neighborhood or going to school together, but the party wasn't as big as it used to be.

"Oh, this is nothing." I told my father. "Wait until you guys leave."

He raised an eyebrow. "Is that so?"

"Alright, my love." My stepmom, Creena, came up beside us. "Leave her alone. She's an adult and is old enough to take care of herself. Remember?"

My dad rolled his eyes which was an odd movement for someone so big. Even though they were now in their fifties, you couldn't tell. Mom was Japanese and hardly aged a day since I was a little girl. And my dad was Italian and still grumpy as hell.

"Doesn't matter how old she is." Dad scowled. "She could be fifty and I'd still beat any fucker who touches her."

"That's why I won't tell you." I winked.

His jaw ticked, his face reddening.

I laughed, patting his arm. "I'm kidding." I stood on tiptoes and kissed his cheek, his graying beard tickling my lips.

"You girls are going to force me into an early grave," he grumbled, grabbing his wife's hand. He leaned down to her ear and whispered something only she could hear.

She choked on a laugh, her cheeks going pink.

I giggled, shaking my head. My parents inspired me. All of the parents did. Us kids didn't know their whole life story. We weren't allowed to know as they wanted to protect us, but I knew they had worked hard for their love. That was what I wanted. Someone to love me like my dad loved my mom.

My real mom died when I was a baby, but Creena was everything I could ask for in a motherly figure. It was amusing when I introduced her as my mother, and we looked nothing alike. Seeing as I was Italian, and she was Japanese. The looks we got were highly worth it.

My dad gave me another hug. "Just be careful. I don't want to go to jail for murder if I find out some fucker touched you."

"I'll behave," I reassured him. "I promise."

"Good girl." He pulled back. "We're going to head out early. Your brother's here so keep an eye out on each other. Alright?"

"We will." My brother was nineteen and had my dad's temper running through him. If anything happened to me, no one would know about it because the culprit would be dead.

Mom pulled me into her arms. "You be careful but also not too careful. You are allowed some fun. You don't do it much."

"I know."

"I hear Zach will be showing up." She held me at arm's length and gave me a wink.

"Really?" I thought he was leaving after dropping me off.

"Yeah." She smiled. "He was talking to Ashton and Aiden outside as your father and I showed up."

"Oh." My cheeks burned. "That's nice."

She laughed. "We'll talk later."

"I look forward to it." And I did. Talking to her was like talking to a best friend but with her being more experienced and older, it helped whenever I needed advice. When it came to Zach though, I imagined I would be needing that advice sometime very soon.

When my parents left, I went back to serving the rest of the drinks.

"Did you hear that Zach's going on a date?" someone whispered.

My hackles rose, my back stiffening.

"Really? I thought he just went out with Luna tonight," someone else responded.

I casually handed out drinks, trying to keep within earshot without looking too noticeable.

"I guess that wasn't a date," the first person said.

"Wow. Poor girl."

My cheeks burned, shame weighing heavily on my shoulders that I thought something was finally happening between Zach and I.

He was going on a date? How could he do this to me? And after we had just gone out for dinner and shared a kiss. My lips tingled, remembering his mouth on mine.

I ran my fingers along my lips, wondering what his deal was. He was known to be a player, never settling down for anything other than casual sex. But I never questioned him about it. We were best friends but that was a subject I didn't feel I had any right talking to him about. I also didn't want to know how many notches he had on his bedpost.

After I finished serving the rest of the drinks, I brought the tray into the house. When I headed back outside, I was stopped short by Zach standing with the twins.

He was beautiful. His hair was more unkempt than when I left him not even an hour before. He had been running his fingers through it. I knew because I had seen him do it whenever he was stressed. What was he stressed about this time? Work? His upcoming date?

Blood burned through me. Did I have a right to be upset? Yes, yes I did. My parents had taught me not to let a guy use me. I was stronger than that. Although a part of me wanted to stomp over to him and demand what the hell he was thinking, I wouldn't. No. I would make him come to me. My mother taught me that as well.

"If a guy pisses you off or hurts you in any way, don't you dare go crawling back to him."

I stared at my stepmom with wide eyes. "Why not?"

"Because if he cares, if he actually cares about you, he'll come crawling to you, Luna. Make him work for your heart."

Mom was right. But hearing that Zach was going on a date, still hurt.

Zach's dark eyes caught mine. He nodded once. The movement had been so sudden, I wasn't sure if I saw him do it. Lifting his hand, he brushed his fingers along his mouth.

My heart stuttered, my skin breaking out into a sheen of sweat. Even though he was going on a date, I knew, I knew to the marrow of my soul, that he wanted me.

"Luna." Gigi came up to my side. "You okay?"

"I overheard someone saying that Zach's going on a date." I shook my head. "Did you know?"

"Really?" Gigi's eyes widened. "No, I had no idea. But you guys just went—"

"Yeah, I know," I mumbled.

"Wow." She paused. "I know that Zach has a messy past with women, but I never thought he would do this to you."

I swallowed hard, the backs of my eyes prickling with tears. Clearing my throat, I stood up taller, refusing to let it show that he got to me.

"Do I have a right to be upset?" I asked her, needing reassurance that I wasn't overreacting.

"Of course." Gigi shook her head. "Girl, could you imagine if a guy did this to Meadow?"

I laughed. "He'd wake up with no dick."

"Exactly." Her gaze softened, her shoulders dropping. "If you need to talk, I'm always here."

"I know." I wrapped my arms around her shoulders, giving her a hard hug. "I love you."

She laughed lightly. "I love you too."

Gigi released me, her eyes scanning the small crowd. "I'm going to go get drunk."

"Have fun." I sighed, wishing I could do the same. Not that I couldn't, it just wasn't what I wanted to do. No. I wanted *him*. Even though I knew I shouldn't and that he didn't deserve it.

Heading to the patio set, I slumped onto an empty chair and waited. It took every fiber of my being not to go up to him and demand to know why he would go on a date with another woman after taking me out for dinner.

"Let him come to you."

My stepmom's words bounced in my head. I would listen to her, even though it was hard as hell.

Zach stood off to the side. He was quiet and brooding. Always watching what was going on around him which was something he did quite often. He kept on high alert. I also noticed how he always faced people, never keeping his back to them if he could help it.

My stomach clenched, wondering what that was about but fearing the answer just the same.

Zach had taken off the suit jacket, leaving him in a white dress shirt and black dress pants. The sleeves were rolled up to his elbows, making the tan in his skin become more pronounced. He had also removed the blood red tie, leaving the top three buttons open.

He caught my gaze.

I glared at him.

He raised an eyebrow.

My body buzzed, my heart picking up speed with each passing second that ticked by. My mouth tingled, remembering full well what his lips felt like pressed against mine.

Crossing my arms under my chest, I lifted my chin defiantly.

His mouth twitched, pulling up into a smirk.

Shaking my head, my palms tingled, itching to slap that smirk right off his face. Cocky fucker.

"Hey, Luna."

I jumped, the back of my neck heating as Ashton sat down beside me.

"How's it going?"

"Not too bad. You?" I was thankful for the distraction, knowing full well that Zach and I would eventually get caught eye-fucking each other across the backyard.

"Oh, you know, living the dream." He stretched his long legs out in front of him, resting his arm across the back of the couch behind me.

"That's a pretty shitty dream," I teased.

"Truth." He winked, taking a swig of his beer. "I don't know what's going on between you two," he said, nodding toward Zach. "And I know your father is a scary fucker. All of ours are, but it's holding Zach back."

"What? Are you a relationship expert now?" I mumbled.

"Hardly." Ashton grunted. "Listen, I have my own shit to deal with but just know, I'm here. If you need to talk. Or have sex." He waggled his eyebrows. "I can help you with that too."

I coughed, choking on a laugh. "Excuse me?"

"It's just sex, Luna." He shrugged. "It's not like we'd be getting married. Think about it. I'm willing to teach you all I know too. I don't pass that information on to just anyone."

I gaped at him. "You're serious, aren't you?"

"This is a very important subject, Luna. A girl has to know how to please her guy. Well I can be that guy. And you can be that girl. I'll teach you."

"I don't know what to say right now." There was no way I would have sex with him. All the power to people who could have random hookups, it wasn't my thing. And even if it was, it definitely wouldn't be with Ashton.

He finished off his beer before he stood. "The offer is there for whenever you're ready." A hint of amusement flashed behind his eyes. "Just saying."

"Go get me a beer." I shook my head, laughing to myself.

"Yes, ma'am." He saluted me and headed back into the house.

"What was that about?" Gigi asked, coming toward me.

"I'm not sure you want to know." My cheeks burned even more at the mere idea of sleeping with Ashton. I had never considered it before. The twins were hot yeah, but they were friends. Was Ashton right though? Could sex just be sex?

"Luna?"

"Sorry," I muttered, meeting Gigi's gaze. "What were you saying?"

"I was just asking what Ashton wanted. Although with him, it probably had something to do with sex, didn't it?"

I scoffed. "Now why would you think that?"

She laughed, gently nudging me in the shoulder. "Because I know him. We *all* know him."

Ashton took that moment to come back with two beers. He handed me one before sitting down right beside me. He was so close, he might as well have been sitting on my lap.

I glanced up, finding Zach staring directly at us. Although he stood across the yard, I could see that familiar tick in his jaw. His body was rigid, his back stiff. My heart stuttered.

I inched away from Ashton. "Thank you for the beer but you really need to learn to give a girl some space."

"Why?" He leaned down to my ear. "Do I make you nervous?"

His hot breath tickled the side of my face, sending a shiver down my spine.

He chuckled.

I glared up at him. "Ass."

He moved away from me, leaving a few inches between us but placed his arm on the back of the couch behind me.

"What are you doing?" Gigi asked, leaning forward and looking between us.

"I have no idea." I took a sip of my beer. "I'm just drinking."

"I meant what I said," Ashton said as he brought the bottle up to his mouth.

"What did you say?" Gigi pointed at him. "Did you ask her to have sex with you?"

Ashton frowned. "How could you know that?"

"Because I know you." She looked at me then. "What did you say?"

"She didn't say anything so that means I still have a chance." He kissed my cheek. "Isn't that right, Luna?"

"Oh God." I pushed him back. "Stop. I am not having sex with you." I met Gigi's gaze. "He offered to teach me."

Gigi gagged.

Ashton's head whipped around. "That's fucking rude."

Gigi and I laughed.

"You know we love you," I told him once I calmed down. "I appreciate the offer, but I'm not having sex with you."

"Yet," he corrected. He nodded once. "Think he would be pissed?"

"Uh…" I cleared my throat.

"On that note." Gigi stood. "I'm going to go get another drink."

When we were alone, Ashton continued, "I mean it, Luna. You've had a crush on the guy since we were kids. And he hasn't made a move. I don't know what his deal is but he better do something before it's too late."

I wasn't sure if I should be pissed at Ashton's honesty or agree with him. I sighed, pulling the label off the bottle.

"I heard he's going on a date," I murmured.

"What?" Ashton's head whipped around. "Where did you hear that?"

"I overheard people talking about it." I shrugged.

"I think you should talk to Zach about that before you start believing what everyone else is saying. Whatever you're thinking, Luna, it's not true." Ashton stood from the couch just as Aiden came toward us. He greeted his brother, then both of them headed over to where Zach stood with a few other guys.

Could Ashton be right? Was there no date at all?

"I think he's checking you out," Gigi said, rejoining me on the couch.

"What?" My cheeks burned. "He's not." But Zach was staring our way.

"Well let's find out." Gigi stood from the couch and held out her hand.

I took it, letting her pull me to my feet.

"Do you trust me?" she asked, her gaze landing on another group of guys that I had seen before at previous parties.

Brody Davies was included in the bunch. Being the mayor's son, I hadn't seen him in a while. He caught my gaze, giving me a little wave.

I waved back.

He ran a hand through his short brown hair, turning back to the guys he was standing with.

"I'm surprised he's here," I told Gigi.

"Who?" She followed my line of sight. "Oh yeah. Brody needed a break from whatever it was that his father was trying to get him to do. Anyway." She tugged me along. "Do you trust me?"

"That's the second time you asked me that," I said, following beside her. "Of course, I trust you. But what are you—"

Gigi pulled me to the group of guys I had only met in passing because of her.

"What are you doing?" I tried tugging my arm from her grasp but her hold only tightened.

"Hey guys," Gigi said sweetly, stepping up beside a tall blond.

"Hey, Angelica," he crooned, licking his lips.

"This is my girl, Luna." She tugged me beside her, ignoring him eye-fucking her. "She's shy."

I snorted.

Gigi winked at me.

I had no idea what kind of game she was playing but I caught movement out of the corner of my eye.

Zach left the twins, coming toward me, his hands clenched at his sides. While he stalked toward us, he stared me down.

My heart jumped to my throat.

Oh. Crap.

(Zach)

These feelings coursing through me were new. Even though we had kissed already, I had never felt possessive of her. She was friends with guys. I knew that. Hell, she was friends with Ashton and Aiden. But when it came to someone I didn't know, I turned into a damn caveman.

Luna had been the first female that I became friends with. Although I was friends with the other girls in our circle, it was never the same with them as it was with her. But now, as I watched Gigi pull her to a group of guys, my feet carried me to her before I knew what I was doing.

I shouldn't care. We weren't official. I wasn't good enough for her. She deserved better.

"You're pathetic. You deserve to spend the rest of your life alone, Toy."

Memories from my past tried to force their way into my head but I shoved them back and let them give me the strength I needed to confront Luna. And why the hell had she been glaring at me? She must have heard something. Or she believed the rumors. I couldn't blame her. It wasn't like I ever denied them.

As I approached the group, Luna saw me first. Her eyes widened, her cheeks turning a bright shade of red.

A tall bastard who was staring down at her lasciviously, followed her line of sight.

"What the hell do you want, Porter?" he asked. What was his name? Brian? John? I couldn't remember, and I also didn't care.

You're talking to my girl.

"I need to speak to Luna," I said and walked away, knowing she would follow. The tone of my voice left no room for questioning.

"You didn't have to be rude, Zach," Luna said from behind me.

The fact that she followed me, stirred something inside of me. That alpha side. That side that wanted to protect her and ravage her all at the same time. The side that wanted to show her I *was* good enough.

I moved across the yard and sat on a patio chair. As much as I wanted to pull her onto my lap, I didn't for fear she would push me away. I couldn't deal with that right now, knowing it would break me.

"Zach," she repeated when I didn't say anything.

"What, Luna?" My cock twitched at the hardness in her eyes. Her defiance always got to me. She was headstrong and knew what she wanted and didn't care what she had to do to get it. Except for when it came to me. It was like there was a wall up between us and no matter what we did, we couldn't break through it.

"Why are you looking at me like that?" she asked, her cheeks reddening even more.

I stood from the chair, heading to the side of the house, needing to put some much-needed distance between us. I should have gone inside but there were too many people. There were too many damn people everywhere. And then they would ask questions. Questions I wasn't ready to answer because I had no idea what the hell those answers were.

"Zach," she pressed, following me. "What's up with you?"

"You were talking to him," I said.

"So?" She frowned. "Why do you care who I'm talking to?"

"Well…" *Words, Porter. Use them.* But I couldn't. Words were lost on the tip of my tongue as Luna stared up at me with those chocolate brown eyes of hers. Fuck me, she was beautiful.

Her cheeks reddened even more.

It took everything in me not to rip her dress in half and see just how far down that blush went. Was she pink everywhere? My palms twitched, begging to run over her smooth skin.

Clearing my throat, I turned away from her and adjusted the semi I was now sporting.

"Hey."

A gentle hand touched my shoulder and that was when I lost it.

SIX

Luna

ZACH SPUN ON ME, his eyes cold and deadly. Before I knew what was happening, he had me up against the wall.

"Zach," I whispered, wanting to reach out to him but holding back instead.

His gaze dropped to my mouth and before I knew what was happening, his lips came down hard on mine.

His kiss was rough, bruising. *Demanding.*

He fisted my hair, holding my head in place as he completely took control and devoured my mouth.

The kiss consumed me, making me dizzy with pleasure and lust.

Keeping one hand in my hair, his other roamed down the side of my body.

I shivered, snaking my arms around his neck.

He growled, forcing his tongue deeper into my mouth. He swallowed my moans and whimpers. He breathed in the air that gave me life and made it his own. He made me feel alive from that mere kiss.

I knew we shouldn't be kissing. I knew that anyone could catch us right now. But I didn't care. He had been holding back for so long, I needed to show him that this was right. That this was meant to be and where we belonged, instead of him going on that damn date.

I grabbed his hand that was on my hip, pushing it lower and up my inner thigh.

Zach stiffened but his own pleasure finally took over. He inched his hand beneath my dress and up my inner thigh.

I cupped the back of his head, deepening the kiss. I needed him. God, did I ever need him. Not that I expected him to fuck me beside the house, but I needed a taste. *Please, just a taste.*

Tease me. Want me. Make me yours.

When his hand reached my center, I jumped.

Voices neared us, getting louder and louder.

Zach maneuvered us, pushing me back into the dark corner between the house and fence. If anyone looked, they would see the shadow of his back but not me.

I broke the kiss, my chest rising and falling with ragged breaths.

His mouth trailed down the length of my jaw, licking and sucking a path to my neck. All the while, his fingers brushed over my soaked panties. He gave me a grunt of approval before slipping a finger beneath the fabric.

"Nice and wet, Moonbeam," he rasped, pushing a finger into me.

I whimpered, the burn of his finger stretching me, heating my skin.

"Fuck," he growled, nipping the side of my neck. "So tight. So perfect."

"Zach," I whined.

"Shhh… the pain won't last long." He slid his finger out most of the way and slowly pushed it back inside of me. He worked up a rhythm, forcing the pleasure coursing through me, higher and higher.

"Oh." I arched against him, my hips moving against his hand as if they had a mind of their own.

"Better?" he asked, lifting his head. The dim lighting of the moon cast a glow around him. It helped me see the beautiful lines of his features but other than that, I couldn't see him in great detail. One day. Hopefully soon. I would see all of him and he would see all of me.

"Yes," I whispered, staring up into his heated gaze.

"Good." He gave me a small smile.

"Zach, I…" What the hell were we even doing?

He leaned his forehead against mine. "I know, Moonbeam."

My heart jumped. I wasn't sure what I wanted to ask him. With his finger deep inside me, I couldn't think straight.

He removed his hand from between my legs.

I whimpered at the loss. "What are you doing?"

"I shouldn't…" His mouth pressed into a firm line.

I grabbed his hand, moving it back between my legs. "Please."

"Fuck." He covered my mouth with his, stealing the very breath from my lungs. "I shouldn't do this. Not here. Not like this. Not with you."

"Why not?" I leaned back, pushing out of his hold. "Is it because you have a date?"

Zach's brows narrowed, his jaw ticking. "What date?"

"The one that you're going on." I huffed, smoothing down my dress. "I hope you enjoy your date," I mumbled, walking past him.

A firm hand grabbed my upper arm, pulling me back against a hard body. "There is no fucking date."

My eyes widened. "What?"

"I want you, Luna. Only you. But not here. Not this way. And the first time you come, I want it to be with my tongue deep inside you. I want to taste your pussy explode."

I swallowed hard at the vulgar words caressing my ears. But I couldn't help but wonder why people were saying he was going on a date. Was he lying to me?

"Nothing to say now?" he crooned, licking along the shell of my ear.

"You want me?" I finally asked.

"Yes." He ground his pelvis into the seat of my ass. "I do. Fuck do I ever. But..."

"What?" I asked, when his voice trailed off. "What is it?"

Zach spun me around, pushing me up against the fence. "There are things holding me back," he said, his voice husky. He ran his hand up my inner thigh, his fingers tickling my skin.

"Is it because I'm not experienced like you are? Or like the women you sleep with?" I panted when his fingers pushed beneath the fabric of my panties once again. "Tell me. Tell me something."

His brows furrowed. Brushing his thumb along my bottom lip, he placed a soft peck on my forehead. "There are no other women. There is no damn date. I don't give a shit what the rumors say. None of them are true."

I leaned back, staring up at him and searching for any signs that he was lying to me. But before I could decide if he was or not, Zach fisted my hair and crushed his mouth to mine.

His finger brushed over my clit, igniting a spark of pleasure up my spine.

He grunted, splitting my lips with his tongue. His finger flicked back and forth, forcing that burn I felt for him into a raging inferno.

I whimpered, grabbing his hand. Was I trying to stop him? Make him go further? I wasn't sure. I wanted him. I had wanted him since I was a kid, but I wanted him to want me just the same. I didn't know what was holding him back. Was it me? My father? Our friends? His career that he's working hard toward?

Cupping his nape, I pulled his mouth down hard on mine at the same time I cupped him over his pants.

He jumped, pushing his pelvis into my touch.

I wasn't sure what I was doing but I figured if I gave him a little taste, maybe he would finally open up to me.

"Fuck," he growled, grabbing my hand. "Stop, Luna."

"But…"

"Listen to me." He brought my hand up to his mouth and kissed my palm. "Whatever questions you have, I'll answer them, but I need time. I promise you that there is no date and I'm not fucking half the town. It's been a while for me. A long while."

"What does that even mean?" I uttered.

"Exactly what you think it means." He kissed the tips of my fingers. "I haven't had sex in over a year."

"Really?" My mouth fell open. "Why not?"

He shrugged. "It's…complicated."

He gave my clit one final flick before pulling his hand from between my legs. Brushing his thumb over my mouth, he pushed the tip between my lips. "You've never been kissed like that before. Have you?"

"I have no idea what you're talking about." Could my inexperience be the true reason he was holding back?

"Whatever you're thinking—" He ran the tip of his thumb over my tongue. The heady scent of my arousal wafted into my nose. "—it's not true."

"You have no idea what I'm thinking." I shoved away from him. "If you want me like you say you do, you would stop pushing me away."

"Luna." His brows narrowed.

"No," I snapped. "What's wrong with me that you're holding back? It can't be the age thing because I'm only a couple years younger than you. Is it because I don't have a career path set out? Or I just work with my mom at the tattoo shop? Is it because I don't know what I want out of life? Tell me, Zach. Tell me something."

"We can't be together," Zach said, but even though the words left his mouth, I could see the inner turmoil in his deep brown eyes.

"You're lying," I murmured.

"Fuck." He raked a hand through his dark hair. "I'm not good enough for you."

I stared at him, my eyes roaming over his face. The anger rushing through me just a moment before, simmered as I watched the man before me crumble with the emotions weighing him down.

"Hey," I said gently, snaking my arms around his neck. I pulled him against me. "You are good enough, Zach. You are more than good enough."

His rigid body relaxed at my words.

"Meet me in my bedroom," I whispered, looking up at him through hooded eyes.

His eyes darkened even more in the shadows of the night. "When?"

I thought a moment. "Ten minutes." It would give us either enough time to cool down or make things worse. I was betting on the latter.

"Alright, Moonbeam," he said, his voice rough. He pinched my chin, leaning down until he was eye level with me. "Ten minutes and then you're fucking mine."

My breath caught.

"Let's go before people start looking for us." He placed a soft peck on my mouth. "I meant what I said."

"Ten minutes and then I'm…I'm yours."

"Yeah, Moonbeam." He released me. Just when I thought he was going to walk away, he reached out to cup my face. "Thank you."

Those two words had been so quiet, I wasn't sure I heard him correctly.

When he turned around and re-joined the party, I let out a breath I hadn't realized I had been holding.

I couldn't believe I had made out with Zach like I did. I also couldn't believe that I took initiative and put his hand between my legs. I was never like this before with other guys. Not that I had many lining up at my door or anything, but with Zach I felt comfortable. Knowing he needed control, I was surprised when he let me take it as far as I did. But he was right, I didn't want to continue this beside the house. In the dark. No. I wanted to see him. *All* of him.

Taking a deep breath, I slipped out from beside the house and found Zach sitting on one of the patio chairs. He caught my gaze, his dark eyes roaming down the length of me.

I glanced down at myself, elated that I looked presentable. But I was sure that my hair was a mess. My body heated, remembering how he had his hands running through it just moments before.

"Luna."

My head snapped up, finding Zach still staring my way. "What?"

"Come here."

I smiled at the rough demand and headed toward him. "Ten minutes, Zach. I told you that."

"Ten minutes until what?" Ashton asked as he walked by us with a tiny little blonde on his arm.

I recognized her from previous parties. "Nothing," I told him.

He looked between Zach and me, and then back down at his date. "Let's go find your friend."

She giggled, running her hand up Ashton's arm. "Okay."

They walked away, leaving me alone once again with the man who stole the very breath from my lungs every damn time he was near.

"Luna," Zach repeated, my name falling from his lips like melted honey.

When I took a step toward him, a couple of guys staggered toward me. They bumped into me, forcing me back until gentle but firm arms wrapped around me.

"Watch where the hell you're going," Zach snapped, his voice laced with venom.

The guys muttered an apology and went into the house.

"Hey," I said gently. "It's fine."

"The fuck it is," Zach growled, tightening his hold on me. He moved back to the chair, keeping his arm around me and pulling me onto his lap.

My body buzzed at being this close to him again. As much as I liked it, I knew that he wasn't ready to let whatever this was between us be known publicly.

"You can let me go now," I said, squirming in his lap.

He grew beneath me, becoming harder as the seconds ticked by. "You need to stop doing that, Moonbeam."

"Doing what?" My cheeks burned. I knew I had gotten a reaction out of him beside the house but feeling him pressed up against me, gave me a sense of power I had never felt before. "Sorry," I muttered anyway.

"Don't be sorry." His mouth brushed along the shell of my ear. "I'm a man and I have a beautiful woman's ass on my lap."

"You put me here. It's not my fault you're..." I swallowed hard. "Reacting to it."

"I'm not reacting, Moonbeam." He pulled me flush against him. "I'm fucking hard."

"Zach," I breathed, shivering against him. "We're not alone and I told you ten minutes. It hasn't been ten minutes yet. We shouldn't be doing this here."

"No, we shouldn't but it didn't stop you a moment ago when I almost fucked you against the side of the house. So, you're into exhibitionism but not voyeurism. Good to know."

I shook my head. "Wait. What?"

Zach chuckled. The sound was deep and rich, promising endless hours of pleasure. "Say it, Luna," he demanded, his voice husky. "Tell me how I'm reacting to you."

"I...Y-You`re..."

"I'm what?" His grip on me tightened. "Say it."

"You're hard," I whispered.

His dark eyes flicked to mine. Something shone behind them, but I couldn't make out what it was.

Just as I was about to ask what the hell he was doing, a large shadow loomed over us.

"Get your *fucking* hands off my daughter."

SEVEN

Luna

I **JUMPED, FALLING OUT** of Zach's lap and landing hard on my ass. A sharp slice of pain traveled up my spine. I winced, breathing through it. That was going to leave one hell of a bruise tomorrow.

Zach grabbed my arm, helping me to my feet. "Are you okay?" he asked, concern apparent on his face.

"I'm fine." I smiled up at him. "Thank you."

"What the hell did I just say?"

"Dad," I snapped. "He saved me from getting trampled." As much as I didn't want to, I pulled myself from Zach's grip and glared up at my dad. "You don't have to be rude." And this was clearly one of the reasons why Zach wanted nothing to do with me.

Dad frowned, his brows narrowing in the center. He looked over my head.

"Don't look at him." I punched him in the arm. "Look at me."

My dad met my gaze, his face softening. "You have your mother's fire," he said gently.

My anger with him simmered. Knowing he wasn't talking about my stepmom but my birth mother instead, I let out a soft sigh.

"I promise he was being a gentleman." Unless you counted the things we did beside the house and what Zach had said to me. I cleared my throat.

"A couple of guys were drunk and stumbled into her," Zach explained from behind me.

Dad crossed his arms over his chest. "That true?" he asked me.

I nodded.

A dark shadow passed over his face but before I could question it, my stepmom came up beside us. "Everything okay?"

"Yeah." My dad looked over my head once again. "How's work going?"

I followed his gaze.

Zach's stiff body relaxed a touch. "Good. It's taking a while to get the hang of things. I don't think my dad actually wants to retire yet."

Much to my surprise, my dad chuckled. "Probably not. He likes having something he can control."

Zach smirked. "He does."

Dad nodded once, staring at Zach. Questions hid behind his dark eyes, but he never asked them. He never demanded to know what was going on between us. But I knew in time that he would. My father had a temper on him. He had used the excuse that it was because he was Italian, but the real reason was because he had experienced things no one should ever have to go through. I was thankful that he was retired from the navy but unfortunately for most of our fathers, those demons still followed them long after retirement.

Mom said something quietly to my dad, pulling his attention away from us.

"Luna."

I looked up at Zach.

He took a chance, reached his hand out, and brushed his finger along mine. "I should go."

"Really?" I looked back at my dad. "Is it because of him?"

"It's because of many things, Moonbeam, but right now it's because it's not our time."

I turned back around. Was he right? Could there be a reason that we were interrupted? Was it fate? Did I even believe in fate?

"I'll talk to you later," he said, pulling away from me.

"You leaving?" Dad asked, wrapping his arm around his wife's shoulders.

"I am." Zach stared him down, waiting. For what, I wasn't sure but the powerplay between them sent a shiver down my spine.

Dad raised an eyebrow, a slow smirk spreading on his face. "Have a good night, Zach."

"Thank you. You as well." Zach turned back to me. "Call me later."

I nodded, watching him leave the backyard and head into the house.

"Did you really have to do that?" I demanded once I was alone with my father.

My dad only grunted.

"What are you even doing here?" I asked. "I thought you guys left."

"Your brother's friend got a little too drunk," Dad explained. "So, he asked me to drive them back to his place."

"Oh." I shivered, wrapping my arms around myself, missing Zach's warm touch.

A soft material slid over my shoulders.

I jumped, finding Vince Junior smiling down at me. "Thank you," I said, pulling the sweatshirt off my shoulders and slipping it on over my head instead.

"Always." Vince turned to me when our parents were out of earshot. "I saw Zach and Dad having a silent showdown. I thought for sure Dad was going to do some kung fu shit and kick his ass."

I rolled my eyes.

"I think it surprised Dad though."

"What did?" I asked my brother.

"When Zach never looked away. You know that look Dad gets when he's pissed or trying to be intimidating. Zach never backed down. I'm sure that impressed Dad."

"You think so?"

Vince shrugged. "I know it sure as hell impressed me."

I sighed, wishing I could go back to the moment where it was just Zach and I in the dark corners beside the house.

"You got this, sis." Vince kissed my cheek. "I promise."

"Just like you do?" I threw back at him, knowing he had a crush on Gigi and didn't do a damn thing about it.

He met my stare. "I have no idea what you're talking about." And with that, he walked over to the twins. Even though he was only nineteen and couldn't drink legally yet, everyone treated him like he could. No one looked at him as just a teen or my little brother.

"Luna?" Gigi came up beside me. "Everything good?"

I took a deep breath, wanting to go inside and curl up with a glass of wine and a good book. "Yeah."

"I saw your brother."

My ears perked up at that. "Oh? Did you talk to him finally?"

Gigi rolled her eyes. "I always talk to him but..."

It's never alone, I wanted to add.

"Anyway, just came to make sure you were good. I saw that your parents stopped by. Vinny's friend couldn't handle his alcohol it seemed." Gigi glanced around the backyard. "I really need to be more careful about who I invite."

I quietly excused myself and headed back into the house. My name was called, I waved but I didn't stop until I reached my bedroom.

Tonight held so many new revelations, I wasn't sure what to do with them.

Watching Zach stand up to my father, even if no words were said, sent a rush of excitement through me.

Dad might not have had everything to do with this, but I knew he was one of the main reasons why Zach held back.

I had to make my dad see that I was an adult and that I was no longer his little girl before it was too late, and I lost Zach forever.

(Zach)

Staring Stone down was something I never thought I would do. He was a large scary fucker, but I refused to let him stand in the way of what I was trying to work toward. Even though I knew that I didn't deserve Luna, I couldn't help but touch her, kiss her, hold her. She had gotten under my skin years ago. It was like she burrowed herself into the marrow of my bones and refused to leave.

I knew Luna had believed the rumors. How could she not when I never denied them myself?

When I told her that there was no date and that I hadn't had sex in over a year, it was like something shifted between us. I could see the relief flood her eyes.

Yeah, sweet girl, I am all yours.

Truth was, I had trouble getting it up in the beginning. The nightmares from my past had become so frequent and overwhelming, that they'd appear in my waking thoughts. Until Luna, my body had a hard time reacting. But it wasn't for lack of trying. I had used sex as a way to numb the pain, but it got to the point that it didn't work. I could hear my stepmother's voice over and over in my head, telling me that I wasn't good enough. It got to the point, I could never finish, so I gave up and stopped having sex. Instead, I worked out. A lot.

I needed to tell Luna this. I needed to explain everything and tell her that it had only ever been her, but fear was a bitch and it stopped those words from leaving my mouth.

I blew out a slow breath and gripped the steering wheel tight in my hands. I shouldn't have left, but I knew that if I would have stayed like I wanted to, I would have ended up spending the night balls deep in Luna. She wasn't ready. She said she was. She acted like she was. But she wasn't. I knew, because I wasn't ready either. I didn't want to hurt her, but our friendship meant more to me than sex.

Even after realizing she had a crush on me, I never acted on it. As much as I wanted to, something always held me back. Her father. Me. My past.

Stone didn't think I was good enough for his daughter. Well, neither did I.

But I could still feel the heat between her legs. The way her pussy clenched around my finger. Her moans on my tongue as I kissed her.

My dick lengthened, pushing against the fly of my jeans. Fuck me. Just the thought of her had me wanting to beg like a bitch in heat. I wasn't used to this. This want. This incessant need where I couldn't do anything else but have Luna at my side.

I was like a caged animal. I craved her virginity and as much as that made me sound like a fucking caveman, I was determined to get it.

My hands white knuckled the steering wheel. Thoughts of Luna sucking me off while I was driving, rushed through my mind.

My cock lengthened even more, pushing against the fly of my pants.

As soon as I pulled up to my parents' place, I sent up a prayer that the lights were off. Either they were out, or they had retired for the night. When I drove into the garage and saw that it was empty, I breathed out a sigh of relief.

My parents were out, enjoying the marriage their love had created. I knew because when I was a kid, I had accidentally stumbled upon some toys they had collected over the years. After the abuse I had endured by the hands of my stepmother, I thought my dad was going to beat me for invading his privacy. But he only sat me down and explained in not so much detail, what the items were. It was only when I got older that he told me about the BDSM lifestyle.

"Isn't this like a no-no for you to be telling me about your sex life?" I should have been grossed out, but I wasn't. I was intrigued. Not with my parents' private life but by how open Coby...my dad was. How no matter what he and my mom had gone through, they talked about it. I had learned very quickly that communication was key.

"Maybe it's not the norm for me to be telling you." Dad shrugged. "But I don't give a shit. You and I both know that life

isn't normal. I would also rather you learn from me than the Internet."

Made sense. "So why now?"

"You're eighteen." And I wasn't a virgin went unsaid. Meaning, I fucked an actual woman and not...I swallowed hard, nightmares from my past trying to take over.

"Listen to me, Son." My dad placed a gentle hand on my arm. "Whatever you do, whatever you're into, just please make sure it's consensual. If it's men or women, I don't give a shit, as long as you have their consent."

I laughed. "Are you trying to tell me that you wouldn't care if I was gay?"

"I wouldn't." He sat back in his leather recliner. "As long as you're treated well, I couldn't give a shit."

I smiled, my heart warming even more for the man I had looked up to for as long as I could remember. "I'm not gay but thank you."

He nodded once. "I just want you happy, Zach." He pointed at me. "And please remember, communication is key."

And somehow, I had forgotten that. There was no way I could tell Luna how I felt. Even though I knew she would return the same feelings for me, she deserved someone not so...broken.

"Ten minutes."

My dick leaked at the memory of Luna begging me earlier in the night. How she told me to meet her in her room in ten minutes. And how her father ruined the chance for me to be with her. To be with the woman I had wanted for what felt like my whole life. I knew she would be good for me but at the same time, would I be good for her?

"Communication, Zach. Remember it."

Some people would probably frown on the fact that my parents were open with me. But I didn't care. It only made me curious and want to explore.

Luna.

My dick lengthened.

Fuck.

Palming my cock, I left my car and ran into the house. It was moments like this where I wished I didn't live in the city. But always having my room at my parents' place, I took advantage of this moment. I didn't think I could make it the hour's drive without jerking it a couple times.

Unlocking the door, I shoved it open and slammed it shut. Falling back against it, I took a deep breath and closed my eyes.

No woman had ever affected me this way. Something about tonight made me realize I couldn't wait anymore.

I wanted Luna and I was going to have her. Even if it was just for one night. I needed to know what she tasted like. What made her breath catch? What made her moan? I wanted her to look at me like I was her everything and nothing all at the same time. I wanted to be hers. But I knew she wasn't ready for me. Hell, was I even ready for *her?*

Reaching into my pants, I almost fell to my knees when my hand came into contact with my swollen cock. I imagined it was Luna. On her knees. Licking those full pouty lips of hers. Her looking up at me with pleading eyes. Waiting. Ready. Begging to taste me.

She would ask for permission and I would willingly comply. I pinched the tip of my dick.

A hiss escaped me.

Fuck me, I was going to hell. I shouldn't have these thoughts about her. I still remembered the way her wet pussy clenched around my finger. It gripped me like a fist, sucking me in even deeper. Her cunt had pulsed, squeezing, vibrating with need for me.

Pre-cum dripped from the head of my cock. I swiped my thumb across it, a shiver trembling through me.

Bringing my hand up to my mouth, I licked the slick tip and swallowed the salty essence that my body produced.

Before I came in the foyer of my parents' house, I trudged to my room, slammed the door shut, and ripped open my fly the rest of the way.

I fisted my cock, gripping it tight and started giving it hard strokes. My breathing picked up. A sheen of sweat coated my skin.

I tried forcing the image of her out of my head, but I couldn't stop it. Luna was in my mind's eye so clear, it was like she was standing right in front of me.

My hand picked up speed. As much as I wanted to prolong the orgasm, my dick ached. My balls were heavy, needing the release they'd been craving since Luna and I kissed earlier that night.

A groan escaped me when my dick twitched as I remembered her tongue in my mouth, dancing along with mine. Her mewls of pleasure. Her begging, hinting. Her grabbing my fucking hand and sticking it between her legs.

Suddenly, my legs gave out. I fell to my knees, still keeping a hold of my dick.

"Luna," I bit out through clenched teeth.

My fingers dug into the carpet, my other hand jerking my cock hard and fast. I chased that orgasm like I never had one before. Like I couldn't get enough. Like I needed it to fucking survive.

A hot shiver trembled through me when my phone vibrated in my pocket.

Pulling it out, I threw it in the floor in front of me as Luna's face flashed on the screen.

Another groan escaped me at seeing her beauty.

My dick throbbed, a blinding light flashing before my eyes. Cum shot out of me, coating my hand and dripping onto the floor.

"*Fuck*," I bellowed out, my whole body soaked from exertion. It had been a long time since I had an orgasm and I knew that because of Luna, maybe I could finally heal.

Not realizing I closed my eyes, I opened them. My gaze landed on my phone with my cum covering the picture of Luna when she called a second time.

No voices sounded in my head. My stepmother's awful words didn't dig their way into my soul. It was because of Luna. It had to be. It all made sense now but still terrified me just the same.

As Luna's face flashed across my screen, my dick lengthened at the sight. It swelled in my hand, clearly ready to go again.

Fuck.

(Luna)

"Yeah?"

I frowned. "Why haven't you been answering your phone?" I had called Zach several times before he actually answered.

He cleared his throat. "I just got in. Didn't hear my phone."

"Oh okay. What's going on?" He was lying. He always answered his phone and had the sound on.

"Nothing, Luna." He cleared his throat again.

"You're lying." I sat up in bed. "Talk to me."

"I'm fine, Luna. It's nothing."

"Alright." I slumped back on my bed. "Are you alone?"

"Yeah, Moonbeam," he murmured. "Just me and my hand. My parents are out for the night."

A breath I didn't realize I had been holding, left me. "Well I just called to make sure that you're—wait. Your hand?" I sat up, leaning on my elbow. "I…what were you doing?"

"Fuck, Luna. You can't ask me shit like that. I've been hard all fucking night. Ever since we kissed. Ever since you stuck my hand between your legs and begged me to finger you. I can still feel your ripe little body sucking me in even deeper."

"Oh…" My cheeks burned at his confession. "I wish you hadn't left."

"I know but I need slow. I don't know what we're doing but I also don't need your dad kicking my ass before I can prove…"

"Before you can prove what, Zach?" That he was good enough for me? That we deserved to be together?

Zach inhaled deeply. "Get some rest, Moonbeam. We'll chat tomorrow."

When he hung up, I stared at my phone, wondering what the hell happened tonight. One moment we were kissing, on the verge of fucking in public and then my dad showed up. They had a stare down and Zach pushed me away. He fell within himself and I had no idea how to get him out of it.

I crawled into bed, thinking about when I was sitting on Zach's lap. His hot breath on my neck. His semi-erection straining beneath my ass. My lips still tingled from the rough bite and kiss of his mouth on mine.

My stomach tumbled, my core needing to be filled by something other than fingers. I groaned and rolled over onto my side, punching my pillow. The longer I thought of what happened and what could have happened, the hotter I became. My heart raced. An ache I never experienced before, settled between my legs. God, what I wouldn't give to feel him harden like that beneath me again.

Mustering up the courage, I dialed Zach's number.

"Moon—"

"Zach," I breathed, not sure what I was getting myself into. "We almost had sex tonight. We were going to have sex. I told you to meet me in my room in ten minutes but then my dad showed up. Would you have come to my room if he hadn't?"

"Luna."

"Answer me." I sat up, leaning against the headboard. "I need to know."

"Yes, Luna. Yes, I would have come to your room and fucked you. It wouldn't have been making love either. None of that romance shit you read about in your books. It would have been pure hard fucking because I…"

"You what?" I whispered.

"I should go."

"No." I gripped my phone tight. "Tell me, Zach."

"It's all I can give you. I wanted to rip your pussy open with my dick. I have no self-control when it comes to you, Luna. You should stay away from me."

My heart sped up. "You know that's not going to happen." I didn't believe him. I knew there was a gentle side to him that he never showed anyone.

"Luna? What are you doing? What do you want?"

"I…I don't know." My breathing picked up. I wanted him. I ached for him. "Something happened tonight. When I fell in your lap. When we kissed. When I felt your finger deep inside me. The things you said."

"You have no idea what you're getting yourself into."

"I don't care. I want more. I want…I want something." I squeezed my breast, pinching my nipple. "Zach."

"Fuck me. Tell me what you're doing. Right now."

I wasn't sure what was coming over me.

"Tell me, damnit."

"I..." *God, get it together Luna.* "I have to go."

"No," he rasped. "You called me, Luna."

I hung up, mentally smacking myself at even calling him in the first place.

My phone rang, indicating a video call this time.

Oh God.

I answered, finding Zach staring back at me.

"I'm going to give you one chance to tell me what the fuck is going on," he said, his jaw rigid.

"Or else what?"

"Don't test me," he said, his voice filled with warning.

As much as I wanted to see how far I could push him, it would wait.

"Tell me what you're doing."

Mustering up the courage from somewhere deep down inside me, I leaned the phone against the headboard and scooted back on my bed.

"Luna." His gaze roamed over me. "Shit."

"You can come over," I said, my voice husky.

"As much as I would love to do that, this is better at the moment." He licked his full mouth. "Touch yourself for me."

I swallowed hard, hesitating.

"Come on, Luna. You initiated this. Touch yourself. Play with that pretty little kitty. Pinch your nipples. I don't give a shit. Just do something."

"I got a better idea," I told him, jumping off the bed. I locked the door and stripped. Moving to the end of the bed, I slid up the length of it, careful not to show Zach any part of me that I knew he wanted to see.

"Luna." His eyes darkened. "Are you fucking naked?"

I grinned, swiping my tongue along my bottom lip. "Maybe."

"Woman." His nostrils flared. "You're playing a dangerous game."

"I don't care." I reached a hand beneath my hips. When my fingers came into contact with my soaked center, I let out a soft gasp. I wasn't sure if it had been the few drinks I had throughout the night or what it was, but this was exhilarating. This newfound bravery was exciting and something I had been looking for.

"More, Luna. Give me more."

"Zach," I purred, flicking my finger along my clit. Pleasure erupted through me, my eyes fluttering closed.

"That's it, baby. Touch yourself for me."

Spreading my legs, I inserted a finger inside of me, imagining that it was Zach. Thrusting in and out, I undulated my hips. Back and forth. Side to side. A moan left me, the ecstasy I felt for the man on the phone, sliding between us.

"Shit, Luna."

My eyes popped open, finding Zach's hand wrapped around his cock. I coughed. "Holy hell."

"This is for you, Luna," he said, his voice rough. "All of it."

"God."

His eyes locked with mine. "Don't come."

I whimpered. "Then you can't come either."

His hand pumping his cock, slowed to a stop. He squeezed the base, blowing out a slow breath.

"You can still come over," I said, rubbing that tiny little bundle of nerves between my legs.

"As much as I want to, I have a long day tomorrow."

"Too bad," I said breathlessly.

"You better not come, Luna. I want you to explode all over me when we finally get the chance to fuck."

"God." As much as I didn't want to, I withdrew my hand from between my legs. Bringing my fingers up to my mouth, I licked the essence of my desire off of them.

He groaned, stuffing his cock back into his pants. "It's going to be a long fucking night."

I laughed. "Good night, Zach."

"Good night, Moonbeam. Dream of me."

And I did.

(Zach)

I was pacing back and forth for the last half hour when a knock sounded on the door.

"Yeah," I called out, still wondering what the hell Luna had been thinking. I never thought she would be brave enough to make a move let alone initiate phone sex. Watching her with her hand between her legs had me almost coming undone instantly. Neither of us had started anything until now. I was confused but I also wanted to take her up on her offer even though I knew we would end up in dangerous territory.

"Hey, Son." My dad stepped into the office that was joined to his. His dark eyes glanced around the room before piercing into me. "Everything okay?"

How he knew when something was wrong was beyond me. It happened every damn time I started pacing too.

"I'm confused," I confessed, not liking the sound of the vulnerability in my voice. After my little chat with Luna, I needed out of my bedroom and went to my office, thinking it would distract me from her. But it didn't help and only made me more wired instead.

"About what?" he asked, sitting on the leather couch leaning against the far wall.

"My friendship with Luna." I joined him. "I think it's growing into something more." A lot of people hated talking to their parents, but I found I needed it. Although I was adopted, I never felt like I wasn't a part of them, and they never made me feel any less than their child.

"You've been close since you were kids and she's always had a crush on you. Are you starting to feel something toward her?"

"I've always cared for her. Is it turning into something more? I don't know but I do know I want to try. Something. Anything. With her." I wasn't ready for a relationship. Never had been. It was too much like giving up control. I wanted to fuck her but at the same time, I didn't want to be with anyone else.

"I get that, but I will warn you, her dad will kick your ass if you hurt her." Dad rose from the couch and grabbed a bottle of water from the mini fridge I kept stocked and handed me one.

"He'll probably kick my ass even if I don't hurt her," I mumbled, wishing I had something stronger than just water at the moment. "He doesn't like me."

Dad scoffed. "Trust me, Son. It has nothing to do with you as a person. It's because you're a man. It doesn't matter if you were some random stranger. He wouldn't like you no matter what."

"You would think he would want someone for his daughter who actually knows her and not some fucking stranger." I pinched the bridge of my nose, trying to ward off the impending headache.

"Yeah." Dad laughed. "I didn't have to deal with parents when I was dating your mom. I just had her brothers to worry about."

I smiled. "And how did that go?"

"Your Uncle Greyson kept me on my toes, but I won her heart." He shrugged. "I would have burnt the mother fucking world down for her."

My heart warmed. I wanted that same love for someone that he had for my mom. I wanted their connection. That trust and communication. "I want the same."

"You'll find it, Zach." Dad cupped my shoulder. "Just be careful. Luna loves her father."

Meaning, she would probably choose him over me. But I wasn't sure if she actually would or not. He seemed to raise her better than that. Especially with someone as headstrong as Creena for a female role model.

"Just take it one day at a time and don't pressure her into doing anything she doesn't want to do. I imagine she isn't as experienced as you."

My dick twitched at her being pure and untouched. The thought of taking her virginity and making it mine, stirred something dark and feral inside of me.

Dad laughed harder. "Yeah. You are definitely my kid."

I only grinned.

"Well." Dad stood from the couch. "I should head to bed and try and get some sleep before your mom starts worrying." He paused at the doorway, turning back to me. "I'm just going to tell you one thing. Don't hurt Luna and lead her on. If you're not into her, stop whatever it is you're doing before it goes too far."

"I like her." I had no intention of leading her on.

"Good." Dad stared at me. "I've heard the rumors. I'm sure she has too."

"It's not true," I confessed.

"How long?"

"Over a year."

He nodded once, left the office, and quietly closed the door behind him.

I sighed, slumping onto the couch.

I needed a drink.

EIGHT

Luna

HEADING INTO THE DOVE Project, I was looking down at my phone when I bumped into someone. "Oh. Sorry."

"Are you okay?"

I looked up, finding Clara Blanco staring down at me. "I'm so sorry." I laughed lightly. "I'm distracted apparently." Add to the fact that I hadn't talked to Zach in a few days and I was a mess.

"No problem." Her bright blue eyes warmed. "I was just leaving." She glanced at her phone, a soft sigh leaving her full red mouth.

"Everything okay?" I always liked her. She had been nothing but nice after signing on to volunteer at the center a couple of months ago.

"I have a blind date coming up and I'm a little anxious." A nervous laugh bubbled out of her. "It's been awhile."

"You got this." I patted her hand. "You're beautiful and kind. I'm sure you'll have the guy eating out of the palm of your hand in no time."

Her grin grew. She fluffed her long blonde hair, giving me a wink. "Well, I am irresistible."

"Now you sound like Meadow." I smirked, shaking my head.

"Well she is pretty awesome." Clara had become friends with all of us but kept mostly to herself. She didn't live in our town, so she never came to the parties that Gigi threw. As much as Gigi insisted. Clara preferred to go to school, work, volunteer at the center, and that was it. It made me like her even more because I would probably be the same way if I didn't live with the girls.

"I hope you have fun on your date, and I can't wait to hear all about it," I told her. "But I should get inside."

"Thanks, girl," she said, walking past me. "Have a good one."

"You too," I called over my shoulder. I headed to the door of the large building and stopped. Turning back around, I saw Clara talking to Aiden and Ashton. They looked my way every so often.

My heart stuttered, wondering what that was about.

"Luna?"

I jumped, spun around, and found my mom and Jay Rodriguez coming toward me. "Hey, sorry I'm late."

"No problem." Jay smiled, the wrinkles at the corners of her eyes becoming more pronounced. "Come. Ainsley's waiting for you."

A few days later, I was getting dressed when thoughts of my desperate phone call to Zach crashed into me. My body heated. Although, I had forgotten what we had done, every time I went to bed at night, he invaded my dreams. I still couldn't believe I had gotten up the courage to do that. And watching him touch himself...my body hummed. Yup. Definitely unexpected.

We were only able to text with how busy we had both been at work. My mom and Jay had needed me to help Ainsley, one of the other girls who worked at The Dove Project, with fixing up the place.

They also had a biker club come into the tattoo shop Jay owned, unexpectedly, who wanted new ink since they were staying in town for a few days. I had set up the appointments and both my mom and Jay were so busy, they had to call in a favor and get help.

Finally getting a day off on Saturday, I slipped into a cute red bikini. It had been the first sunny day all week, so I wanted to take advantage of it while I could.

Throwing on a white sheer button up shirt, I pulled my hair back into a ponytail. Just as I was about to leave my room, my phone dinged.

Zach: You free today?

I smiled.

Me: Yes.

Zach: Good.

My heart thumped. I wasn't sure if it would be awkward, knowing what we had done a week ago. Add to the fact that we almost had sex too. I was thankful he turned down the date. When he cleared the air about the rumors, I wondered why he didn't do that when they first started spreading. Maybe he found it easier not to. I was sure it could get tiring after a while and he probably just gave up.

Zach and I hadn't talked about it but clearly, there *was* something going on between us. Something that neither of us could deny. Not that I wanted to anyway, but I knew even though Zach wanted me, and I wanted him, something was holding him back. I just didn't know what it was.

A knock sounded on the door.

"Come in." I gave myself one last glance in the mirror and let out a soft sigh.

"Holy shit, girl."

My head whipped around. I squealed when I realized who was standing at the door.

Piper Michaels laughed, closed the distance between us, and pulled me into a hard hug.

"How are you? When did you get back? Your parents must have missed you something fierce. It's been way too long."

She giggled at my badgering of questions. "I'm good. I got back last night and yes, they missed me but also understood that I had to come see my favorite people. God, I've missed you girls."

I wasn't sure how Piper did it, but she convinced her parents, Maxine and Dale, to let her backpack across Europe for the past three months for her birthday.

"But how are *you*?" She spun me around. "You look good. You've lost weight."

"You think so?" I had always been curvy thanks to my father's cooking and Meadow's constant baking. But I decided in the last year to become more active, so I took up running.

"Girl, Zach is going to eat you up when he sees you in this."

My head snapped up. "Why would he care?"

She laughed. "We all know you've had a crush on him for years. But I heard you're becoming closer." She winked.

"Gigi has a big mouth," I muttered.

"I heard that," Gigi yelled from the hallway.

"You were supposed to," I called back.

We all laughed.

"Tell me about your trip," I told Piper, hooking my arm in hers and leading her out of my room.

"It was so good." Her cheeks reddened. "Really good."

I paused in my steps, forcing her to stop beside me. "How good?"

"Uh…" She coughed, a light laugh leaving her. "I met someone. I don't want to talk about it just yet but…" She shrugged. "Anyway. Don't tell the twins. I need to talk to them still."

"I won't." I searched her face.

She averted my gaze.

"Well, I can't wait to hear about everything you saw," I said, changing the subject.

She glanced my way, a grin spreading on her face. "I've never taken so many pictures in my life."

I laughed. "Come outside with me. I'm going to soak up this sun while I can."

She nodded, telling me about the food she ate, the sights she saw, and the places she went to.

As I listened to her tell me all about her trip, I couldn't help but wonder how it would go with the twins. She was the only girl Ashton and Aiden dropped everything for. They enjoyed threesomes and were not discreet about their exploits. Piper was their best friend, but we all knew it went beyond that. But we also knew that Piper wasn't into it as much as the guys were. I had a feeling the person she met on her trip, had something to do with this, whether she liked to admit it or not.

I left Piper in the house and headed out to the backyard. Grabbing one of the loungers, I took off my cover up.

Resounding whistles erupted around me.

I laughed. "Thanks guys."

"You look good girl." Gigi handed me a bottle of water.

"I know." I winked, taking it from her.

She grinned. "I think our families want to have dinner next week at my parents' place."

"Oh," Meadow exclaimed. "Backyard barbeque."

I jumped. "Where the hell did you come from?"

She rolled her eyes. "I'm small but I'm not that small. You guys just don't pay attention." She spun on her heel and headed back to the house. "I'll start planning out some new desserts."

"I swear your sister's a ninja," I told Gigi.

She laughed, shaking her head. "She takes after our father that way." She paused. "How's your brother doing?" she asked me while I sprayed on some sunscreen.

"Good." I passed her a glance. "Why?"

She shrugged, sitting on the lounger beside me. "No reason."

I bit back a laugh.

"Is he seeing anyone?" she asked, averting my gaze.

I smiled. "Why don't you just admit that you have a thing for him?"

She gasped, feigning shock. "I have no idea what you're talking about. Besides, he's only nineteen. And I'm still dating Matt. But God, I feel like a dirty old woman."

I laughed. "He won't be nineteen forever you know."

"That's true." She sighed.

My brother worked with Ashton and Aiden's father's construction company now that he was done school. Although he had no idea what he wanted to do with his life, he liked getting his hands dirty.

He had planned on becoming partners with Ashton and Aiden whenever their dad was ready to retire as well. Aiden was in the navy and was having problems. But none of us knew what those problems consisted of. It took him to a dark place whenever it was brought up, so we never questioned it further.

"I'm just curious if there's someone else," Gigi continued.

"No, but you do know that he's had some psycho exes. So just be careful," I warned.

"He's too young to have psycho exes." She scowled.

"I know." I continued setting up the lounger, getting ready for my tan.

"Um...Luna." Gigi cleared her throat. "Zach's here."

My heart jumped when I remembered the last phone conversation we had.

"That's nice." I swallowed hard.

"He's coming this way."

I followed her gaze.

Zach was coming toward us. His stride was long, his body stiff. His eyes were dark, taking in my form.

"He looks pissed." Gigi rose to her full height. "Good luck with that one, girl."

"Gee, thanks," I muttered, keeping my gaze locked on his.

My heart raced the closer he got.

When he reached me, he grabbed my upper arm in a rough hold and pulled me to the side of the house.

"Zach." I tried prying his fingers off of me, but he was too strong. "What the hell is your problem?"

"What the fuck are you wearing?" he demanded, his voice strained.

"It's called a bathing suit," I said slowly. "Have you never seen one before?"

"Not like this. Not on you. Fuck me, Luna. You're practically naked." He pushed me, backing me up against the wall.

"I am *not* naked. I'm completely covered. I'm trying to enjoy this weather while we still have it." Not that I needed to explain this to him. "And besides, you didn't seem to complain last week when I was naked."

"You need to cover up," he said, ignoring my comment.

"No." I pulled from his grip. "I don't. You are not my father."

"Your father would demand for you to put clothes on too." Zach's gaze traveled down the length of me.

"Well he's not here, now is he?" My breathing picked up the longer Zach stared at me.

"No." He brushed a finger over my shoulder, hooked it beneath the strap of the bathing suit top, and pulled it lower. "He's not. If he was, I don't think he would appreciate me doing this."

"Doing what?" I asked, licking my lips.

"Touching you." Zach backed me up even more, pushing me into the dark corner at the side of the house.

"Zach," I breathed, itching to touch him but keeping my hands at my sides instead. Something nudged at me and told me to wait for him to give me permission.

"I don't like knowing the twins can see you in this." His thumb ran over the fabric covering my nipple. "I don't like knowing that anyone can see you in this."

My breath caught in my throat. "They're focused on Piper." I wasn't sure if that was true or not but either way, it didn't matter.

"I don't give a shit." Zach pinched the nub.

I whimpered, arching into him.

"This doesn't leave much to the imagination." He pulled the fabric covering my breast lower, his gaze falling to my exposed skin. He licked his lips. "I can't wait to taste every inch of you."

I swallowed hard. "Who says you can?"

He grinned. "Trying to play hard to get, sweet girl? Who called me last week? Who initiated the phone sex?"

"I'm not like the other women you've been with," I blurted.

"No, Moonbeam. You definitely aren't." In a quick move, Zach spun me around and shoved me up against the brick wall. "You're better," he growled in my ear, rubbing his erection against my ass. "I've been so damn hard for you all week. I keep touching myself, but I won't come. Not until I can explode inside of you."

I shivered. "Geeze, Zach. Do you always talk this way to women?"

He chuckled, the sound dark and inviting. "I haven't talked this way to a woman in a long time. But I know there's a slutty little girl inside of you." He cupped my breast, rubbing his pelvis against the seat of my ass. "You like my dirty words."

"Zach," I breathed, pushing back into him. "This is...this is too much. I can't..." My head fell back against his shoulder.

He gripped my hip, giving my nipple a pinch with his other hand. "You're so fucking beautiful."

Getting another moment of bravery, I grabbed his hand on my hip and moved it to the spot just above my bathing suit bottoms.

His fingers brushed beneath the fabric. "I want you. I want you so fucking much." His voice was rough, the delicious timbre sliding over every inch of me. He was losing control, on the verge of snapping, and I couldn't wait to help him pick up the pieces.

"Zach," I whispered, pushing back into him. I knew that we shouldn't be doing this out here. I knew that anyone could catch us at any moment, but I didn't care. It was like Zach and I were stuck in our own little world and no matter what happened, it would always just be him and I.

"Fuck, Luna." He cupped my breasts in both hands, pushing his pelvis into me. "You make me so fucking hard." His hands ran down the length of my body. "I can't wait to fill you up. To make you scream my name. To make you *beg* for more."

A breath left me. I couldn't wait for any of that either.

Zach turned me around, pinched my chin, and forced me to look up into his dark eyes. They seared into me, promising me endless hours of mind-blowing pleasure.

With the back of his hand, he ran it down the center of my torso. A path of goosebumps followed, sending a hot shiver racing down my spine.

I licked my lips, staring up at him. Waiting. Hinting. Begging for him to take it further. My body vibrated, my soul screamed for him to make it his own.

"You want me," he said, his voice rough.

"Yes," I croaked.

His lips pulled up into a smirk. He moved his hand lower, brushing his thumb over the fabric covering my clit.

I jumped, a shot of electricity hitting me square in the center of my very being.

His eyes darkened. Running his thumb back and forth, he grabbed onto my hip with his other hand, holding me in place.

I chewed my bottom lip to keep from crying out. The pleasure consumed me. The more Zach rubbed, the higher that pleasure climbed.

"Zach," I whimpered, closing my eyes.

"No." Zach grabbed my chin in a rough move. "Look at me."

My eyes popped open.

"I want to watch your face when you come." He released my chin and slid his thumb beneath the fabric of my bottoms.

I shivered, leaning my head back against the fence. "God."

He chuckled, slowly inserting his thumb into me. "You're perfect. Did you know that?"

I laughed. "I'm not but thank you."

His dark eyes fell to my waist. "Definitely perfect." Hooking his fingers into the crotch of my bottoms, he pulled them to the side. "Christ, you're wet." He removed his thumb, brushing it gently over my throbbing clit. "So fucking wet."

"Zach," I whined, grabbing onto his shoulders. "Please."

"Shhh…" He leaned his forehead against mine. "Come for me, sweet girl." The rough pad of his thumb pushed and prodded, running back and forth over the swollen nub.

A tingle started in my toes, sliding up my legs to the center of my soul. My thighs trembled, my knees threatening to give out on me. A breathless gasp escaped me as the unexpected release rocked through every inch of me.

"That's it." Zach pushed two fingers into me. "Keep coming, Luna."

"Oh God." I cupped the back of his neck, digging my nails into his skin. "So good."

"So fucking good," he added, removing his hand from between my legs. He righted my bottoms, giving my hip a light tap. "I can't wait to fill this pussy up."

I shivered at the idea of him being inside me.

Seconds ticked by. Maybe even minutes where we just stared at each other.

"Zach, I…" I chewed my bottom lip, not sure what I was about to say. So rather than speaking, I lowered to my knees.

His eyes widened. "Luna."

"I've never done this before. But I want to. With you. No one will catch us." Even if they did, at the moment, I didn't care. "Please let me return the favor."

"You don't have to do this," he said, his voice raspy.

"I know." I reached out for him, grabbing onto his pants and undoing his belt buckle. "But I want to."

(Zach)

I didn't make Luna come to get something in return. My father taught me better than that. I had learned how to respect a woman and make her give me everything I had wanted just by using her body, but I still never expected anything out of it.

With Luna staring up at me with those bright eyes of hers, I couldn't help but reach out and run my thumb along her bottom lip. The same thumb that had been inside her tight body. The same thumb that she could smell her desire on. The same thumb that had given her what I could only assume was her first orgasm that wasn't by her own touch.

"Zach." My name was husky on her tongue. That single word falling from her lips forced a drop of pre-cum from the very tip of my cock.

Instead of speaking, I dropped my hand to my side and gave up the very control I had spent my whole life taking advantage of. But could I really give up that control? Could I really open up completely and allow Luna to know the real me without getting hurt in the process? I told myself that this was just physical. Luna had an itch and I was the one who would scratch it. We would do our thing and she would move on. I knew because once she found out how deep my damage went; it would scare her away.

Shaky fingers undid the button on my pants, tugging me out of my thoughts. Lowering the zipper, she pulled the fabric apart and moved the waist of my boxers low enough so she could get access to the part of my body that ached for her.

Her tongue swiped along her lip, a flush of red hitting her cheeks.

Leaning a hand against the fence, I clenched the other at my side. It took everything in me not to take control of the situation, but this was for her. All for her. I wasn't sure why things had changed so suddenly but at the moment, I didn't care. I couldn't for fear that this would end before I could feel her hot mouth wrapped around my cock.

"I don't know what I'm doing," she said, staring up at me through dark lashes.

"Fuck." My cock jumped. "Your innocence is going to kill me."

A sly grin spread on her face. Reaching out, she ran her thumb along the length of my swollen cock. "I know we could get caught at any moment but I..." Her cheeks reddened even more. "I find that I don't actually care about that."

My dick jumped at her words. "No one will see you." I shielded her from any unexpected viewers.

She nodded slightly, lowered the zipper all the way, and reached a shaky hand into my pants. "I want to make you feel good."

Geeze. I was going to come in my pants like a prepubescent boy if she kept talking like that.

A part of me felt I should stop this. The part that wanted to devour every inch of her. To savor her. Taste her. Make her moan my name. This should be happening in private. Not at the side of her house where anyone could walk in and catch us with my dick down Luna's throat. But that other part took over. It controlled my actions. Igniting the desire, I had for the woman kneeling before me. The dark part. The depraved part. The part that wasn't good enough for her. I ignored everything inside of me that said to stop this and just felt.

Luna pulled my aching cock out of my pants, licked her lips, and slid her mouth down the length of it.

I groaned, latching a hand onto her hair. Taking a deep breath, I reined in on the control I currently didn't have. I didn't want to scare her by doing what I really wanted to do.

Her throat closed around my cock. She gagged, sucking me in even deeper.

For someone who had no idea what she was doing, she was fucking incredible.

"I'm not going to last long," I said through clenched teeth. My balls drew up into my body, a hot shiver raking over every inch of me.

Luna moaned, releasing me with a wet smack and licking along the slit in the head of my dick.

"Fuck," I growled, tightening my hold on her hair.

Lowering her mouth back onto me, her cheeks hollowed out, sucking me even farther between her lips.

A hot tingle shot up my spine. "I...Luna..." I gripped her hair, pulling her against me and began pumping my hips. I couldn't control this need, this desire, this damn urge to fuck her face. I wanted to be gentle. I wanted to show her that I could be what she needed but the pleasure coursing through me took over.

She gagged again, her hand clasping onto my hip, but she didn't push me away. She took what I gave her and submitted completely.

(Luna)

I couldn't believe I was doing this—giving Zach head at the side of the house where anyone could walk in at any moment. I never thought I could be adventurous but clearly, when it came to him, I wanted to explore every kinky fantasy both of us had.

"Luna."

My name fell from his lips on a hard growl. Before I could stop to take a breath, his cock swelled, releasing into my mouth and down the back of my throat.

I choked, swallowing every drop of him.

"Fuck me." Zach gripped my hair, pulling my head back and falling from my lips. He wrapped a hand around his cock, pumping a couple more times. The rest of his release landed on my chest.

My core clenched that we had done something so...*dirty*.

Once Zach calmed down, he stuffed his cock back into his pants. Helping me to my feet, he crushed his mouth to mine and backed me up against the fence. "Thank you," he murmured against my lips.

"You don't need to thank me," I said breathlessly.

Zach leaned his forehead against mine, running his thumb through the drops of his release on my chest. "I'm sorry for being rough."

"Don't be."

He gave me a lopsided grin before he released me and headed back to the lounger I had intended to tan on.

Coming back a moment later with a towel in hand, he ran the soft material over my chest.

Something flashed in his dark eyes.

"Zach?"

He cleared his throat. "I want you." He met my gaze then.

My heart jumped. "I want you too but…I can't compete with the other women you've been with. I'm not experienced."

"There's no one you need to compete with, and I don't give a shit that you're not experienced, Luna. I want you. I'll teach you what I like but I have a feeling that you'll be able to figure it out all on your own."

"Really?" Was that even possible?

"Yeah, Moonbeam." He kissed my nose and then my mouth. "I can't wait to fill you with every inch of me."

I shivered at the thought. "What if it hurts?"

He chuckled, sinking his teeth into my shoulder. "You'll enjoy it, baby. I promise you that."

"I'm not one of your whores, Zach," I blurted.

He leaned back, searching my face. "I already told you that I haven't had sex in over a year. What do you take me for?"

"I'm sorry." I took a deep breath. "I've seen the women you've been with. I have known you forever, remember?"

He sighed. "I deserve that. But people can change, Luna. Remember that."

"I'm not experienced, and I don't want you to be disappointed," I confessed.

His face softened. "I could never be disappointed." He brushed the back of his hand down the side of my face. "Not with you. Never with you."

(Zach)

Luna raised an eyebrow. "I guess you'll need to prove it then," she threw back at me.

Voices sounded close by, so I released her. As much as I enjoyed the feel of her beneath my hands, I had to pull it back and rein in the beast inside of me.

"Zach." She looked up at me with lust in her dark eyes.

"As much as I want to fuck you, I don't want a show." I brushed my thumb over her bottom lip. "I'll end up killing any fucker who sees you or even hears your screams." I kissed her forehead. "Go tan."

I'll come for you later, sweet girl.

NINE

Luna

I DID AS ZACH said and laid out in the sun. It ended up only being for half an hour when I was pulled from my lounger by Gigi and Piper.

The three of us jumped into the pool, followed by the twins and Meadow while Zach stood off to the side. He said he needed to make some business calls but no matter how much work he had to do, he was always watching me.

He had a small smile on his face. I thought he was keeping an eye on all of us when I realized he was specifically watching only me. Every time I moved, his eyes followed me. Knowing what we had done not too long ago, stirred something inside of me. I didn't know what my desires were. Or what kind of kinky fantasies I had but going down on him and in public no less, was hot as hell.

Once the sun was close to setting, I got a chill and excused myself from the group, so I could take a warm shower and wash the sunscreen off of me. Fantasies of Zach rubbing the sweet scent into my skin, stirred through me. My body tingled, an ache throbbing between my legs. I still couldn't believe I had given him head beside the house. A laugh escaped me, pride resonating on my shoulders that I was brave enough to do that sort of thing.

Thoughts of his cock deep in my mouth made my nipples pebble. I shivered, let out a hard sigh, and finished washing up.

Turning off the water, I wrapped a towel around me and left the shower. I didn't know what was going on between Zach and I, but I knew it was something I wanted. I wanted to see what could come of this. If anything at all.

Pulling the towel off of my body, I ran it through my hair and left the bathroom. Humming a soft tune to myself, I was stopped in my tracks when a throat cleared.

Zach stood by the door, leaning against it with his arms crossed over his chest. His dark eyes roamed down the length of my naked body.

My throat dried. I was half-tempted to shield myself. No man had ever seen me completely naked before. Especially not him. The man I had a crush on since I was a kid. The man who gave me my first orgasm only hours before. The man who had invaded my dreams for as long as I could remember.

My heart jumped. My stomach tumbled. My core heated.

Dropping the towel I used to dry my hair, I waited.

Zach closed the distance between us in three long strides. When he crashed into me, I couldn't help but notice how right this was. With his hands in my hair, he covered my mouth with his.

I moaned, opening to his rough kiss. My lips tingled, my hips undulated against him. He groaned, tugging my head back and fucking his way between my lips.

Zach ran a hand down my side, cupped the back of my leg, and wrapped it around his waist before backing me up against the wall. The pictures behind me, rattled at the rough movement. Every inch of him pushed into me.

His clothing covered erection rubbed against me, lengthening against my soaked center.

I whimpered, sliding my core along his rigid length. Although he was still fully dressed, I could feel every part of him.

Our breathing picked up. He wasn't even inside me and the pleasure was almost too much.

I released his mouth, unable to take it anymore. "Zach. I...holy shit."

He gripped my inner thigh, spreading me wide and picking up speed with his hips. "Come all over my pants, Luna. I want to smell like you."

"I need you inside me." I cupped his nape. "Please, Zach."

His eyes darkened. "Tell me, Luna. Tell me what you want." He leaned down, his mouth finding the soft spot beneath my ear. "Tell me how much you want me inside this greedy little cunt."

My body vibrated, pleasure burning through me. "Please," I whined.

"Say it, Moonbeam," he growled, nipping the side of my throat.

"Fuck me," I cried out, a fast release crashing into me.

Zach lifted me in both arms, slamming me up against the wall and crushing his mouth to mine.

Running my hands down his chest, I pulled his shirt from his pants and slid my fingers beneath the fabric.

He shivered, his muscles jumping under my touch.

Zach reached between us, unbuckling his belt and lowering the zipper to his pants.

I broke the kiss, watching, waiting for what he would do next.

He glanced down at me through hooded eyes, the lust billowing between us. "Take out my cock, Luna."

Reaching into his pants, I wrapped my fingers around him and pulled the thick length free.

"Fuck." A deep growl rumbled from his chest. "Shit." He leaned his forehead against mine, letting out a slow breath. "Your hand feels so fucking good."

A slow grin spread on my face. "Better than my mouth?"

"You're a naughty girl, Moonbeam."

I kissed his chin, running my thumb over the slit of his cock. A drop of pre-cum coated the tip.

Wrapping his hand around mine, he helped me guide the tip to my center.

"Please," I begged, trembling in his arms.

"I shouldn't be fucking you against the wall," he rasped.

"Then put me on my bed," I told him, tightening my legs around his waist. I didn't care that I was against the wall. I didn't care that I was a virgin and that no matter what position we were in, it would hurt. I knew that he would make me feel good. He would kiss away the pain and replace it with pleasure I had never felt before. I knew because I trusted him. Although we had shit to work through, I didn't care about any of that and just wanted to feel him instead.

Zach blew out a slow breath, rubbing the tip against my clit.

The shock of pleasure erupted through me. "Oh..."

"Come against my cock, baby," he murmured, pushing the tip of him into me at the same time a knock sounded on the door. "Fuck," he growled, stopping us from going any further.

Dammit. "Yeah?"

"*Piccola*," came a deep voice from the other side of the door.

My eyes widened. "Daddy."

(Zach)

Son of a bitch.

I tried pulling away from Luna, but she only latched on tighter. "Luna," I said through clenched teeth.

She gave me a look, her cheeks flushed with lust. For me. But she wouldn't let me pull away. "I'll be out in a moment," she called out. "He can wait," she told me.

"Not going to happen, sweet girl." As much as I wanted to fuck her, there was no way that I was doing that with her father standing on the other side of the door. I couldn't remember locking it. If I didn't, he could come in at any moment, see me between his daughter's legs, and kick my fucking ass.

"Luna." The doorknob jiggled.

I breathed out a sigh of relief that I had in fact locked the door even in my lust-filled state.

"I'll be out soon," Luna told him. "I'm getting dressed."

"Hurry up," Stone demanded. "I have a date with your mother."

"Wait for me out in the living room." Luna ran her thumb over the tip of my dick.

A low groan escaped me.

She grinned.

"Not happening, Luna," her father bit out.

Fuck. He knew. He fucking knew that she wasn't alone. I wasn't sure how he knew but Stone was a smart man. And a lethal one at that.

"Luna." I grabbed her hands, but she pulled them out of my hold. "I'm not doing this with you when he's clearly not leaving."

"He can wait." Luna wrapped her hand around me, pumping hard and fast.

"Luna," I grit out, leaning my forehead against hers. "What the hell are you doing?"

"Playing." She tilted her head, licking along my bottom lip. "I know you want me."

"Baby, you have me in your hands. I've never been so damn hard. Of course I want you."

She kissed my chin. "Good. Then come for me."

As soon as those words left her mouth, my release shot onto her stomach. "Fuck," I groaned.

Luna stared up at me with those dark brown eyes of hers.

I shook my head, clearing my throat. "I have no idea what the—"

"Luna," her dad barked.

I jumped, backing up and dropping her onto her feet. Righting my pants, I gave myself a good shake. That shouldn't have happened. Not like that. Not against her fucking wall.

"You better be fucking alone in there," her dad continued.

Luna rolled her eyes. "Hide in my bathroom," she said, picking the towel up off the floor and wiping it over her stomach.

The alpha inside of me roared, knowing that although she wiped up my release, she would still smell like me.

"Are you going to tell him about this?" I blurted. "About us?"

She frowned. "Is that what you want?"

"I—"

"Luna! Get your fucking ass out here."

Luna huffed, pushing me into her bathroom and shutting the door without so much as giving me an answer.

Voices sounded from the other side of door. One deep. One high. Both aggravated. I liked her dad. I respected the hell out of him but the fact that I let him control my actions when it came to his daughter, pissed me off.

Suddenly the door swung open, revealing a red-faced Vincent Stone.

I swallowed hard, backing up a step.

His dark eyes traveled down the length of me before jumping back to my face. "Should I kick your ass now or later? Or should I go to your parents and let them do it for me? Your mom is a violent little thing and I bet if I played the story just right, she would put you in her chair."

I frowned, not understanding what he meant.

"You see, I like your parents and I respect the hell out of them." Stone took a step toward me. "But the fact that you're in my daughter's bathroom is making me not give a shit about any of that."

"Daddy." Luna came to his side. "Will you stop, please? I told you he was helping me fix my toilet."

"Oh?" Stone glanced between us. "Is that so?" He chuckled. "You must think I'm a moron, *Piccola*." His gaze met mine. "I don't know what's going on between you two but whatever it is, I don't like it."

I crossed my arms under my chest. "I was helping her with the toilet like she said." I was taught to respect my elders, but a guy could only take so much before he snapped.

Stone gave me one final glance before he turned and left the bathroom. "Luna, I need to talk to you."

"I'm sorry," she muttered.

"It's fine. I should go anyway." I went to walk past her when she touched my arm. I glanced down at her.

"I *am* sorry," she repeated.

I only nodded, pushed past her and left her room without so much as giving Stone a second glance.

(Luna)

"Did you really have to do that?" I demanded of my father, placing my hands on my hips.

He sat on the edge of my bed, scrubbing a hand down his face. "You have to be careful. We've taught you that."

"What? You think Zach's going to hurt me?" I rolled my eyes. "Come on, Daddy. Seriously. I've known the guy since I was a little girl."

"Yeah." Dad dropped his hand to his side. "Exactly. He's not healthy for you."

"And some stranger is?" I cried, frustrated that my father felt the need to butt his nose into my business all the damn time.

"Be careful how you talk to me." Dad rose to his feet, towering over me. His dark eyes peered into mine.

"Then you need to stop this."

We stared each other down.

I let out a hard sigh, knowing that there was no point in arguing with him. Once my father had an idea in his head, that was it. He wouldn't see reason. Maybe I could talk to my mom. She could hopefully try and convince him that Zach and I were right for each other. That he was right for *me*. Before it was too late and I lost him to some other woman.

TEN

ZACH

I COULD STILL FEEL Luna trembling against me. Feel her hand wrapped around me. See the need in her eyes. She wanted me, that much was clear. But her father was a problem. A large problem and I had no idea how to get him to understand that I would go through him to get to his daughter. I didn't give a shit how big he was.

While Luna was dealing with her dad, I decided to leave her room and give them some privacy.

"Hey, Zach," both Ashton and Aiden said, coming toward me.

"Hey," I said, heading to the kitchen to grab a bottle of water.

"Are you going on that date?" Ashton asked.

I stopped, peering at him over my shoulder. "I told you I wasn't."

"Are you dating Luna yet?" he threw at me.

My jaw clenched so damn hard, a sharp pain shot up the side of my face. "That's none of your fucking business."

He laughed. "Didn't think so. If you aren't, do you mind if I ask her out?"

My brows narrowed. "Is that why you tried setting me up on that date? So, you could date Luna instead?" Thoughts of them together invaded my mind. Ashton was a good guy, but while the rumors about me weren't true, they were when it came to him.

Ashton smirked. "It was just—"

"Listen." Aiden stepped forward, giving his brother a glare. "Ignore him. We just want you happy. Both of you happy and if that's not together, well, I think this woman could be good for you. And if something comes out of this thing with Luna. Well…look at this date as a last hurrah before you're tied down."

"I'm not going on that date," I said, sounding like a damn parrot. "Besides, what's in this for you? Are you wanting Luna for yourself?" I took a step toward the twins. "Is that your thing? Sharing women? I know you've had a little thing with Piper, but I don't think Luna's willing to share. In fact, I know she's not."

A knowing glance passed between the twins.

"If you don't get your head out of your ass and make a move, I'll make mine. With or without your permission." Ashton lifted his chin. "I love you like a brother. You're family. But that girl deserves to be happy after pining over you for years when neither of you are doing a damn thing about it."

"Are you fucking kidding me right now?" I grabbed Ashton by the collar of his shirt and pushed him up against the wall. "You stay the fuck away from her."

"Make me," Ashton spat. "You can't date someone and not expect her to do the same. That's not how this shit works."

"I'm not dating anyone. Why the hell won't you believe me?"

"Because we know how you work. I've heard those rumors, Zach." Ashton's brows narrowed. "I know you like your women."

"That's why you set me up on the date all along, isn't it? Say it, Ashton," I demanded, tightening my hold on his shirt. "Say that's what your intention was."

"I have no idea what you're talking about."

I pulled him away from the wall and pushed him back against it, hard. "Tell me."

"Hey!" someone cried but I ignored them.

A strong hand clapped my shoulder. Knowing it was Aiden, it still didn't stop me from spitting the words to his twin, "What the fuck do you want with Luna?"

Ashton grinned. "I want to make her happy because clearly you're not doing fuck all about it. You're too fucking scared to do anything about your feelings for her."

"She deserves better," I blurted.

"*You* deserve her," Ashton said gently. "But it won't stop me from making my move."

Leaning toward his ear, I tightened my grip on his collar and lifted him onto his tiptoes. He may have been a few inches taller than me, but I was bigger. "You touch a single hair on her head, and I will gut you where you sleep. My black eyes will be the last thing you see before you take your last breath."

"Challenge fucking accepted," Ashton mumbled.

I released him roughly and took a step back. The hairs on the back of my neck tingled. I looked to my left and found Luna staring at me with wide eyes. But it wasn't her that bothered me. No. It was her father. He stood right behind her, his dark eyes telling all. What he just witnessed was all the proof he needed that I was nowhere near being good enough for his daughter. And I just slammed the last peg in my coffin. There went my fucking chance.

Good job, Porter.

Turning on my heel, I trudged back down the hall, ignoring the stares of the onlookers and Luna calling my name. I left the house, jogged to my car, and drove home before I did something really stupid. Like driving my fist through one of my best friend's faces.

I was running and that pissed me off even more.

Fucking hell.

(Luna)

"What the hell was that?" I cried, stomping toward Ashton. "What did you say to him?"

"Luna," my father said from behind me.

I ignored him and stabbed a finger against Ashton's chest. "What did you do?"

"I didn't do anything. But I said what he needed to hear." He shrugged like it was no big deal. Well it was. It was a very big deal.

"You're friends. You shouldn't be this way toward each other." Not unless a woman was involved. My eyes widened. Oh God. Was I that woman? Remembering the offer Ashton gave me not too long ago, I wondered if Zach found out about that. "Ashton," I murmured.

He opened his mouth to speak when he glanced over my head instead.

"I'm heading out," Dad said, cupping my shoulders and spinning me toward him. "I was supposed to fix your toilet remember? But Zach beat me to it." His dark eyes met mine. "You still pissed at me?"

I sighed, hugging my arms around his hard middle.

"I'm just looking out for you, *Piccola*," he said low enough for only me to hear.

I nodded. "Yeah." I pulled away.

He said his goodbyes and left the house. As soon as the door shut behind him, I spun on Ashton. "You and I need to talk."

A cocky grin spread on his face. "I'm all yours."

I bit back an eye-roll and headed to the backyard. When Ashton joined me, I placed my hands on my hips. "This shit needs to stop."

"I have no idea what you're talking about," he said, holding his hand out in front of him like he was checking his nails.

"Ashton." I stomped my foot when he didn't look at me. "Seriously."

His gaze flicked to mine. "I'm looking out for you." His face turned serious, his shoulders pulling back. "If Zach isn't going to make a move, I will. Plain and simple."

"Since when? You're sleeping with Piper."

"*Was* sleeping with her," he corrected. "Besides." He shrugged. "I like you."

"No, you like me because you can't have me." I slumped on the patio couch. "And since when are you attracted to me? This isn't like you. You don't go after what's not yours." Not that I belonged to Zach either but that was beside the point.

"Listen." Ashton sat on the couch beside me and took my hand in his. "I'm not doing this because I feel like being a dick to Zach. But like I told you before, he needs a push. Both of you need one. Or a kick in the ass. I'm not sure which. But if he's going on a date, you can too."

"He's not going on that date. Or any date for that matter."

"Not yet, he isn't."

I sighed, leaning my head back against the couch. "I don't understand what's going on. You're not helping, and neither is my father."

Ashton chuckled, releasing me and mirrored my pose. "Do you think your father would react the same way if it were me going after you?"

"Probably. It's clearly why I'm still a…" I clamped my mouth shut, not needing to talk about my virginity with someone other than Zach.

Ashton shot me a look. Clearing his throat, he stood. "Zach's a lucky fucker," he mumbled. "Anyway, Luna. It's been fun as always."

"Wait." I jumped to my feet. "Will you leave him alone?"

Ashton looked down at me. It was like his deep blue eyes were peering into my soul. "I will. For now." He walked past me and headed back into the house, leaving me alone once again.

(Zach)

As I was driving home, my phone rang. I pressed the button on the steering wheel. "Yeah."

"Hey."

"Gigi?" I frowned. "What's wrong?"

"Nothing. There's a dinner at my parents' place next week. Are you coming? I don't know what's going on between all of you, but I know my parents want you there. And your parents will be there so…yeah."

Shit.

"You forgot, didn't you? Listen, Ashton's an ass. We all know he does this shit just to get a rise out of people. You should know that."

"I do." But it still didn't mean I liked it.

"But I want you there and I know Luna does too." Gigi paused. "Will you come?"

"Yeah, I'll be there," I mumbled.

"Good." Her voice lifted. "I'm glad."

"Really? Why?"

She hesitated. "Well…"

"You have an ulterior motive, don't you?"

"Who me? See you later, Zach," she said, hanging up.

I sighed.

Women.

ELEVEN

Luna

"IS HE COMING?" I asked as Gigi came into the house from the backyard. She had called Zach after he left abruptly thanks to my father and Ashton.

"He is." She wrapped her arms around me, giving me a hard hug. "Who's the best?"

I laughed. "You are." I pulled away from her and sat at the kitchen table.

"Can you try these?"

I jumped as Meadow placed a plate in front of me. "Where the hell did you come from?"

"I was in the kitchen. Not my fault you guys always forget I'm here," she said, heading back to the part of the house she's only ever in, besides her bedroom.

"We do *not* forget you're here," I called out, glancing at the plate. "What is this?" I asked as Gigi sat down beside me.

"I don't know but it looks and smells delicious." She grabbed a pastry off the plate.

"Where's Piper?" I asked, still analyzing the pastries staring back at me. I was all for food but when I didn't know what it was, it took a lot for me to give it a chance. Almost like my personal life. Taking a chance on new things was terrifying.

"She went home to see her parents," Gigi replied, stuffing the tiny ball of dough into her mouth. "Holy shit," she said around a mouthful. "Meadow, this is amazing."

"Yeah?" Meadow came back to the table and sat across from us. "It's new and I wasn't sure how it would taste."

"What is it?" I tentatively picked up a pastry off the plate and gave it a sniff.

"Oh, stop being a pussy and just eat it," Meadow chided.

"Who mentioned pussy?" Ashton sat beside me. "Ooooh, what do we have here?" He picked up a ball of dough and shoved it into his mouth. A low groan followed soon after.

Meadow's grin widened. "See? Everyone likes it."

"Why do I feel like you're testing me?" I asked her, taking a bite of the small pastry. Flavor exploded onto my tongue. It was a mix of apples, strawberries and... "Lemon."

"Yup. I mixed up a batch of apples, strawberries, a couple of blueberries, and threw in some lemon as well. I even made the dough gluten-free and vegan." Meadow shrugged. "I'm glad it turned out."

"So, it's semi-healthy. Good." Gigi shoved another one into her mouth.

All of us laughed.

"Not like you need to worry about that. How many hours a day do you work out?" I teased, eating the rest of the pastry and licking my fingers.

"That's exactly the point." Gigi patted her stomach. "But the parents won't send their kids to a chubby dancer, so I have to stay lean."

I rolled my eyes at that. Gigi never liked to talk about it, but she blew her knee out and lost her chance at having a career in professional dance. So, she taught instead but even then, I wasn't sure how she did it. The parents of her students were rich snobs if you asked me.

"You do too much for those kids," Meadow said.

"At least I get paid for it." Gigi popped another pastry into her mouth. "I think after I'm done with this class, I might start teaching for the less fortunate. At least they'll appreciate what I do for them then."

"I like that idea," I told her.

"Me too." Meadow stuffed a pastry into her mouth. She sighed, patting herself on the back.

I giggled, eating another pastry.

Ashton took the empty plate and lifted it to his mouth. Giving it a long lick, he paused when he caught all of us staring at him. "What?"

"You're not a dog." Meadow took the plate from him and stood from the table. "Geeze, no wonder you're still single."

Ashton passed me a glance.

My cheeks heated. "I'm going to go read. Meadow, make some more of those yummy treats. Pretty please."

"I will," she called from the kitchen.

"Hey, Luna."

My eyes shot up, finding Aiden coming toward me. "Hey, where have you been?"

"I was in Gigi's room, making a business call. Trying to take over our father's business is proving more difficult than I thought." He sighed, shoving his phone back in the pocket of his jeans. "My brother still here?"

"Yeah. He's in the kitchen."

"Okay, thanks," he said, walking past me.

Heading to my room, I opened the door.

"Oh, Luna?"

I stopped, glancing down the hall toward Aiden.

"Ignore Ashton. Whatever is going on between you and Zach, will work itself out. I know it will."

"You should probably tell your brother that," I said, heading into my room without waiting for a response from Aiden.

I wasn't sure what had possessed Ashton to start that shit in the first place. Add to the fact that he never apologized.

My phone dinged, indicating an incoming text. I pulled it from my pocket, my body heating.

Zach: You good, Moonbeam?

Me: Yeah. I'm sorry about what happened. With Ashton and my father.

My phone rang then. "Hello?"

"You don't need to apologize for them," Zach said.

I frowned. "What number are you calling from?"

"I'm in my dad's office. My battery died."

"Oh." I sat on the edge of my bed. "I *am* sorry though. My father means well but he needs to mind his own business. I'm a big girl."

"Maybe you should listen to him."

"What?" I barked a laugh. "Are you serious right now?"

"I just mean that what he's saying is true. I'm not good enough for you, Luna. I never will be."

"He never said any of that. Is that how you feel?" I couldn't believe him right now. "You didn't seem to mind that you weren't good enough for me when I gave you a blowjob outside, Zach. Or when we almost had sex this afternoon."

"That shouldn't have happened. None of that should have happened."

I jumped to my feet. "Zach."

"Luna, he's your father. He knows—"

"He doesn't know shit," I snapped. "I'll see you later." I hung up the phone and tossed it on my bed. God, what the hell was wrong with the men in my life?

Scrubbing my hands down my face, I let out a huff before rising from the bed. Taking a quick shower, I rinsed the day off of me. As much as I didn't want to, I washed what Zach and I had almost done off of my skin.

We had been so close. So damn close to having sex and now he didn't want more? Well screw him. I would prove to him that he was wrong.

TWELVE

ZACH

SITTING AT THE BAR of the small Italian restaurant, I waited for my takeout order and felt the hairs on the back of my neck tingle. Glancing around me, I found a woman sitting at the bar a few stools down.

I frowned. Something about her was familiar.

She met my gaze. "Do I know you?"

"I don't know. I was just thinking that you look familiar."

Her brows furrowed. "I was thinking the same thing. I saw you come in. Are you waiting for someone?"

"Just my takeout. I ordered dinner for my parents." My dad had a long day after helping me tie up some business and I was repaying him. Not that I needed to, but I decided anyway to give them a break. And my mom loved the food here, so it was a win-win.

"Oh, that's sweet." The woman smiled. "I was waiting for someone, but it seems that I've been stood up." She sighed.

"I'm sorry to hear that." I had never been on many dates, but I could imagine that being stood up was embarrassing as hell.

"It is what it is." She took a sip of her martini, her gaze flicking to mine. "Do you ever come into The Dove Project?"

"I do. My mom is one of the owners."

"Yes!" she cried, snapping her fingers. "That's where I've seen you before. Can I be forward and ask what your name is?"

"Zach Porter." It explained how she looked familiar. I used to spend a lot of time there before I became busy with work.

"Are you fucking kidding me?"

My head whipped around. "Excuse me?"

"Do I look stupid to you?" the woman seethed.

I shook my head. "What the hell are you talking about?"

Her face turned red. "I was supposed to go on a date...with *you*, asshole."

My eyes widened. *Oh shit.* "I told Ashton I wasn't going on the date." I was going to kill him.

"Well he never told me that." The woman scrubbed a hand down her face. "I can't believe this. I can't believe I was stood up and then the guy still shows up. God, I'm so stupid."

"No, this is not your fault or mine. It's Ashton's."

"He said he talked to you but never told me that you said no." She turned to me, crossing her knee over the other. "You really said no?"

"Yes. There's someone else and it wouldn't be fair to her or you, for me to go on this date. That's why I said no. I can be an asshole but that's a dick move and even I would never do that."

She pursed her full lips. "Fine." She let out a heavy sigh, her shoulders dropping. "I'm sorry."

"No." I signaled the waiter over. "Let me buy you a drink. And then I'm going to murder my friend."

The woman laughed. "Well, since we're here. I guess I should introduce myself too." She rose from her stool and came toward me, sitting on the one beside me. "Clara Blanco." She stuck out her hand.

"It's nice to meet you." I returned the handshake, half-expecting to feel something. A jolt of excitement. A newfound energy. But there was nothing. Years ago, Clara would have been the type I had gone for.

Blonde. Blue eyed. Tanned.

Now, her type didn't do it for me.

Luna.

My body stirred.

I bit back a smirk. *She* definitely did it for me.

"So how long have you known Ashton?"

"Since I was a kid. How did you meet him?"

"Uh…" Her cheeks reddened. "We met at The Dove Project. He had just finished up some work and one thing led to another." She laughed. "I'm not usually that type but I was bored. Anyway, it was fun with him, but he ended up telling me about his single friend who needed a kick in the butt. I guess you're that friend."

"Yeah. I guess so." I still wondered what his true intention was with Luna and why all of a sudden, he was acting this way when he never made a move before. "I am sorry for the misunderstanding."

"Not your fault." Clara gave me a small smile. "Whoever this woman is, she's very lucky. Most guys these days would still have gone on the date with me."

"A couple years ago and I probably would have but I'm not that guy anymore." I shrugged.

"Good." Clara finished off her first martini and brought the second one to her lips. "Thank you for the drink."

I lifted my glass of water. "To a new friendship."

She smiled, clinking her glass against mine. "Cheers."

(Luna)

"So, he didn't go on the date."

"Nope." I leaned against my dresser, letting out a slow breath of relief.

"You're sure about that?"

I met Meadow's gaze. "Why wouldn't I be?"

She shrugged. "In my experience, guys lie."

"No." I shook my head. "I know there are rumors about Zach but they're not true. He actually told me he hasn't had sex in over a year."

Her eyes widened. "Really?" She sat on the edge of my bed, leaning back on her elbows. "Huh. So I guess when you guys finally have sex, it's going to be hot as hell."

"Uh…" My cheeks burned. "I don't think…"

She laughed. "Come on. I've seen the way you two look at each other. It's hot. So damn hot." She fanned herself.

I grinned, shaking my head.

A soft knock sounded on the door. It slowly opened, revealing Piper and Gigi.

"Are we having a party?" Gigi asked, jumping on the bed beside her sister while Piper stood off to the side.

"Ha. Just talking to Luna about Zach and his deliciousness." Meadow waggled her eyebrows.

"You're so weird." I laughed.

"So, what are you going to do about Zach?" Piper asked, joining the girls on the bed.

"I don't know." I shrugged. "He texted that he went to grab his parents some food on the way home from the city."

"Has your dad left you alone?" Gigi curled her long legs beneath her Indian style.

"He has. For now, anyway." I rubbed the back of my neck. "I'm just glad Zach never went on that date."

"Same." Meadow sat forward. "I could see Ashton doing something like that but not Zach. Not when he loves you. It's not how he's wired."

I coughed. "He does not love me."

"Right," the three of them said slowly.

"You guys are insane. He doesn't love me." I needed to do something though. I knew what we had was moving past just a friendship, but I needed him to see that as well.

"I think you should go see him. Maybe wear something sexy." Meadow shrugged. "Get him to beg."

I laughed. "I can't do that."

"Why not? I know he loves you. Hell, we all know it." She lifted her hand, stopping me from speaking. "You can argue all you want but if what you say is true and that he hasn't had sex in over a year, think about it, Luna. Why is that? The guy's hot. He was a whore in high school and then all of a sudden, he stopped? Come on. It's because of you."

"Alright, if all of that is true, why hasn't he made a move?" Although, she did have a good point.

"Maybe he's scared," Piper offered.

"Scared of what?" I asked.

"Relationships can be scary." Gigi shrugged.

"Either way, we know something's happened between you two. I saw you the other night. You were flushed and your hair was a mess," Meadow pointed out. "You can't stand there and tell us, your best friends, that nothing is starting between you two."

My eyes flicked between them. All three pairs of eyes stared back at me, waiting.

"Fine." I threw my hands up. "Yes, something has started but I don't know what else to do. It's my father." I scrubbed a hand down my face. "It has to be. I don't know..." I hated not knowing what was going on. Zach felt he wasn't good enough for me. But what gave him the right to decide that?

"Your dad is scary as fuck, Luna." Meadow sat forward. "But he is hot."

I grimaced. "Seriously?"

Meadow smirked. "I can't help it. Older men turn me on."

"Ew." I pushed off the dresser. "Please don't talk about my father that way."

"What? He's only thirty-something years older than me. But I bet he can still fuc—"

"Stop!" I cried, throwing a bottle of lotion at her.

She laughed, catching it in the air.

"You are a twisted individual." As confused as I was about the whole thing, I couldn't help but laugh.

"Okay, now that we've come to understand just how messed up my sister is, what are you going to do about Zach?" Gigi asked, taking all the fun out of the conversation.

"You had to go there, didn't you?" Piper nudged her. "Couldn't we just let Meadow lust over Stone?"

"Blech." I stuck out my tongue at them. "I don't know what I'm going to do. Maybe I should just let him go because clearly he doesn't want to be with me."

"Please." Gigi snorted. "He does want to be with you but obviously something is stopping him. We all know he's had a shitty past. That's no secret."

"I just wish he would tell me. Or maybe I'll just go to his place and talk to him."

"Talk." Meadow waggled her eyebrows. "Right. That's what I always do when I meet up with guys. They really love talking to me."

"Stop being a slut and let's focus on our friend's love life." Gigi placed her hands on her hips.

"Okay, Mom." Meadow rolled her eyes. "My sister, the buzzkill."

"Focus, ladies." I started pacing. "What would you do?" I stopped when no one answered me. "Nothing? Really?"

"Well…" Meadow looked between all of us. "All of us would say something different, Luna."

"She's right." Piper stretched out her legs in front of her. "I'm also in no position to voice an opinion seeing as my love life is non-existent."

"Same," Gigi murmured.

"What about Matt?" I asked her.

"Uh…" Gigi looked away. "We broke up."

"Good," Meadow and Piper said at the same time.

"Thank you for your sympathy." Gigi threw a pillow at them.

"Whatever." Meadow hugged the pillow against her chest. "Matt's a dick anyway."

"I'm sorry, Gigi. I really am." I looked at Meadow. "What would you do then? If you were me?"

"I would go to him and fuck his brains out but that's not you. You can't do casual sex. It's not in your blood. You need to tell him how you feel."

"But I don't know how I feel. That's the problem."

"No." Meadow pointed at me. "You just don't want to admit to your feelings. But either way. I would go to him and offer just casual sex then. Show him a good time. Let him know what he's missing out on. Make him see that he needs you and only you. Make him crave that hot little body of yours. But again, that's not you. That's me. Or it was. Anyway." She shook her head. "I'm not suggesting that. Don't do that."

"That confused me even more," I mumbled. "I'm a virgin. You girls know that. I can't just offer it up to him and be on my merry way." I raked a hand through my hair. "That's not how I am."

"We would never suggest that. That's what *I* would do. But I would never expect you to do the same." Meadow slid off the bed and came toward me. "Listen to me." She grabbed my hands. "You and Zach are the first of us to finally start something. To get somewhere. Whatever you have to do, whatever it takes, you *will* get there. Because you are meant to be."

"When did you become such a romantic?" I asked, shocked at my friend's words.

She shrugged. "Just go to him. Talk to him. And see what happens from there."

"I agree with her," Gigi said.

Piper nodded. "Same. Casual sex is dangerous anyway. Look at what happened with me and the twins. And besides, you deserve more than that."

"And I don't?" Meadow threw at her, raising a perfect eyebrow.

Piper rolled her eyes. "That's not what I meant." She looked back at me. "Talk to him."

Talk. I could talk. Couldn't I? Looked like it was time to find out.

Later that evening, I was standing at the back of Zach's parents' place like some damn creeper. I really couldn't believe I was going to go through with this. It didn't take much to slip out of my house and drive the few blocks here. I parked a few houses away, so I could go unnoticed. I just hoped that Zach was home and hadn't gone back to the city after dropping the food off for his parents.

Taking a deep breath, I stepped out from the shadows and ran up the backyard, thankful they didn't have one of those security lights. No, they had Brogan and Coby instead. Both of them were lethal and didn't need a security light to tell them when they had an intruder.

Once I reached the sliding glass doors leading to Zach's room, I paused. Peering into his bedroom, I saw that he wasn't in there. My heart raced.

Please be home.

Pulling a key from my back pocket, I unlocked the door. Memories of Zach giving me the key years ago, invaded my mind.

"If you're ever in trouble, you come here. Alright?" Zach held out his palm, a gold key laying on top of it.

"I'm fine," I said softly.

"I don't give a shit if you're fine, Moonbeam. Take the damn key."

I took that key and kept it on me at all times. No matter what happened or where Zach was, I knew I always had a safe place to go. Not that I had a bad childhood, but my father was overprotective. Sometimes I just needed to get away. But I never actually used the key until now.

Slowly opening the glass door, I waited with bated breath for Zach to appear out of thin air. When he didn't, I shook my head and forced myself to get it together.

I still wasn't sure what I was doing but I knew that I needed something. Anything. I needed to prove to him that this was right. That whatever connection we shared as kids, was turning into something more. Something that neither of us could deny no matter how much we tried to fight it.

Slipping into Zach's room, I quietly shut the door behind me and locked it. Taking in his room, I let out a breath I didn't realize I had been holding.

I had been in his room once but that was only because he needed me to grab his phone. I couldn't even remember when that was, but I did remember feeling elated that I was in Zach Porter's bedroom.

My eyes flicked to the large bed sitting against the far wall. It had two nightstands on either side of it. A tall dresser sat against the wall opposite me with a desk to my left. All of the furniture was dark. I imagined that was how his condo in the city was. Dark but inviting. Much like the owner himself.

Shaking my head, I dropped my bag onto the ground and took a step forward at the same time the door opened.

My eyes widened, my heart jumping to my throat.

Zach came into the room, holding his phone to his ear. "Yes, that's right." He shut the door behind him and leaned against it. "I know but I met him for dinner. That wasn't what he agreed on." He pinched the bridge of his nose. "Fine. I'll contact my lawyer." Zach laughed. "No. I'm not bothering my father with this. He already helped me enough today. Yeah, I grabbed him and my mom food tonight." He glanced up then, his gaze landing on me. "He has better things to do anyway than deal with a rich pompous..." He laughed again, the deep sound sliding over every inch of me. "Alright, I'll talk to you later. Thank you for everything. Oh, and I won't be available the rest of the night." He hung up the phone and placed it on his end table. "I assume you're here for a reason."

"You assume correctly." I walked over to his desk, pulled out the chair, and sat. "How was your date?" I didn't know why that question came out. I knew he hadn't gone on the date, but I still asked anyway.

Zach slowly turned toward me and began rolling the sleeves of his white dress shirt up his thick forearms. "There was no date. You know that. I did see her though."

My heart jumped. "Y-You did?"

"I did. She wasn't told that I cancelled the date. I still have to talk to Ashton about that but that's what happened. I bought her a drink for her trouble." His dark eyes locked with mine. "Before you jump to conclusions, I was being polite."

"I would never jump to conclusions." I couldn't imagine going on a date and not being told that it had been cancelled in the first place. I hoped the woman kicked Ashton's ass.

"Good." Zach took a step toward me. "What are you doing here, Luna?"

"I wanted to talk but now…" I stared up at him as he neared. "I'm not so sure what I'm doing."

"Are you sure you didn't come here to try and finish what we started a couple days ago?"

"I have no idea what you're talking about," I said, staring up at him as he closed the distance between us.

"No?" Zach stopped in front of me, placing his hands on the arms of the chair and leaning down toward me. "I think you do. So, tell me, Luna. What is it that you want exactly?"

"To talk," I repeated, unsure as to why I couldn't just tell him that I wanted to finish what we started. But a part of me wanted to see how this would play out. Call me a masochist but I rather enjoyed driving Zach crazy.

"Luna," he growled, inching closer.

"What?" I reached out to touch him. My fingers grazed along his jawline, down his thick neck and to his shoulder. "Can't we just talk? We are friends and all, Zachary," I purred, knowing he liked it when I used his full name.

His nostrils flared. "What do you want to talk about?" he bit out through clenched teeth.

"Hmm…" Getting a moment of bravery, I brushed my fingers down his chest to his waist. "Tell me why you haven't had sex in over a year."

"Luna."

"Tell me. Were you waiting?" I needed to know. I wasn't sure why. But I needed to know that there *was* something between us.

"Yes." He grabbed my hand, giving my palm a gentle bite. "I was waiting for that special woman."

"Really?" My heart skipped a beat. "Have you found her yet?"

"I have." He kissed my fingertips.

"Is she pretty?" I breathed.

"She's beautiful." His dark eyes became even blacker. "She has dark hair, curves that could make a grown man weep. Freckles. She's perfect."

My heart started racing. "You think I'm beautiful?"

He smirked. "Who says I was talking about you?"

A laugh escaped me. "Well, I know this guy."

"You know lots of guys," Zach said, which came out more as a growl.

"Jealous, baby?" I asked, kissing his chin.

"Nah." He fisted my hair, tugging my head back.

I gasped.

"You see." He leaned forward, licking up the length of my throat. "I know you don't want anyone else but me and *I* don't want anyone else but you."

"Prove it," I demanded, pulling his shirt from the waist of his black pants. "Prove to me that you want me." I reached my hands beneath his shirt. His abs jumped when I came into contact with his hot skin.

Zach's body shook like he was trying to rein in on that control he craved. His mouth brushed along the line of my jaw. "It's been a long time, baby."

"I know." I could hear vulnerability in his voice. He was nervous. My chest tightened. But I took a deep breath because if I had to initiate this, I would. "Zach."

His tongue licked along my ear, sending a hot shiver racing down my spine.

I started unbuttoning his shirt. "What did you tell her when she realized who you were?"

"That I was trying to start something with someone else and that was why I didn't agree to the date in the first place."

"Good."

He chuckled. The sound was dark and delicious as it vibrated through me from where his mouth touched my throat.

When I reached the top button of his shirt, I pulled it free and pushed the fabric off his shoulders.

"You came here to talk." He shrugged out of the shirt and let it drop to the floor, keeping his mouth at my ear. "What are we doing?"

"I-I…"

"Are we about to have sex, Luna?" he purred. "Are we about to take that next step? Go from friends to lovers?"

I whimpered at the way he growled *lovers*.

"It'll be your first time and it's been over a year for me. I don't know how gentle I can be. Are you ready for that?"

"Yes."

He held my head, staring me straight in the eyes. "Are you sure? Because if I do what I want to do, it'll be pure." He fisted my hair. "Hard." Tugged my head back. "Fucking." As soon as the last word left his mouth, he crushed his lips to mine.

THIRTEEN

Luna

ZACH'S TONGUE INVADED MY mouth. It was wet. Hot. And it took control much like the rest of him. His hand gripped my hair tighter, forcing my head back even more.

I gasped, taking him even farther into my mouth. His tongue danced with mine. Owning. Taking. Igniting this need inside of me that I never knew I had before.

Scratching my nails down his chest, I ran my hands around his sides to his back and pulled him closer.

Zach released my hair and wrapped his arms around me before lifting me from the chair.

Snaking my arms around his neck, I deepened the kiss, showing him that I wanted this as much as he did.

Carrying me to his bed, he laid me gently on the mattress.

I broke the kiss, staring up into his dark eyes. "I thought you said this would be fucking?"

"I haven't started yet," he rasped, wrapping a hand around my jaw.

"Then hurry up," I demanded.

A wicked grin spread on his face. Gripping my hips, he flipped me onto my stomach and ground his pelvis into my ass. "You're impatient."

I grabbed the blankets beneath me and spread my legs for him. "You have no idea."

He chuckled, sinking his teeth into the back of my neck. "Fuck, you're perfect." He inhaled. "So fucking perfect."

"Show me," I whispered.

"What?" He ran his hand down my side and slid it beneath the fabric of my shirt. "What do you want?"

"Show me what you would do if I wasn't a virgin."

He paused in his path. "What do you mean?"

I lifted onto my forearms, looking at him over my shoulder. "I know you've been with several women. Even if it's been awhile. You still have more experience than me. Have any of them been a virgin?"

His dark eyes met mine. "They haven't."

"Then show me."

"No."

"Zach."

He shook his head. "No, I'm not fucking you like I've fucked them because you're different. You don't deserve that shit."

"But what if I want it? What if I want to know what it's like to be fucked by every side of you?" I turned onto my back and sat up. Cupping his face, I placed a hard peck on his mouth. "Your angry side." I licked along his bottom lip, forcing a shiver to tremble through him. "Your happy side. Your loving side." I reached for his belt and started unbuckling it. "The side of you filled with rage. The side of you that's been dormant for over a year."

A soft growl rumbled from somewhere deep inside of him.

"What if I want to know what you feel like when you're angry and inside of me?" I wasn't sure where these words or thoughts were coming from, but I didn't give a shit what Zach said. I wanted all of him.

Something inside of him snapped. Before I knew what was happening, I was on my back with a hot mouth fused to mine. Zach roamed his hands roughly over my body. His fingers dug into my hips, the muscles tightening beneath his hard touch. He pushed between my legs, rubbing the thick part of himself against me. It ignited a burn I had never experienced before. Even when we previously messed around, it was nothing compared to this.

My heart raced, my skin became clammy, but I knew he would put my safety above anything. He wouldn't hurt me, even though I knew I had finally pushed him past that breaking point.

(Zach)

She didn't want me. Not like that. But her words, her teasing, it tickled the beast until he took control and shoved the rational part of me aside.

With my mouth fused to Luna's, I rubbed my pelvis into hers. I swallowed her soft mewls of pleasure and let my hands speak for me.

But it wasn't enough.

Breaking the kiss, I cupped her breasts and pushed them together. I gently bit a nipple through the fabric.

Luna gasped, arching beneath me.

Gripping the hem of the shirt, I pushed it up her torso, revealing… "Fuck." My gaze popped to hers. "You're not wearing a bra." I was lost in my lust for her that I never even noticed.

Her cheeks reddened. "I was trying to make it easy for us."

My dick jumped. Covering a nipple with my mouth, I sucked the hard nub between my lips and bit down.

She yelped. "Zach."

I released her with a wet pop and blew across the swollen peak.

She shivered, her dark eyes meeting mine. "Please stop teasing me."

"Where is this girl coming from, Luna?" I moved back up her body and towered over her. "This isn't you."

"You don't know if it's me or not because you've never been with me."

Fuck, she got me there. "Luna."

"Please, Zach. I'm not asking you to marry me. Just fuck me. That's all I want."

"You're a virgin."

She rolled her eyes. "Yeah, thanks for the reminder."

Her sass shot to the tip of my dick. Before I could comprehend what I was doing, I had her on her stomach and her pants ripped down her legs faster than either of us thought possible. My hand landed against the cheek of her rear. Again. And Again.

She cried out, lifting her hips into my swings. "Zach," she whined.

Swat. Swat. Swat.

My palm burned but I didn't care. I landed one final blow on her ass before pulling her to all fours. "Hmm…" Running my hand over the red flesh, I watched the way she trembled into my touch. "You want me." I pushed my pelvis against her, rubbing my thick length over her naked center. "You want every side of me."

"Y-Yes." Her body shook.

Pushing the fabric of her shirt up and over her head, I kissed her hairline and tossed the shirt to the side. She knelt naked before me.

I brushed a finger down the length of her spine, mesmerized by the path of goosebumps it left.

Luna shivered, arching her back like a cat. "Zach," she whispered.

"Are you sure you want be fucked like I fucked them?"

"Yes," she said but her voice shook.

"Turn over and lay on your back. Spread your legs for me."

She did as she was told, a flush spreading over her skin at being on display for my feasting eyes.

"I'm not doing that to you. Not for your first time." Even though she said she wanted me that way, I refused because I fucked them, to get the evil bitch out of my head. And now that I was with Luna, this would be a new me. A new us. No matter how much either of us fought our feelings for each other, I knew that there would be no going back from this.

(Luna)

"Zach?" I reached out to him.

He took my hand and kissed my fingertips. The touch was so gentle, it brought a lump to my throat. "Tell me you're sure."

"I am," I answered automatically.

"Luna, please be fucking sure because you're giving me a gift." Zach's body trembled. "I don't deserve your virginity. You should be saving it for someone special."

"I am," I whispered.

His eyes darkened. Releasing my hand, he towered over me and crushed his mouth to mine. But the kiss wasn't like before. It wasn't rough. It wasn't aggressive. No, this one was sweet. Gentle. But it bordered on desperate. Like Zach was trying to kiss everything away. But he didn't make a move to take it further. So I did.

Reaching between us, I lowered his zipper and pushed a hand inside. When I came into contact with his thick cock, I pulled it free from his pants.

He broke the kiss, leaning his forehead against mine. "Fuck," he whispered.

Lining up the tip with my soaked entrance, I wiggled farther beneath him and pushed it against my opening. My breathing picked up.

"We need a condom," I said, rubbing him back and forth over my sex.

He groaned. "No, we don't. I'm clean. I got tested a couple months ago. I want you bare, Luna."

Remembering the first time we almost had sex, we didn't use a condom then either. "I'm on the pill," I whispered.

His eyes dropped to mine. "Why?"

"Because they regulate my periods," I confessed, brushing my thumb over the slit in the tip of his cock.

"Fuck." His nostrils flared. "This is going to hurt," he mumbled, blowing out slow, even breaths.

"I don't care." I tilted my head and kissed his chin. "I know you'll make it feel good eventually."

Zach took my free hand and linked our fingers. "Tell me when."

I pushed the tip of him into me. A little more and the head would be inside me. I wiggled some more, taking the crown farther into my body. The size of him stretched me. I bit my lip to keep from crying out at the burn of something foreign invading my body.

"Luna," he bit out. "I'm not going to fucking last."

"Now," I demanded.

Zach lunged forward, pushing into me in one smooth thrust.

A sob escaped me, my eyes welling as the pain burned through me.

"Shhh…baby." Zach kissed my face. "I'm sorry."

"No. You're fine." My body shook beneath him. "Just move. Please."

He slowly pulled most of the way out and slid back into me slowly. He repeated the movement. Slow. So achingly slow. The pain turned to a dull roar but was soon replaced with…

"Oh…" A tingle shot through me, heating every inch of me. "…My."

"There it is." He squeezed my hand, pushing forward and then pulling back. He kept up the movements but never took it faster or harder.

"Please," I whispered, spreading my legs farther for him.

Zach got the hint and sped up his hips. Cupping my inner thigh, he pushed my knee to the mattress and drove forward. "Fuck me."

"God, Zach. I…" An electric current rushed through me, exploding into pleasure I had never felt before. Spots danced in my vision, his name leaving my mouth on a soft cry. The release slammed into me.

"So fucking tight," he growled, pushing his face into the crook of my neck. "So perfect." His cock swelled. Warmth spread from him and into me.

Running my hands down his sweat soaked back, my heart stuttered. My fingers ran over bumpy ridges. "Zach?" I kissed his shoulder.

He lifted his head, brushing my hair off my face, our lower bodies remaining connected. "I'm not normally a two-second man."

"Oh." I glanced down between us before meeting his gaze. "I didn't realize it was that fast."

He smirked.

"How long can you usually go for?"

Zach slowly pulled out of me.

I winced, a tinge of pain spreading through my sensitive flesh.

"Hours, Luna," he said, leaving the bed and heading to his bathroom. He came back a moment later with a cloth in his hand. He laid down beside me, running it between my legs. "This will help with the swelling."

My heart warmed. "Thank you." I covered his hand, keeping it between my legs. "You good?"

He nodded, staring at our joined hands.

"What is it?" I asked, lifting onto my elbow. "Zach." I nudged him when he didn't answer me.

"I made you bleed." His brows furrowed. "I've never…" He cleared his throat.

"Hey." I kissed his cheek. "I'm fine. I promise that I'm fine."

He turned his head, his lips finding mine. He pushed me back onto the bed and knelt between my legs. "I've never been with a virgin before and it's taking everything in me not to fuck you again. Not to fuck you how I really want to fuck you."

"Oh." I cupped his cheek. "Maybe in time?"

A cocky grin spread on his face. "You want me again?"

I swallowed hard, my cheeks heating. Would I sound desperate if I told him that I did? "If you want. I mean…"

He chuckled, lying down beside me. "I want whatever you want, Moonbeam."

I blew out a slow breath. Pushing away from him, I slid off the bed and picked up my clothes.

"What are you doing?" he asked, sitting up and leaned against the headboard.

"I'm leaving." Wasn't that the rule? "Isn't that what people do after?"

"Yeah, if they're having a one-night stand. Sure." He leaned forward. "Is that what you think this is, Luna?"

"Maybe?" I said, suddenly feeling exposed.

"Well, I don't know about you, but I want you again. And again. Tonight, wasn't a one-time thing for me and I can bet on my life savings that it wasn't the same for you either. Am I right?"

"I guess."

A sly grin spread on his face. "Drop the clothes and come here."

I dropped them and took a step toward the bed. Once I reached the edge, he lifted a hand.

"Kneel on the bed," he demanded, his voice husky.

I knelt like he instructed.

"Crawl to me."

My body heated. I placed my hands on the mattress and crawled toward him.

"Fuck." Zach wrapped a hand around his cock. "Yeah, baby. Just like that."

I laughed, crawling into his arms.

He wrapped himself around me, kissing my throat and laying us down on the bed. "I'm not letting you leave anytime soon, Moonbeam."

"Okay." I brushed the bangs off his forehead. "Then I think you should convince me to stay."

And he did.

FOURTEEN

Luna

THE NEXT MORNING, I woke to a soft kiss on the forehead. I smiled, stretching my arms out beneath the pillow. Opening my eyes, I found Zach staring down at me with a huge grin on his face.

"I'm sorry for waking you."

I sat up. He was already dressed. Wearing a dark red dress shirt tucked into black pants, he looked good enough to eat. The blood red of the shirt enhanced the natural tan in his skin. My stomach tumbled. God, he was beautiful.

"What time is it?" I asked, my voice rough from lack of sleep. We had sex two more times before he let me go to sleep and he made sure to be gentle every time. But no matter how gentle he had been, my body still ached.

"It's almost seven thirty. I have to head into the city, or else I'd still be sleeping beside you."

"Oh okay." I sat up, scrubbing my hands down my face. "How do I look?"

His eyes darkened. "Fucking perfect."

I laughed, gently smacking his arm. "Right. My hair's a mess and I need to have a shower and brush my teeth."

"Maybe so." He kissed me roughly on the mouth. "But you're still perfect if you ask me."

"You're too sweet," I told him, my heart warming.

He pulled back, something flashing in his eyes before he turned away. "Get dressed. My mom made breakfast."

"Uh…" My cheeks burned. "Isn't that weird? I mean…"

"Not weird at all. She always makes breakfast."

"I mean—"

"I know what you mean, Luna." Zach picked my clothes up off the floor and handed them to me. "Trust me, it's not weird."

"Have you had other women over?" I couldn't help the jealousy running through me that he had shared his bed with someone else.

"No, Luna." Zach chuckled.

"What's so funny?" I demanded.

"You're jealous."

"I am not."

"Yes, you are." His laugh deepened. "I told you I haven't been with a woman in over a year."

"Alright." I sighed. "I'm jealous. I can't help it."

Zach leaned over me and kissed me softly on the mouth. "Any woman I fucked before you, was either at their place or a hotel. So I've never even shared this bed with anyone else but you. And no woman has ever been over to my apartment in the city. Does that make you feel better?"

I breathed out a sigh of relief. "Yeah. It does." I cupped his face. "Does it make you feel better knowing you're the only man who's ever been inside me?"

"Fuck." He shivered. "You can't ask me shit like that when I can't do anything about it." He pulled away. "Get dressed."

I giggled.

Zach shook his head. "Women."

"Do you think your parents know I'm here?" I asked, sliding off the bed and quickly getting dressed.

A soft knock sounded on the door. "Your mom made breakfast," Coby called from the other side of the door. "And tell Luna, she's welcome to join us."

My eyes widened. "How…"

Zach only shrugged, a hint of amusement flashing in his eyes.

"How does he know that I'm here?" I asked Zach as we headed to the door.

Zach opened it and I stepped out into the hall, finding Coby leaning against the wall.

"I heard you both talking," Coby said. "That's how I knew you were here." His eyes flicked to Zach. "Luna, will you excuse us a moment?"

I looked between the both of them and nodded. "I'll see if your mom needs any help."

(Zach)

"You're going to lecture me, aren't you?" I asked my dad, leaning against the wall across from him and mirroring his pose.

"Nope." He crossed his arms under his broad chest, staring pointedly at me.

"Are you going to tell me that I'm making a mistake? That I should have ended things before they even began? That I should have kicked her out before you woke up so we wouldn't be having this conversation?"

"Nope," Dad repeated.

Frustration coursed through me. "Then what is it?"

"I'm just going to ask you one question. A question that I've learned over the years is a hard one to answer." Dad pushed away from the wall. "Do you know what you're doing?"

I opened my mouth to answer but snapped it closed.

"That's what I thought." Dad walked down the hall toward the kitchen, leaving me alone to stew in my thoughts.

He was right. I really had no idea what the hell I was doing. Whatever was going on between me and Luna would never be the same. We could never go back to being just friends. Even if we never slept together again, everything had changed. And I wasn't sure if it was for the better or worse.

Taking a deep breath, I started walking toward the kitchen when I was stopped short by laughter.

Luna placed a plate on the table, laughing at something my mom had said. She threw her head back, the boisterous sound coming from somewhere deep in her body. It wasn't a light laugh. No, it was full-bodied, and it stirred every cell in my body.

I decided right then that it was definitely for the better.

Joining Luna and my parents in the dining room, I cleared my throat.

Luna's eyes snapped up, a wide smile spreading on her face when she saw me approach.

It took everything in me not to pull her into my arms and kiss the very breath from her lungs. But I couldn't. Not that it bothered me to kiss her in front of my parents, but I wasn't sure what she wanted out of this. Whatever it was we were doing.

(Luna)

I had worried that it would be weird, but Zach's parents didn't say anything about me being there. They weren't stupid. They must have known what had happened between us, but I was thankful they didn't ask questions. I just hoped they didn't mention anything to my father. Oh God, my dad. My stomach twisted. He would lose his shit if he found out that his little girl had been defiled.

"You good, Moonbeam?" Zach asked, coming behind me and placing a soft kiss on my hairline.

I smiled, looking up at him and nodding. "Yeah."

"Good." His hand brushed down my arm, linking with my fingers.

"Are you?" I asked him in return.

He winked. "Oh yeah. Best sleep of my fucking life."

A breath left me on a whoosh. "Good." I looked around us, nervous that his parents would magically appear but soon realized that they were in the kitchen.

"Did my mom say anything to you?" Zach asked, his voice low.

"No. Just good morning and she was telling me a story about you."

"Oh?" Zach raised an eyebrow. "What was it about?"

"I was trying to pry information from your mom about your first crush."

"My first crush was a couple years younger than me." Zach leaned down to my ear, his mouth brushing along the shell of it. "So I really couldn't do anything about it."

"Is that so?" My heart jumped. "Well, she was a lucky girl either way."

"She was a very lucky girl, Luna. A very lucky girl indeed." Zach brushed his fingers over the seat of my ass, giving it a light pinch.

I jumped, smacking his hand away.

He winked and sat at the dining room table.

When I sat beside him, he cupped my knee, brushing his thumb back and forth. "Breathe, Luna. We'll take this one day at a time."

I nodded, did as he said, and let out a slow breath. His parents took that moment to join us.

Brogan sat across from me, her deep blue eyes meeting mine every so often.

I shifted in my seat, unsure what to do or even say. I had never spent the night at a guy's house before. When I showed up last night, I never even thought what would happen the next morning or how I would face his parents. I had one focus and that was on Zach.

"When are you heading to the city?" Coby asked Zach, breaking the unnerving silence.

"Soon." Zach checked his phone. "Actually." He stood. "I should head out now."

I stuffed a piece of bacon into my mouth and rose to my feet.

"Already?" Brogan asked, glancing at the spread before her. "Looks like we'll have to eat this all ourselves, my love."

Coby chuckled. "That's a lot of calories, little one."

"Hmm…" Brogan tapped her chin. "Wonder how we can work them all off."

I coughed, my eyes widening.

Coby grinned while Zach laughed.

"On that note." He kissed his mother on the head. "Have fun." He passed me a glance. "Luna."

"Thank you for breakfast," I murmured, rushing to follow him out of the house.

Once we were outside, Zach reached a hand out to me.

I slipped my fingers in his, letting him lead me down the driveway.

"Where did you park?"

"A few houses down. I didn't want to get caught sneaking in." I shrugged. "It worked."

A sly grin spread on his face. "I guess it did."

We walked to my little beater of a car. Once we stood beside it, I leaned against the driver's side door and crossed my arms under my chest. Waiting. Wondering.

"Will I see you tonight at Angel and Jay's?" I asked him, needing to break the unnerving silence between us.

"Yes." Zach closed the distance between us. He gripped my hip, running his thumb back and forth.

A shiver trembled through me. Leaning my forehead against his chest, I breathed him in.

"Luna, last night..."

I leaned back, staring up at him. "Yeah?"

He smirked. "It was fucking incredible."

A breath left me on a whoosh. "It really was."

A goofy grin spread on his face. He cupped my cheek. "I want more."

"Really?"

"Yes." He brushed his thumb over my bottom lip. "I want slow, Luna. I need it but...I want slow with you."

My heart stuttered. "I'd like that." I grabbed the collar of his shirt, pulling him toward me and placing a hard peck on his mouth.

Zach cupped my nape, deepening the kiss.

I moaned, breathing in the scent of his spicy cologne.

He chuckled, breaking the kiss and placing a peck on my nose. "Until tonight, Moonbeam."

My cheeks heated. "Have a good day."

"You too." And with that he walked away.

My gaze followed him, noticing the extra bounce in his step. My eyes trailed down the length of him, landing on his ass.

"Stop checking me out," he yelled over his shoulder.

I laughed, shook my head, and headed home.

FIFTEEN

Luna

TRYING TO SLIP INTO a house when you lived with three other girls, was hard. Especially when two of them were early risers. And to top it off, the twins were there as well.

"Well look what the cat dragged in finally," Meadow said, sitting at the dining room table. She grinned and patted herself on the back. "I'm so proud of myself right now."

I rolled my eyes, shut the door behind me, and joined everyone in the dining room. "Are we having a party or something?" I asked, sitting beside Meadow.

"Looks like Zach finally got his head out of his ass," Ashton said, leaning back in his chair. A smug grin spread on his face but there was something else there. Something dark, something unknown. Was he jealous?

"So…" Meadow sat forward. "I need to know. How was it?"

"Meadow," Aiden scolded. "We don't need to know about her sex life."

"I'm going to go take a shower," I mumbled, rising from the table and heading to my bedroom. As soon as I entered the room, I went to close the door when Ashton appeared. "What do you want?"

"Did you enjoy yourself?" he asked, coming into my room and forcing me back a step.

"Why do you care?" My heart jumped.

His deep blue eyes glanced around the room before landing back on me. "Is he still going to date other people?" he asked, ignoring my question.

"He hasn't dated anyone. Not for a long time." I snapped my mouth shut, not sure if Zach actually wanted that piece of information made public.

Ashton stiffened. "Seriously?"

"I don't know what's gotten into you, but this shit needs to stop," I said, glaring up at him.

"I like you, Luna," Ashton confessed, shoving his hands in his jean's pockets. "And I don't want to see you get hurt."

"You only like me because Zach showed an interest. You never even made a move before him." I turned around to head to my dresser and get some clothes when a firm hand grabbed my upper arm. "Ashton," I murmured.

He spun me around, cupped my face and did the unexpected. Something I never thought he would ever do. Especially not with me.

Ashton crushed his mouth to mine.

My eyes widened.

He backed me up until I hit the wall, keeping a firm grip on my face. His tongue peaked out, licking along my bottom lip before giving it a gentle nip.

A shiver trembled through me but before he could take it further, I pushed him away. "Stop this," I said, my cheeks burning.

He only gave me a cocky grin. Reaching out, he ran his thumb over my bottom lip. "If he hurts you, I'll kick his ass." Leaning down to my ear, his hot breath scorched the side of my face. "And once he's done with you, I'll be here to pick up the pieces, *Moonbeam*."

My heart jumped to my throat. Before I had a chance to respond, Ashton pushed past me and left my bedroom, quietly shutting the door behind him.

Reaching a hand up to my lips, my fingers grazed over them. They tingled from the kiss. A few days ago, no guys were interested in me and now there were two. What the hell was going on?

A soft knock sounded on the door.

Oh God. Now what? "Come in."

The door opened, revealing...

"Piper? Listen, I have no idea what's happening right now, but I promise, nothing is going on between Ashton and I," I said all in one breath.

"I'm not with him. I haven't been with the twins for a while," she said, coming into my room and shutting the door behind her. "But I just wanted to warn you."

"About what?" I asked, leaning against my dresser.

She sighed, running a hand through her dark hair before pulling it back into a high ponytail. "Ashton is a player. I'm not sure what his intentions are with you, but I overheard him talking to Aiden and a couple other guys."

"Is he only interested because Zach is?" I knew Ashton had gotten around but I never thought I would ever be his latest conquest.

"I'm not sure. Just be careful. Ashton has no interest in settling down. I...I hurt him. I hurt both him and his brother and I didn't mean to." Piper let out another sigh and pushed away from the door. She moved to my bed, sitting on the edge of it. "The guy I met in Paris…well…it was intense but, Luna, it was fucking amazing."

"That's good. Is it not?"

She shrugged. "I'm not sure."

"Well, meeting someone in Paris *is* romantic and all," I added.

She laughed lightly. "I don't think romance had anything to do with it. But it…God, Luna, it was the best night of my life, but it also scared the shit out of me."

I frowned. "How come?"

"Because if he hurts me, I don't think I could ever come back from that."

I thought a moment. "Do we know this guy?"

A nervous laugh left her. "I…he's been around. Meeting up in Paris was super random. I don't even know how it happened. But he was there. I was there. And the next thing I knew, I was leaving his hotel room the following morning."

"Wow. I…uh…went to leave last night. After everything…"

"Oh?" Her gaze shot to mine. "And?"

"He wouldn't let me leave." I shrugged. "I'm not experienced like all of you are, but I had assumed that's what you do after and he wasn't having any of it."

Piper smiled. "It's different for you. Sure, you can leave after if there's nothing there but for you and Zach, something has always been there."

"You think so?" I asked, my stomach tumbling.

"Yeah, I do." She hesitated. "I heard he never went on that date."

"No. He didn't." I sighed. God, if he found out that Ashton kissed me… "I need to know. Did the twins ever get jealous of each other?"

"No." Piper looked away. "It wasn't supposed to happen. Not like that. We got drunk and one thing led to another, but it was supposed to be one time. That was it. But I needed more. And then Paris happened, and my wish came true. So I ended things with them."

"How did they take it?"

She pulled the elastic from her hair and put it back into a ponytail. I realized she did that whenever she was nervous or was talking about something she didn't actually want to talk about.

I moved to the bed, sitting beside her and taking her hand in mine.

"God, Luna. I like this guy. I like him so damn much, but he also terrifies me. And my dad's going to lose his shit…" She grimaced, shaking her head. "Anyway." She stood. "I just wanted to warn you about Ashton." She quickly left my bedroom, not giving me a chance to respond.

I really had no idea what the hell just happened. I knew something was up with Piper and the twins, but I never knew that it went that far. And then for Ashton to hit on me and tell me that he wanted more. Something was definitely in the water.

(Zach)

Today was long as hell. I couldn't get thoughts of Luna out of my head, so all damn day, I was sporting a semi. And I couldn't tell you what my meetings were about. My father was going to kick my ass.

While I was sitting in my office, waiting for the clock to tick down to the time I could leave without it being frowned upon, my phone rang.

Sticking the ear piece in my ear, I pressed connect. "Porter."

"Hey."

My dick jumped.

"Hey, Moonbeam," I greeted, my voice coming out husky.

A breathless laugh left her. "How's your day going?"

"Long and boring," I grumbled, sitting back in my leather chair. "How about yours?"

"Not too bad. I went to The Dove Project and helped out there for a little bit and then did a few hours at the shop."

I smiled. The Dove Project had been set up by all of our mothers, years ago. It was to help human trafficking victims get their lives back after the trauma they endured. "How's it going there? I know everyone's working on getting it ready for the extension my mom wants to do on the place."

"Good. Really well actually. Oh wait. You're working. Am I bothering you?"

"Never, Moonbeam." In all honesty, even if I was busy with work, I would drop everything to talk to her.

"Oh okay. Good." She went on to tell me about the center and how she loved volunteering there. It was something she had been telling me for quite a while, and it made me wonder why she never actually worked there.

"Luna," I said when she paused for a breath.

"Sorry." She laughed. "I'm talking your ear off and you have things to do before dinner."

"No." I sat forward. "It's not that. Have you ever thought of working at the center?"

"I…no. It's not something I want to do. I love working with my mom and Aunt Jay. That's my job. But the center is just something I do for fun. And that's…" She cleared her throat. "Anyway, I should go and let you get back to work so I can get ready. See you later, Zach."

"Luna." A click sounded in my ear. I frowned, wondering what that was about. As soon as I was about to take the ear piece out, another call came in. "Porter."

"That sounds so professional."

I grunted. "How are you doing, Clara?"

"Good. You?"

"Oh, you know. Living the dream."

She scoffed. "Right."

"What's up?" I stood from behind my desk and gathered up my things. No sense sticking around if I couldn't focus on work. The sooner I got out of there, the sooner I could get a work out in and head back to Luna.

"I was just wondering if you've accomplished anything with your girl."

"Uh…we're making progress I guess you could say." I didn't usually give my phone number out to just anyone but when Clara mentioned how her brother was trying to get an internship, I gave her my business card and told her to tell him to contact me.

I shut down my computer and leaned a hip against the desk.

"Well, that's better than nothing." Clara laughed. "We should go on a double date."

"Oh? Are you seeing someone?"

"I am. After you turned me down, I was feeling sorry for myself and met someone."

"I…that's not…"

She laughed harder. "I'm kidding. I actually met up with a guy I dated in high school. It was so weird, Zach. I found out that he'll be living in the same area as me."

"Life has a funny way of throwing these things in your path. Obviously, you two were meant to be."

"We're taking it slow but…" She sighed. "I would really like to meet her."

"I'll set it up."

We continued talking about school, work and our upcoming double date. I liked Clara, but she would never be more than a friend. Although we had a lot in common, it wasn't the same as it was with Luna. With Luna, it just felt…right.

Later that night, I arrived at Luna's place. Stepping out of the car, I walked around it and leaned against the passenger side door. I sent Luna a quick text that I was there and started reading through my emails. I could have gone inside but I was sure that it would have been weird for her already since she didn't spend the night before there. Knowing how our friends worked, I would bet on my life that everyone knew we fucked.

"Hey, Zach."

I glanced up from my phone, finding the twins coming toward me. Aiden chanced a look at his brother before meeting my gaze once again.

"How's it going?" Aiden asked as both he and his brother stood on either side of me.

"It's going fine. What's up?" I went back to my phone.

"How was your date?" Ashton asked that time.

"There was no date, but Clara actually didn't know that. Did you forget to tell her that I never agreed to the date in the first place?"

Ashton shrugged. "I have no idea what you're talking about."

"You need to stop this shit." Because it was really starting to piss me off. I spun on him, getting in his face. "Are we having this fucking conversation again?"

"Zach." Aiden clapped my shoulder, pulling me back.

"I never pegged you for a hothead." Ashton pushed away from the car and jogged up the sidewalk to the house before slipping inside.

"What the hell is his problem?" I murmured, pinching the bridge of my nose to ward off the impending headache.

"He's hurting."

I slowly turned to Aiden. "What?"

He shrugged. "Believe or not but Ashton was in love with Piper and she ripped his heart out."

"Wasn't she fucking you too?" Not that I liked talking about my friend's sex lives, but he was the one who brought it up.

Aiden shrugged. "She has her own shit to deal with but there will be a time where she needs us." He started walking away before he stopped and looked at me over his shoulder. "I would snatch up Luna while you can. My brother isn't a patient person and I know with persistence, he could make Luna fall in love with him." And with that, he headed toward the house and slipped inside it much like his brother did.

I didn't have a lot of time to dwell on Aiden's words because the door opened again. Luna stepped out onto the front porch, followed by the rest of the girls.

My breath caught in my throat, my mouth going dry at the sight before me.

Her black wavy hair was pulled back in what looked like a braid. I couldn't overly tell from where I was standing. But the dress she was wearing almost brought me to my knees.

The floor length material was a deep green with a high collar and when she turned around? I almost whimpered like a baby. The back was completely bare.

I placed my hands in front of my lap, trying to shield the bulge in my pants. But before I knew what I was doing, I was heading her way.

She caught my gaze. "Hi."

"Hey." I glanced at her mouth, wanting to kiss her but not wanting to let whatever this was between us, made public yet. "I'll drive you."

She nodded, walking past me. The scent of her followed. It smelled like roses and vanilla.

Gigi walked past me, giving me a wink.

While Meadow walked past me and muttered a, "It's about fucking time."

I grunted, following Luna to my car like a lost little puppy.

"Who's coming with me?" Gigi asked, stopping in front of her SUV.

"We will," Ashton said with Aiden following behind him. He cast me a look. Sympathy? Confusion? I had no idea, but I knew not to get between two brothers. I just hoped I hadn't lost Ashton as a friend because of all of this.

"Are you coming with me?" Gigi asked Meadow.

Meadow made a face. "Obviously. I don't want to watch them suck face."

Luna's cheeks reddened. "We wouldn't do that in front of you."

"Oh." Meadow pouted. "And why not?"

Gigi shook her head. "We'll see you at our parents' place." She slipped into the vehicle and drove off, leaving Luna and me alone.

"Where's Piper?" I asked Luna when I realized that we were missing a person.

"She's meeting us there." Luna opened the passenger door. "Coming?" she asked, letting her gaze travel down the length of me.

Every inch of me buzzed at the heat in her eyes.

I grinned. "I'm not sure we have time for that, Luna."

She laughed, sitting in the passenger seat.

I grabbed the door, leaning on the frame and peered down at her. "You look beautiful."

"Yeah?" Her smile grew. "Thank you. It's a little dressy but it's comfy." She gave her shoulders a small shrug.

"I like it." I shut the door, blew out a slow breath and made my way to the driver's side of the car. This was going to be a long night.

Finally joining Luna, I gripped the steering wheel. I needed something to take the edge off, but I knew the only way to do that would be by throwing Luna in the back seat and showing her exactly what it was that I wanted to do to her.

"Everything okay?" she asked, cupping my arm.

I grabbed her hand, kissing the tips of her fingers. "I want you sitting beside me at dinner. I won't be able to handle it if you're not close to me."

Her brows furrowed. "Of course," she whispered. "But I don't know what that means."

Neither did I but I said it and I meant it. "Just please sit by me."

She nodded. "I will."

"Good." I dropped her hand, placed mine on her knee, and drove us to Angel and Jay's place.

I wasn't sure where those words had come from or why I felt that way, but I knew that if Luna sat anywhere else, I would lose my shit. How I knew that was beyond me. But I didn't need to cause a scene, especially when her dad was going to be there.

Add to the fact that trying to keep my hands to myself while her father was nearby was going to be the hardest fucking thing I had ever done.

SIXTEEN

ZACH

THE DRIVE TO ANGEL and Jay's place was a quiet one. Shortly after we sat in my car, Luna grabbed my hand and placed it on her lap. For the rest of the way, she stared out the window, lost in her own thoughts.

I wanted to ask her what she was thinking about. Or ask what her plans were. Would she ever go back to school? What sort of career was she looking for? Would she consider dating me? My jaw clenched at that last thought. I had to sort through my own shit first.

When we arrived at Angel and Jay's place, I had to park a couple of houses away because the street was lined with cars.

"Wow. It's busy tonight," Luna said, sitting forward.

"Looks like Angel and Jay, aren't the only people having company over." I killed the engine. "Ready?" I asked Luna.

She gave me a small smile. "I guess so."

"What's wrong?"

"Whatever my dad says or whatever anyone says for that matter, don't listen to them. Alright?"

"If you're referring to Ashton, I don't give a shit what he says but he needs to keep his hands to himself."

Luna looked away but not before I caught it.

Guilt.

My stomach twisted. "What happened?"

"Nothing." Luna placed her hand on the door and went to open it when I cupped her shoulder.

"Luna," I said, trying to keep my voice gentle but firm. "Tell me."

Luna glanced at me over her shoulder. "Will you keep your fists to yourself if I tell you?"

"What?" I shook my head. "Tell me."

He kissed her. Touched her. He did worse.

"Tell me because the thoughts rushing through my head are not helping me any."

"He kissed me," she whispered.

My vision clouded. Instead of answering, I left the car and went around to her side as she slipped out of the vehicle.

"Zach," she said gently.

"Let's go," I bit out. I was going to kill him. I was going to drive my fist through the fucker's face. I didn't give a shit that we were supposed to be friends. That ship had sailed long ago when he decided to kiss my girl.

"I'm sorry."

I spun on Luna, forcing her back a step.

Her eyes widened.

"Did you ask him to kiss you?" I asked, my voice calm and even.

"What? N-No." She shook her head. "I would never do that."

"Did you beg for it? Plead? Give him any hints that you wanted his lips on yours."

"No." She stared up at me with wide eyes. "Of course not."

"Was this after you spent the night with me?"

"Zach, I—"

"Tell me," I snapped, grabbing hold of her upper arm.

"Y-Yes." Luna placed her hands on my chest. "I'm sorry. I'm so sorry."

I kissed her forehead and then her nose. "You have no reason to be sorry." I grabbed her hand and led her up the driveway to Angel and Jay's place.

"Zach." Luna rushed to keep up with me. "What are you going to do?"

"Nothing." Not yet anyway. I wouldn't approach Ashton until I could get him alone. He would be expecting me to confront him in front of everyone. But I wouldn't. I didn't need to give Stone any more reason why I shouldn't be with his daughter.

When Luna and I made it to the backyard, she pulled her hand from mine.

I glanced down at her.

"I'm sorry," she whispered. "Hi, Daddy."

I slowly turned around, finding Stone coming toward us.

His dark eyes flicked to mine. They were cold. Deadly. But when they landed back on his daughter, they shone with love.

"Zach." My mom came toward me.

I let out a breath. "Hey, Mama." I leaned down and kissed her cheek.

She smiled up at me, her dark curly hair piled high on top of her head in a messy bun. "How are you doing?"

"I saw you this morning. I was fine then and I'm fine now." But I had a large fucker breathing down my neck and it was only going to get worse when he found out I had spent the night before balls deep inside his daughter.

Something flashed behind Mom's eyes. "Whatever happens, you're strong. You got this. But if you need me, I'm here." She raised a hand. "I don't give a shit how old you are. You're my baby."

My heart swelled with even more love for this woman. A woman I had put through hell along with her husband when they adopted me as a boy. But no matter how much of an asshole kid I was, they never gave up on me.

"Everything will be fine." It wasn't like I was going to cause a scene in front of our friends and family.

She nodded. "Good." She searched my face. "Any nightmares?"

"Not since before last night," I told her. Truth was, I had the best sleep of my life when Luna was beside me.

A slow smile spread on her face. "I wonder why that is."

I chuckled and kissed her head. "I think you know why."

"Yeah." She sighed. "I do. Your dad is the same way. He always tells me that he sleeps better when I'm beside him."

"It makes sense."

Her eyes searched my face. Cupping my cheek, she chewed her bottom lip. "Don't let the bitch live rent free anymore. Kick her ass out and take your life back, Zach. She doesn't own you."

Bile rose to my throat. My parents had been the only ones who knew that I could hear my stepmother in my head.

Mom gave me a soft smile. "Well I should go see what your dad is doing." She went to walk away just as my father came out of the house with two water bottles in hand.

"Hey." He nodded toward me. "Jay said she has fake wine if you want to try it," he told Mom.

She grimaced. "Um...no. And that's too tempting anyway. Wine is wine. Whether it has alcohol in it or not."

Dad grunted. "True." He clapped my shoulder. "Everything good?"

"Oh yeah. Fine and fucking dandy." Besides the fact I could feel Stone throwing icy daggers into the side of my head. I was perfect.

"Why is Stone glaring at you?" Mom asked, crossing her arms under her chest.

"Why do you think, little one?" Dad grumbled, glancing over his shoulder.

Stone was still talking to Luna. His back stiffened, his dark eyes looking our way. He nodded once, no doubt making nice since I wasn't alone.

"Want me to kick his ass?" Brogan asked.

"Uh...I'm not sure I should answer that since you taught me to respect my elders and all." I rubbed the back of my neck. This night was turning into a shit show and it had only just begun.

"Brogan." Coby grabbed her hand, linking their fingers. He brought her hand up to his mouth and kissed her knuckles. "Zach can take care of his own battles. You know that."

"I know but it doesn't mean that I can't protect him."

"If I need you, I'll tell you." I kissed her cheek. "Thank you."

She chewed her bottom lip before letting out a hard breath. "Fine. I'll behave."

"Good girl." Dad rose to his full height.

"I'm going to go mingle." Mom stood on her tiptoes and kissed his cheek before she headed into the house.

Dad's hard gaze met mine. "Remember where we are, Zach. And also, remember that these people are our family and friends."

"I know but I—" Laughter sounded, stirring something inside of me. Something dark. Something feral. Something I had never felt before with anyone I had ever been with. And I didn't know how to deal with these emotions running through me.

"I know, Son." Dad clapped my shoulder. "I get it," he said low enough for only me to hear. "I know you would do anything and go through anyone to have her but be careful. She loves her dad. I'd hate to see her have to choose between the two of you."

Before I had a chance to respond, he pulled away and went back to my mom. He linked their fingers once again and kept her at his side before she went and did something everyone would regret. Although, I had a feeling my mother wouldn't regret it too much.

I let out a hard sigh and moved to the wall by the patio doors. Leaning against it, I crossed my arms over my chest and watched. It had been what I always did. No matter how old I was, I couldn't help but pay attention to what was going on around me.

Memories poked their way at my mind, trying to break free but I shook my head, forcing them back.

A laugh brought me back to the present. My gaze landed on Luna standing with her brother, Piper, and the twins.

Ashton looked my way and nodded once.

I nodded back, wondering if he was going to do something stupid. But when he didn't and only went back to the conversation going on around him, I let out a breath of relief.

"Remember where you are."

I jumped, the back of my neck heating at being caught staring by my father. "I remember. It's not like I would do anything here anyway." I looked around the yard. Stone was nowhere to be found but it didn't mean that he wasn't keeping an eye on me. I knew how all of our parents worked. They liked for us to think they were all sweet and innocent, but I knew that back in the day, they were lethal as fuck. Some more than others but lethal just the same.

"When did this all start?" Dad asked me, leaning against the wall beside me.

"She's always had a crush on me," I told him.

"I know. When did everything else start?"

"I…A week or so ago." I shrugged. Give me a board meeting and I could talk circles around it but when it came to Luna, I was a blubbering fool.

"Are you using her?"

"What?" My head whipped around. "No. Never."

"I love you, Zach. You may not be mine by blood, but you are still mine." Dad turned his head toward me. "But if you hurt her, I can't protect you."

"I don't plan on hurting her," I said, the hackles on my neck rising that he would even suggest such a thing. "She's the first woman I've been with in a long time. Whatever rumors you've heard, they're not true."

"You already told me that. But why didn't you say something?"

I shrugged. "What's the point? People are going to believe what they want to anyway. As long as she doesn't believe them, I don't give a shit what anyone thinks."

"Good. Keep it that way but just don't hurt her. You have a temper."

"I would never fucking hurt her," I said a little too loudly.

Several heads turned our way.

I coughed. "I would never hurt her," I repeated, quieter that time.

"I'm not saying that you would hurt her physically. Fuck, Zach. I know that would never happen." Dad turned to me, leaning his shoulder against the wall. "But I know that when you're pissed, you don't think. So promise me, if something happens, you come to your mom and I. You don't act out on that anger. You hear me? You come to us."

I searched his face, frowning. "What are you getting at?"

"Just come to us." He cupped my nape, leaning his forehead against mine. "Promise me."

"Okay." My heart jumped. "I promise."

He pulled away, gave me a final look, and joined Angel who was standing around a BBQ. A minute passed and both of them were looking my way.

I sighed, pushed away from the wall and moved to one of the loungers.

Luna was still chatting with her mom and little brother. Although, he wasn't so little anymore. He was a couple of years younger than Luna, but he still towered over her.

She laughed at something he said, the sound shooting through every fiber of my damn soul.

I sighed, scrubbing a hand down my face. I had to get it together for fear that Stone would kick my ass. Or her brother. I wouldn't put it past him either. He was probably lethal as hell just like his father.

I noticed for the first time that Luna had lost weight. Why I never noticed the night before was beyond me. Oh yeah. Because all I could think about was sticking my dick in her. My stomach twisted. I was such an asshole.

She still looked good though. With her curves more toned, I could see the hint of muscle in her slender frame.

Especially the way her back dipped into a tight ass that I had my hands on last night.

"Stop staring."

My head snapped up, finding Gigi slumping down on the lounger across from me.

"I'm not staring," I grumbled, my gaze flicking to Luna.

Gigi laughed. "Right. And I'm not lusting after my friend's younger brother."

I raised an eyebrow. "Really?"

She shrugged. "I can't help it."

"I get that. So I can only assume you're talking about Vince Junior." I sat back in the lounger. "Am I right?"

She shrugged again, her cheeks turning pink. "We can't help what the heart wants, I guess. Have you seen Piper?" she asked, quickly changing the subject.

I scanned the backyard, finding her standing with Meadow and the twins. "She's over there."

"Oh okay." Gigi shook her head. "I didn't even know she was here yet. We had to make a stop at The Dove Project. One of the pipes burst. The guys couldn't get there quick enough, so Piper and I were dealing with it." She laughed lightly. "That was fun."

"I bet it was. Tell me something." I leaned forward. "Why doesn't Luna want to work there? She's good at what she does there. She loves helping those women."

"She does but I don't think it's what she wants to do in life." Gigi ran her fingers through her long dark hair before pulling it over one shoulder.

"What do you mean?" Luna had said the same thing, but I never got any more information out of her.

"I mean just that." Gigi shrugged. "Luna isn't like the rest of us. She wants more. She wants to be able to give what she knows to someone else. She wants a…"

"What? What does she want?" I would give it to her. Whatever it was.

"A baby, Zach." Gigi sighed. "She wants a baby."

My dick twitched. Every alpha instinct in me, boomed. A baby. She wanted a fucking baby.

Gigi laughed. "I can see by the expression on your face, you had no idea."

I swallowed hard. Opening my mouth to speak, I snapped it shut when I realized I had no idea what to even say to that. Luna and I had known each other since we were kids. And this thing between us was new, fresh, and way too damn soon to even consider having kids. But if that were the case, why the hell did it just sound so...perfect?

"Listen." Gigi moved to the empty spot beside me. "Whatever happens, just don't hurt her. She's been in love with you since we were kids. I know I know." Gigi fluttered a hand in front of her. "It's only a crush but we're not stupid." She glanced up at me then. "She loves you, Zach. And I know her father is against this whole thing too. Hell, all of our fathers are. You boys have it easy. You can date and fuck whoever you want."

"Meadow doesn't seem to have a problem getting whoever she wants," I said, finally able to speak after the blow that was laid on me.

"My sister is one of the lucky ones. She just doesn't care. She's always been that way." Gigi laughed. "I'm jealous."

"That makes two of us. Not that I've ever really cared what anyone thought but..." Having to deal with a grumpy overprotective father held me back. Although, I wasn't sure if Luna could handle everything I wanted to do to her.

"I know her dad is crazy protective." Gigi patted my hand and stood. "Prove to him that you are good enough for his daughter and he might just leave you both alone. And please be careful and for the love of God, do something about this thing between you two before Ashton does." She shook her head and walked away.

Looked like everyone knew about Ashton. Probably more so than I did.

After Gigi left me to stew in my own thoughts, I headed into the house to see if any help was needed.

"Ladies," I greeted.

"Zach." Jay smiled, reaching her arms out.

I chuckled, wrapping her up in a hug.

"How are you?" she asked, leaning back but keeping her hands on my shoulders. "You good? Your mom said that you've been working a lot."

"I have but I'm doing well. This company won't run itself," I joked, absentmindedly hooking an arm around Max's shoulders as she came up beside me.

"You've been working out." Piper's mom, Max, patted my stomach. "Or your parents aren't feeding you enough."

"Leave him alone. The boys are active. All of them are." Jay laughed. "You're just jealous because Dale's letting himself go."

"He is not," Max cried, stepping away from me and placing her hands on her hips. "He's still hard as—"

"On that note." I slowly backed away before I could hear any more about how hard Piper's father was in any capacity.

While Jay and Max continued to playfully argue, I quickly went to the bathroom. When I was done, I was about to head back out into the hall, when I heard voices. Slowly opening the door, I found my mom standing with Stone out in the hallway. I inched the door closed a little more but kept an ear against it. I shouldn't have been eavesdropping, but I was curious.

"You care to tell me why you're giving my son a hard time, Stone?"

My back stiffened. My dad told her that she shouldn't say anything to him.

"I don't want him with my daughter."

My stomach twisted. Although I knew he didn't want me with Luna, it still hurt to hear him say it.

"Yeah. Well, you have no control over that, sweetheart."

"Actually, I do. Zach's going to run this business and be too busy for her. Luna will move on."

"You can't honestly believe that's what will happen?" Mom laughed. "You're smarter than that. Look at what happened to the rest of us. You know how it works. You fall in love, you fight, you make up but no matter what, you will always be together because that's how this works. That's how all of this works."

"Doesn't matter," Stone grumbled.

"What issue is it that you have with my son? You know Zach's turned into a wonderful man even after all the shit he went through as a kid."

I shoved my hands in my pockets, not enjoying the nightmares of my past being brought to light. Although only my parents knew the full extent of what I went through, everyone had an idea on what happened. I was abused by my stepmother. Nothing really to hide there but my parents wanted it to remain hush-hush until I was ready to tell people.

"Doesn't matter. He's not good enough for my daughter. No one is."

"Stone, I love you like a brother but right now, you're lucky I don't kick your ass."

My heart warmed, knowing my mom had my back.

"You're retired, Brogan," Stone pointed out.

"Fine, I'll just go to the one person, probably the only person, who can put you in your place."

He hesitated. "You wouldn't."

"I would."

"Brogan, I—"

"Stone."

I opened the door a little more, peeking out in the hallway.

My mom was staring up at Stone with her hands on her hips. "You tell my husband that we had this conversation and I'll come out of retirement just for you." And with that, she spun on her heel and walked away.

"Fuck." Stone rubbed the back of his thick neck and followed her.

This couldn't happen.

You're worthless.

This could never happen.

You don't deserve happiness.

What I did with Luna shouldn't have happened at all.

You're nothing. Absolutely nothing.

My stepmother was right.

Luna should never have fallen in love with me. She was getting too close. This just proved what I had known all along. What had been ingrained in my head since I was a kid.

I deserved to be alone.

(Luna)

I wasn't sure what changed over the last half hour or so, but Zach seemed off. When we sat down at the table that was sitting outside because there were too many of us for indoors, Zach's jaw was clenched tight. I had come to know over the years that he did that whenever he was stressed or thinking about something. Either way, it meant something, or someone pissed him off.

We sat at a large table in Gigi's parents' backyard with his hand on my inner thigh. I had used the excuse that I was cold, so he gave me his jacket to place in my lap. He quickly realized what I was doing, the heat in his eyes becoming more pronounced.

I may not have been experienced but I knew what I wanted, and I wanted him. Hard. Fast. Soft. Gentle. I didn't care. I wanted Zach to take me to new heights and show me what it was like to truly let go. Even though we had already been together, I had a feeling that I didn't experience the true him. The real Zach Porter.

With his thumb brushing back and forth over my thigh, he let out a slow breath, his stiff body relaxing.

"Everything okay?" I asked him, inching my hand beneath his jacket and linking my fingers in his.

"Yup." He looked down at me.

"You're lying."

"Doesn't matter if I am or not." Meaning, he wouldn't tell me.

"Zach." I pulled my hand away and shoved him gently. "Tell me."

"Not now," he bit out.

I huffed. "But—"

"So, Zach," my father barked.

He was sitting to the right of us, across the table and a few chairs down. Not directly in front of us and thank goodness for that. I was sure he would be looking under the table, making sure Zach kept his hands to himself.

"How's the business going?" my father asked.

"Very well," Zach said, sitting up straighter.

"I heard you're trying to grow the business," my dad added.

"Zach's going to be taking over the business when I retire," Coby explained, nodding to his son across from him. "He's also going to expand it. His grandfather would be proud."

"We're all proud," Brogan added.

"How do you want to grow it?" Dad asked, leaning forward. For once he was actually interested in what Zach had to say.

I loved my father, and I knew he was only giving him a hard time because he was showing interest in me. But now, he seemed like he actually wanted to know more about the man who was adopted into our large extended family at a young age. I didn't know why though. Dad clearly had an ulterior motive.

Zach shifted beside me when he realized everyone was looking at him.

"Tell him, Zach," I coaxed, squeezing his hand.

His hand gripped my thigh in a firmer hold. "I want to add hotels and all-inclusive resorts to the business."

"That's amazing."

"Good job."

"You will do really well."

Praise sounded around the table.

My heart swelled for the man sitting beside me.

"Be proud," I whispered, squeezing his arm. "I am."

He relaxed a little more at that.

My dad looked between us, something flashing behind his dark eyes. But the moment I saw it, it was gone. I prayed he could see what I saw in Zach. I didn't want some fling. I had feelings for him, and he would be stupid not to see it. Hell, *everyone* could see it.

A motion caught my eye. I glanced down the table, locking eyes with Ashton.

My lips tingled, remembering the kiss. I wondered if Zach had approached him yet.

Ashton narrowed his brows.

Aiden punched him in the shoulder, muttering something to him.

Ashton glared at his brother and I looked away before I could catch him staring at me again. I didn't know what had gotten into him, but I did know that I didn't want to find out.

SEVENTEEN

ZACH

I WAS PROUD OF my work but hated being the center of attention. It was why I always stayed off to the side. I would rather watch and listen than be the one who did the talking. Unless I was in a boardroom directing the meetings, I preferred to remain silent.

"Hey." Luna came up beside me later that evening when we were sitting around the campfire. "You okay?"

I nodded, wanting to pull her in my arms and tell her how I felt. But instead I kept my hands to myself and my words remained silent.

She sat beside me, wrapping a blanket over both of us.

I pushed it off of my lap, knowing that her father would think something was happening beneath it.

"Keep your hands to yourself, Porter," a deep voice growled in my ear. "I may be retired but I have no issues breaking every single one of your fingers." Stone clapped my shoulder. "We clear?"

"Crystal," I muttered, pushing his hand off of me.

"Careful. I like your parents, Zach. I'd hate to lose that friendship over something that could have been prevented."

My jaw clenched. It was so damn tight, a sharp pain shot up the side of my face.

"I'm glad we've come to an understanding." He clapped my shoulder again.

"Daddy," Luna snapped. "Stop threatening him and go home already."

"Watch the tone, Luna."

She huffed.

"Luna," Stone barked. "Walk with me."

"I'll be back," she whispered and left with her father.

He had every right to be concerned. I was just waiting for the day he found out I had already defiled his daughter. If he only knew the nasty, dirty things I wanted to do to her. He would do more than break my fingers.

Luna came back about ten minutes later. She dropped hard onto the patio couch beside me and pulled the blanket up and over us. "He left."

"Everything good?" I asked her, taking that as my chance and reaching a hand beneath the blanket. Cupping her inner thigh, I blew out a breath I didn't realize I had been holding.

"My dad's an asshole." Luna sighed. "But I love him." She met my gaze. "He won't bug us for the rest of the night," she said, waggling her eyebrows.

I laughed, shaking my head.

She grinned. "I like this."

I kissed her temple. "Me too, Moonbeam." I brushed my nose over the shell of her ear. "I like this a lot. More than I could ever tell you."

"Really?" Her breath caught.

"Yeah." The hairs on my nape tingled. Someone was watching. And I would bet my life savings that it was Ashton drilling daggers into the side of my head. I was too old for games, but a little playing wouldn't hurt. "Your dad's no longer here. Isn't that right?"

She nodded, chewing her bottom lip.

"What would you do if…" I grazed my hand higher up her inner thigh. "Your damn dress is too long," I grumbled.

She laughed, the sound full-bodied and shaking through her. "Were you going to try something, Zachary?"

I shrugged, leaning back and rubbing my nape. "I guess you'll never know now."

"Aww." She leaned into my side. "Too bad. I guess I shouldn't tell you that I'm not wearing any panties."

My back stiffened, my cock leaking at her words. "Wha—"

Suddenly, Piper jumped on the seat beside Luna, startling her.

They laughed.

"So…" She looked between us both. "How's it going?"

"Good," I answered, imagining Luna's bare pussy at the moment. I wondered if she was lying. Maybe she was. She was still naïve when it came to sex. Nah. My girl was a brazen little thing.

Luna stood, bent her knee and sat back down. She leaned forward, moved her hand beneath the blanket, and pushed mine beneath the fabric of her dress.

My fingers slid up her thigh with her guidance until they reached her core. So bare. So soft. Completely uncovered like she had said.

She shot me a look, a sly grin spreading on her face before she turned back around to continue talking to Piper.

"I keep hearing how close you two are getting and I'm happy to see it." Piper kicked her long legs out in front of her. "It's about time anyway."

"How was your trip?" I asked her, getting the subject off of us.

With my hand at Luna's bare pussy, it was hard to concentrate on Piper's retelling of her trip, but I had to keep it to cool. I didn't want to embarrass Luna.

"It was amazing. I met so many people. Tried so many different types of food. Saw every museum I could." Piper sighed, a smile growing on her face. "It was heaven. I only came home because I was missed." She glanced at Ashton and Aiden who sat on the other side of the bonfire.

Piper met my gaze, her cheeks reddening. She gave a small shake of her head.

I nodded once. All of us knew they had been a thing but having a relationship with one person was hard enough, let alone with two people. I wasn't sure how people who lived in polyamorous relationships did it but if it worked, all the power to them.

Luna grabbed my hand, pushing it out of her lap. "I have to use the bathroom," she told me.

I leaned toward her ear. "Don't even think about getting yourself off. If you do, I will find out. And, Luna?"

"Yes?" she whispered.

"I will make you regret not telling me that you weren't wearing any panties." I sat back, the shiver trembling through her making my dick twitch.

Luna stood, smoothing down her dress, then headed back into the house. Once Piper and I were alone, I nodded toward the twins.

"How long?"

"Too long," she muttered. "You heard the rumors. I'm not stupid. Although, they're not really rumors anymore. Fact is fact. I slept with them. A few times when it was supposed to be a one-time thing. We were drinking and one thing led to another. Now they want more but I..." She met my gaze that time. "I met someone."

"While in Europe?"

"Yeah. Paris actually." Her shoulders slumped. "But he probably wants nothing to do with me ever again. I don't know. It was...intense. I was just convenient for him while he was on his trip."

It was on the tip of my tongue to ask who it was, but I thought better of it.

"She likes you," Piper said, changing the subject. "She likes you a lot. Always has but I see it more now. I know I haven't been home in a while, but you have her heart, Zach."

"I like her too," I confessed. How could I not? Luna had been the only woman to make me drop to my knees and beg for her to do whatever she wanted to me.

"She's liked you for years but I'm sure you knew that already."

"I did." And I felt the same way. I had always felt the same way, but I also had to protect myself and her from the vileness that threatened to bleed from me.

Luna took that moment to sit back down beside me. "Miss me?"

I did. I did more than she would ever know.

(Luna)

"I'm going to take Luna for a drive," Zach told Gigi as she stepped out of the vehicle.

"Okay." She waited while the twins, Meadow, and Piper were out of earshot before she opened my door. She leaned in toward me and gave me a hug. "Be safe."

"Always." I was expecting Zach to just drop me off and that be it.

"Have fun kids," she told us both. "And don't do anything I wouldn't do."

"That doesn't leave me many options," I teased.

"I'm not my sister," Gigi joke.

Laughter erupted around us.

She shut the door, gave us a wave, and headed toward our house. We waited for her to enter before Zach drove away.

"Where are you taking me?" I asked him, taking off my shoes. Rubbing the balls of my feet, I winced as a sharp slice of pain shot up my calf.

"Somewhere neither of us have been." He tapped my hip. "Lean against the door and put your feet in my lap."

I did as I was told.

He cupped my foot, massaging his thumb into my heel.

I moaned, a hot shiver racing down my spine.

"Feel good?" he asked, his eyes twinkling in the dim lighting of the moon.

"Mmmhmm." I sighed. "God, you're so good with your hands."

He chuckled. "You seem surprised by that. Remember all the times I've made you come already, Moonbeam."

"Oh. Yeah." My cheeks burned. "Well either way, it feels good."

"Good." He kept up the movements, massaging the pain from the shoes out of my feet.

"Where are we going?" I asked him, my eyes fluttering closed.

"Just for a drive. I need to get away." That familiar tick in his jaw beat in tune with my heart. This would be the first time we would be alone. Truly alone.

"We're here."

I jumped at the deep voice in my ear.

"You fell asleep," Zach said, brushing his thumb along my jaw.

"Oh." I shivered at the soft touch.

He sat back, letting me up.

Stretching my arms up and over my head, I dropped them when I realized we had parked somewhere that I had never been before. "Sorry for falling asleep."

"Don't be. You were obviously tired."

I was. All of these new unknown emotions running through me were not the norm for me, and I didn't know how to deal with them.

"Whatever you're thinking, Moonbeam. I won't hurt you." He kissed me softly on the mouth. "Any pain I cause you will be because you ask for it."

My core clenched at that thought.

He grinned, running his thumb over my bottom lip. "Look." He pinched my chin, turning my head toward the front of the car.

My eyes widened. "Oh, Zach." I opened the door and slid out of the vehicle before he had a chance to respond.

We were on top of Stanley's Peak. I knew because I had seen the pictures from Meadow's phone.

"Do you like it?"

"Like it?" I repeated, rushing to Zach's side. "It's beautiful."

"I agree." Yet he wasn't looking at the scenery, but at me instead.

My cheeks burned. "I've never been here before," I said, turning around and gazing out at the scenery before us. It was late into the night and the moon had risen just above our small town. If you looked close enough, you could see all of our homes in the far-off distance.

"You know what it is?" Zach grabbed my hand, pulling me back against him.

"Stanley's Peak," I answered.

His body stiffened. "Have you been here before?"

"No." I frowned. "Have you?"

"No," he growled. "I've never thought anyone was worthy of coming up here with me until now."

"I'm not sure if I should think you're cocky or take that as a compliment."

Zach turned me in his arms. "I am cocky, Luna, so take it however you want. But I earned that shit." He pushed me up against the side of his SUV.

"Zach," I breathed gripping his jacket. "I'm not accusing you of anything."

He gripped my hips, pulling me against him. "I never said you were."

I cupped his nape, running my fingers through the soft hair.

His dark eyes met mine. Something switched between us. I was close with everyone else but when it came to Zach, our friendship had always been deeper than what I shared with the rest of our friends. He liked my quirks. Never teased me about enjoying my food or was on me when I decided to start running. He may have been quiet with everyone else but he sure as hell talked to me.

"Thank you for bringing me here," I whispered, pulling his shirt from the waist band of his pants.

His brows narrowed but he didn't stop me.

Pushing my hand beneath the fabric, I ran them over his abs and up to his chest. Reaching around him, I grazed my other hand up his back. His skin was bumpy from what felt like scars. His body stiffened but he still didn't push me away.

"I never felt these the other night," I murmured, looking up at him then.

"That was the point," he said, his voice raspy.

"You were keeping them from me?" I asked, pulling my hands free from beneath the fabric and starting to unbutton his shirt.

"I was." His hands wrapped around my wrists, stopping me. "I was trying to make it so you wouldn't worry about me because I knew you would. If I told you all the shit I've been through..." His voice became thick. "You would worry."

I met his gaze.

His eyes pierced into me.

Getting a sense of bravery, I pulled my hands from his and continued unbuttoning his shirt. When I reached the last one, I licked my lips. I couldn't see him in great detail because of the darkness but I remembered him from the night before. Although I had never known about the scars on his back. A flutter of disappointment traveled through me.

Zach reached around me and opened the back door. "Get in and lay down."

I did as I was told, laying on the back seat of his SUV.

He crawled in after me, leaving the door open to keep the light on. "Touch me."

My breath caught in my throat. Brushing my fingers inside his shirt, I pushed it off his strong shoulders. I swallowed hard. Bumpy ridges coated his back like he had been stung by hundreds of bees. My heart jumped, my chest tightening at what could have happened to him.

"I was burnt over and over again. By lighters. Cigarettes. Candles. That's why they're all different sizes," he explained, his voice strained.

A hard lump lodged its way into my throat. "I had no idea. I'm sorry."

"Don't be, Luna. You weren't the one who burned me."

"No...I wasn't but I'm still sorry." I pushed the shirt farther down his back, replacing it with my hands. Placing a soft peck on his shoulder, I trailed soft kisses along the strong muscle to the side of his thick neck.

"I've never let anyone touch me before," he murmured, his breath fanning my face. "When I had sex, I would be in control. I would pin them down and not let them run their hands over my body but you..." His breath caught. "With you, Luna, I want your hands on my skin. Your nails in my flesh. I want to feel you all over me."

"Is that why you never go swimming?" I asked, brushing my thumbs over his nipples.

"Yeah." His teeth sunk into my shoulder. "And why I don't like being naked."

"Why are you showing me then?" I didn't want him to feel like he had to.

He leaned on his elbows on either side of my head and brushed a hand over my hair. "I trust you, Moonbeam."

EIGHTEEN

ZACH

LUNA'S EYES SHONE AS soon as those words left my mouth. "I'm sorry for what happened to you," she said, the sadness in her eyes quickly becoming hard with fury.

I swallowed over the lump that had suddenly lodged its way in my throat. I never had a woman sympathize with what I had been through. Unless it was my mom, but she didn't count. As much as I appreciated what she and my dad had done for me, it was never enough. All the women I had been with didn't want to know me. They wanted my dick and that was it. I always assumed Luna would be the same way and I knew I shouldn't have when it came to her. She wasn't like the rest.

She still didn't know my whole history and I wasn't sure if I would ever be able to tell her. But one day at a time, piece by piece, I would try and open up. I would try and show her that I was good enough. That I deserved her, no matter what.

"You're getting this one for—"

I winced but when Luna's hands came into contact with my bare skin, that soft touch drowned out the noise of my stepmother.

My body tensed as Luna's fingers continued to trail along my chest.

"I like the way your muscles feel beneath my touch," Luna whispered, kissing my collarbone.

The lack of control suddenly slammed into me. In a quick move, I wrapped a hand around her throat and forced her head back.

She gasped, her eyes dilating at the rough move.

Hooking my hand around her thigh, I pulled her farther beneath me and pushed her dress to her hips.

Licking along her bottom lip, I sucked it between my teeth and ground into her.

She panted, arching beneath me.

"Do you want more?" I asked, my voice deep and raspy.

Her eyes landed on me. They were wild, needy, and filled with so much damn lust, it took my breath away. "Yes."

It was all the consent I needed.

(Luna)

"Sit up and lean against the door," Zach instructed, closing the other door behind him. The interior light turned off, but I could still see him in the glow of the moon.

I did as he said, leaned my back against the door, and waited.

He leaned over, placing a soft peck on my forehead.

I tilted my head back.

He smirked, placing an even softer kiss on my lips.

I shivered at the gentle contact, wondering exactly what he was going to do but waited with bated anticipation just the same.

"Bend your knees," he murmured, keeping his mouth against mine.

I did as I was told, pulling my dress to my hips and spreading my legs.

He leaned back, glancing down at my lap. His tongue swiped along his bottom lip. "So fucking beautiful." He reached out, trailing the back of his hand up my inner thigh.

My heart raced. "Zach."

"Shhh…" His eyes popped to mine. "It's just us here."

I nodded, chewing my bottom lip. Placing my hand on his shoulder, I held him for support. Although we had sex already, we were never technically alone. This was different for us and pushed our friendship into unchartered territory.

"I want to taste you, Luna." He licked his lips. "Will you let me do that?"

"Yes," I breathed, never feeling a mouth on me before. It wasn't like our night together held a lot of foreplay.

"I'm going to lay down." He pinched my chin, tilting my head back. "And you're going to ride my face."

I swallowed hard, my body leaking at what he was suggesting. I sat up and hugged the back of the passenger seat so he could lay down behind me.

Lifting my dress to my hips, I straddled his chest.

"Trust me, Luna. You'll enjoy this, but I can guarantee you that I'll enjoy it even more." Zach lifted the hem of my dress, his eyes falling to the apex between my thighs. "Take this off."

My cheeks burned but I lifted the dress even higher and slid it up and off of me before throwing it behind me.

"Fuck." Zach ran his hands up my thighs and gripped my hips. "I should have done this the other night, but I couldn't…"

"You couldn't what?" I asked, staring down at him.

"I needed you too much, Luna." Zach kissed my knee. "Now stop talking. Come up here and let me taste this pretty pussy."

"God, Zach." I slid farther up him, his hot breath washing over every inch of me.

"Fuck me, you smell good." He ran his hands up the length of me, cupping my breasts. "Drop this cunt on my tongue, Luna," he demanded, his voice strained like no matter what happened, he wouldn't be able to move on until I gave him what he wanted.

"What will you do if I don't?" I asked, my body vibrating.

"I don't suggest testing me, little girl."

A sly grin spread on my face. Lifting to my knees, I placed my foot by Zach's head on the bench and my other on the floor. The move opened me up even more to him.

"Fuck, Luna." His eyes dropped to my center and back up to my face. "Please."

My heart raced at the sheer desperation in his voice.

"Now. Please. Fucking hell. *Now.*"

Doing as I was told, I lowered onto his mouth.

He growled, piercing his tongue into me.

A hard cry left my lips, the abrasiveness of his beard scratching at my center. "Oh, God. Zach," I whined.

He hummed against me, the sounds vibrating through every morsel of my being.

I had never felt a pleasure this great. Even the times we had been together, this was something else. It was on a whole other level. His tongue thrust into me, swiping from my center to my clit and back again.

Holding me in place, he ate at me like he was damn near starving for that sustenance only my body could provide him.

"Zach," I breathed, undulating my hips against him. "Please. More. God, give me more." I threw my head back, closing my eyes and just felt. No part of me went untouched by him.

Zach shook his head, forcing his tongue even deeper. Releasing me with a wet smack, he inserted two fingers inside of me.

A low moan escaped me.

"Look at me."

I met his gaze.

"You're going to come and you're going to come fucking hard. I want you to scream for me. Let it all out, Luna. Let me hear how good your man is making you feel."

A breath left me. He referred to himself as *my man*.

"Do you understand me?" he asked, thrusting his fingers slow and deep inside of me.

"Y-Yes."

"Good girl." He kissed my inner thigh. "It's just you and me, Moonbeam. Let it all out." Before I had a chance to brace myself, Zach dropped me back onto his mouth and sucked my clit between his teeth.

A shattered gasp left me.

He growled against me, spreading me open with his thumbs, and sucked and pulled. Flicking his tongue against the swollen nub, he thrust his fingers back inside me.

A hard moan left me that turned into incoherent sounds. Pleasure shot up my spine. An electric charge singed my skin. The hairs on my body tingled. My toes damn near curled.

"Oh God." His name left my lips on a hard cry when the release slammed into me. Stars danced in my vision. "Zach," I moaned, cupping his head and running my fingers through his hair.

Much to my surprise, he released me and pushed me back.

I wiggled down him, trying to let him up without kneeing him in the groin.

Zach sat up and grabbed my hands, pulling me back into his arms. Cupping my ass, he covered my mouth with his. The acidic scent of my desire coated his lips. I moaned, tasting myself on him.

Reaching between us, I undid his belt and lowered the zipper to his pants.

He lifted me onto my knees, breaking the kiss. "I need you," he whispered.

I pulled his cock out of his pants and lowered onto him, a hard shiver trembling through me.

He groaned.

Wrapping my arms around his shoulders, I leaned my forehead against his. "You have me. Always."

(Zach)

I almost lost it when Luna lowered onto me. Her pussy gripped me tight, squeezing and sucking me in even deeper.

"You have me. Always."

A hard shiver trembled through me at her words. Her sweet delicious words that I had longed to hear. From her. From anyone. I spent my childhood feeling unwanted. And now I was wrapped in a woman's arms who had wanted me since she was a little girl.

Running my hand down her arm, I linked our fingers.

Luna moved against me, tilting her hips forward and back. She gave us both what we wanted, mind blowing pleasure erupting between us.

"Zach," she whispered, covering my mouth with hers. "Come for me."

Wrapping my arms around her, I held her against me and did as she demanded.

I came. I came fucking hard.

NINETEEN

Luna

SOMETHING HAD SWITCHED IN Zach. He had been desperate to taste me and when I gave us both what we wanted, he closed up completely after. But I wasn't sure why or if maybe I had done something wrong.

Now both of us were sitting in the back seat. I had quickly put my dress back on, feeling embarrassed that I wanted him so desperately.

"Luna." Zach brushed his fingers along my nape. "I'm sorry."

I looked away, smoothing out my hair.

"Don't be mad at me," he murmured, kissing my shoulder.

"I'm not mad." I looked up at him then. "Concerned, yes. But not mad."

It was his turn to look away. He sat back, raking a hand through his hair. He glanced out the window, the dim lighting of the moon casting an eerie glow on his handsome face.

"Thank you," I said softly, unsure what to even talk about now. I could feel him dripping out of me. I was sure that most would think it was gross, but I found that I liked it. I enjoyed being able to feel him.

"I should take you home."

My stomach sunk. "Already?"

He turned to me then. "It's getting late, Luna."

"Can we stay for a little longer?" I asked, hopeful. "Please."

He searched my face. "Okay."

"How has work been?" I asked, deciding that it was best to keep the conversation off of us because obviously something had taken a turn for the worse inside of him. I just wished he would talk to me.

"Busy. As much as I think I can do it all, I know I can't." He smiled softly. "I wish my dad wasn't retiring but I could never ask him to work alongside me."

"You know he would if you asked him."

"I know and that's why I won't ask him."

"Makes sense."

"Thank you," Zach said, bringing our joined hands up to his mouth. "For tonight. For everything. For just being you. Thank you for showing me that there are women in this world who aren't out for blood."

My breath caught. "I…I don't know what to say to that."

"You don't have to say anything." He leaned his forehead against mine. "Just thank you."

"You're welcome." I cupped his nape, my eyes fluttering closed. Breathing him in, I got the faint scent of sex and his spicy cologne. "But I really haven't done anything," I said after a minute or so had passed.

"You have." Zach sat back and rested his arm across my lap. "Do you remember that girl I dated in high school? It lasted for less than a second."

"I believe so." Truth was, I remembered most of them because I was too shy to make a move, or he was too stuck in his head to do anything about it.

"She spread it around school that I wouldn't take no for an answer. My parents had to step in before her older brother kicked my ass."

"Wow." My eyes widened. "Why would she accuse you of something like that?"

"Because she was drunk and wanted me to fuck her, but I said no. I may be a lot of things, but I don't take advantage of women. I know how that feels and I didn't like it. So why the hell would I do it to someone else?" He shrugged. "Anyway, that's one of many stories but I don't want to bore you with that shit."

"You could never bore me." I thought a moment. "Tell me something no one knows." I turned toward him.

"Really?" He raised an eyebrow. "Why?"

"I want to get to know you more than I already do." My cheeks burned. "That's all."

Zach pinched my chin, placing a soft peck on my mouth. "I like this girl who I wish I could have given my virginity to instead of it being taken from me without my...." He cleared his throat. "Yeah."

"I..." Bile rose to my throat. "I didn't know."

"It doesn't matter." He cupped my cheek. "It's in the past. As much as the shit I went through, sucked, I like to think I came out stronger in the end."

My throat closed up, knowing he never had a choice who he gave his innocence to. Even though he had never said it, I could only imagine that was what happened to him. "Zach." My voice wavered.

"Hey." He brushed his thumb over my bottom lip. "I didn't mean to make this...I didn't...Fuck. I'm not used to this. I've known you for years. Since we were kids. You are my best friend, Moonbeam. I know your dad feels you could do better, but I promise, I will try my hardest to be the best for you and prove him wrong."

"I don't care what my dad thinks," I blurted.

"Yeah, you do, Luna. And that's fine. I get it. He's your father. I understand."

"So, just because he feels that you don't deserve me…is this ending between us?" My stomach was doing flips, waiting for Zach to give me his answer.

"I don't want this to end but he's right."

"No." I pushed him. "Don't say that shit to me. I don't care what he thinks." I raised a hand when he went to speak. "Listen to me, Zach. I like you. Alright? If you haven't figured it out by now, I've liked you since we were kids, but I know you know that. Everyone knows that. But I don't know what I'm doing. I'm new. Naïve. Whatever you want to call it, but I do know that I want more. From you. From this."

"You do deserve better, Luna," Zach told me.

"You just said that you would do your hardest to be the best for me." I grabbed his shirt, pulling him against me. "You are the best for me. You are." I covered his mouth with mine when he went to argue. "You are," I whispered against his mouth.

His body stiffened. "Luna."

"Shut up." I leaned back. "I'm in love with you. I don't expect you to say it back to me. I may be new at this but I'm also not stupid. I'm just telling you how I feel. The heart wants what it wants and all that shit, so no, Zach. I don't care what my father says because I want you. So yeah, you can take that how——"

A hot mouth captured mine in a deep, bruising kiss.

I broke the kiss. "Zach."

"Shut up." He fisted my hair, holding my head in place. "Just shut up." Crushing his mouth to mine, he devoured every inch of it. Slipping his tongue between my lips, he stole my breath.

"Zach," I whispered against his lips. I didn't expect him to say those words back to me. Hell, I hadn't expected to say them myself, but I was sick of this shit with my father. He couldn't control who I wanted to be with. That wasn't his choice to make.

Zach broke the kiss, leaning his forehead against mine and took ragged breaths. "I..."

"Shhh...you don't have to say anything back to me, Zach. I'm not that type of girl if you haven't noticed. I just want you to know that I'm not going anywhere."

His breath hitched. "Fuck, I like you. I like this. Being with you. Touching you. Holding you. Having a fucking conversation with you." He cupped the side of my neck. "But I can't say those words back. Not yet. I care about you. You have to know that."

"I do." I looked up at him then, placing my hand against his cheek. "Don't."

He leaned into my palm. "I'm not doing anything."

"You're feeling guilty." I brushed my thumb along his full bottom lip. "Don't feel guilty, Zach. I know you care about me."

"I...I would go to hell for you. I've been in fucking hell, but I would go back there, just for you. Just to have you at my side. Just to have you with me."

"No, Zach. You're never going back there again. Ever. Do you understand me? I'm here. Even if nothing comes of this and we just remain friends, I want you happy. That's all I've ever wanted."

"Fuck, Luna."

I couldn't help it. The tears started to fall. My heart hurt for him. For what he went through as a boy. And I didn't even know the whole story, but I still ached for him.

"Shit." He pulled me against him. "I didn't mean to make you cry."

"I just...I can't..." I hiccupped. "I don't know what you went through, but I know it was brutal. God, I don't know what's wrong with me." I laughed lightly. I hiccupped again.

"Breathe, Moonbeam," he coaxed. "Shhh..." He petted a hand over my head. "Talk to me."

"I want to know everything about you, but I imagine that it's hard to talk about." I shrugged. "So, I just..." I shrugged again, picking at a fuzz on my dress.

He cleared his throat a couple of times before kissing my temple. "There were times I wished it would have been me who died instead of my dad. I even tried searching for my real mom but after looking for what felt like fucking ever, I found out she had passed away from cancer."

"I'm so sorry." I cupped his knee.

"Don't be." He kissed my temple again. "I had Brogan and Coby at this point."

"Do they know you tried looking for her?"

"They were the ones who told me to." He paused. "I never thought I would get parents like them. Most people want to adopt babies. Not children and especially not ones like me."

"I'm glad they did." I looked up at him that time.

"I'm glad they did too. I not only got them as parents, I got a whole family too. But..." He looked out the window, his eyes dark. Hoping. For something that I couldn't quite put my finger on.

"It's not enough," I answered for him.

"No." His jaw clenched. "It's not."

"What is it that you want?"

"I'm not sure anymore," he murmured.

We sat in silence. It felt like an eternity had passed before either of us said anything.

"Let's go." He opened the door. "I'll drive you home."

"Oh." My stomach sunk. "Do we have to?"

He gave me a soft smile. "It's almost three in the morning."

"Already?" My eyes widened.

"Time flies when you're having fun." He winked.

My cheeks burned.

He took my hand, helping me out of the back seat.

I moved to walk around him when he stepped in front of me. "Zach?"

He stared down at me, the muscle in his jaw, ticking. "You're beautiful," he murmured. His voice was so soft, I almost didn't hear him. Using the back of his hand, he brushed it down my cheek. "So damn beautiful."

My breath caught in my throat.

He shook himself, clearing his throat. "Let's get you home."

(Zach)

I had to be careful with Luna. If I let myself go, if I let her see the true error of my ways, it would only scare her. Would she still want me then? She loved me. She said so herself. I knew she had feelings for me, and rumors had gone through our group of friends and family that those feelings were more than just a crush but to hear her say it, stirred something inside of me. Something that was dark. Something that had never been unleashed before until now. I grew up needing to protect her. I wasn't sure why. But now that I knew exactly how she felt, this protection bordered on insanity.

Once we reached Luna's house, I put the car into park and sat there. I just fucking sat there. I had a beautiful woman sitting beside me who had confessed her love for me, a woman that I'd fucked several times already, a woman who *knew me* inside and out and yet, I still fucking sat there.

"Zach?" Luna gently touched my arm. "Will you spend the night with me?"

My gaze snapped to hers. "Why?"

Her mouth fell open. "What do you mean *why*? I spent last night with you. You took me for a drive tonight and we had sex in your car. I confessed my feelings for you." She lifted her hand when I went to speak. "I'm not done."

My dick twitched at the sass.

"I'm not proposing to you. I'm not being clingy. I don't give a shit what happens anymore."

I raised an eyebrow. "You don't?" I wasn't sure where this was going but I was curious just the same.

She pressed her lips into a firm line before blowing out a slow breath. "Fine. I do care. Alright? I can't help it. Either way, that doesn't matter. I'm just asking you to spend the night with me. That's it. It's not like I just told you that I'm pregnant or anything."

"It would be scientifically impossible for you to find out this soon," I blurted like the asshole that I was.

She scowled. "I know that, Zach. Thank you very much for letting me know how my own body works."

"I mean." I rubbed the back of my neck. "Luna, this isn't ending how I want it to. That all came out wrong."

"It's fine." She sat up straighter and cleared her throat. "I know I'm not like the usual women you've slept with. And I understand that it's been awhile. I get that. I'm new but have you ever stopped to think for just a second that maybe I'm willing to learn? Hell, I gave you a damn blow job. Outside. Where anyone could have walked by." She shook her head. "But it's fine."

"Luna."

"It's okay." She opened the passenger side door and slid out of the vehicle.

"Luna, I didn't mean—"

"Zach, it's fine." She smiled but it never reached her eyes. "Thank you for a wonderful evening." She shut the door and walked up the path to her house.

Shit. What the hell had I just done?

TWENTY

Luna

ONCE I REACHED MY room, I grabbed my pillow, shoved my face into it and screamed. God, how stupid was I? I couldn't believe I had told Zach that I loved him. It was the dumbest thing I had ever done.

I sighed, slumping on my bed and dropping my bag on the floor. This could not be happening.

Rising to my feet, I picked my bag up off the floor and tossed it on the chair in the corner of my bedroom. Maybe I should wake the girls up. Grab some wine and talk. I glanced at the clock. It was pushing four in the morning. The house was quiet, so I was stuck wallowing in my own self-pity.

A lump lodged its way into my throat, but I refused to cry. My mom taught me better than that. But I was pissed. No. I was furious. How the hell could Zach fool around with me only to throw it all back in my face?

A knock suddenly sounded on the door.

I frowned.

Rushing to it, I opened the door, finding Zach staring down at me. "Zach," I breathed. "How did you get in?"

"I have my ways," he muttered.

I glanced past him, finding Meadow walking back down the hall. She gave me a wink before slipping into her bedroom.

"What do you want?" I asked him, keeping a firm grip on the door.

His hands were shoved into his pockets, his dark hair was messy and unkempt. My body heated, remembering I had run my fingers through it not too long before.

Zach cleared his throat. "Luna."

I swallowed hard at the husky tone of his voice and moved out of the doorway. Needing to put some distance between us, I headed to my dresser and pulled out some pajamas. "What are you doing here, Zach?"

"I came to apologize."

"Why?" I turned on him. "Because you felt guilty? You felt sorry for the girl who was stupid enough to confess her feelings for you? Or better yet, you felt like it was the right thing to do because your parents raised you well." I rolled my eyes, slamming the dresser drawer closed.

"Careful, Moonbeam."

The delicious undertone of his threat washed over my skin. "Or else what, Zach?" I met his gaze in the reflection of the mirror. "I'm not perfect. I'm not tall. I have curves that will never go away no matter how many miles I run. I have freckles because I love the sun. Oh, and my hair will never be perfect either. Is that the issue?" I couldn't stop the word vomit from leaving my mouth.

"Luna." He shut the door and took a step toward me. "You *are* perfect. More than perfect. You're damn near flawless."

"Then why the hell did it take you so long to make a move?" I threw at him, spinning on my heel. "Why after all this time?"

"Because I was fucking scared," he said, his voice raising. "And I'm scared for you too. I'm scared what my darkness will do to you. You've always been too damn important for me to risk it. I've been selfish because I've needed you so much but was scared to risk a relationship and losing you. Is that what you wanted to hear, Luna? You want to hear how a grown man is fucking terrified because of these feelings. Or how lately I can't do anything because you fucking distract me. I don't want to hurt you but fuck me, I want to rip open your soul. I want to fuck you so hard, you feel me for the rest of your damn life." He took another step in my direction. "But right now, all I can think about is shoving my cock down your throat to shut your sassy mouth up. Is that what you wanted to hear?"

My heart jumped, my skin tingling under his intense scrutiny, but no words left my mouth.

"Nothing to say now?" He closed the distance between us but didn't touch me. "Don't want to accuse me of anymore shit?"

"I'm not one of your sluts," I whispered.

He chuckled, the sound dark and inviting. It was as if the devil himself were standing in front of me and saying, *'Come here, little girl. Let me give you a piece of candy.'*

"No." Zach leaned toward me, brushing his nose along the side of my cheek. "You are definitely not like the previous women I've been with. None of them were brunette."

I frowned. "So you fucked women who didn't have brown hair?"

"Exactly." He grinned.

"Why not?" But I already knew the answer.

"Because then they couldn't remind me of you."

"But now you want me." I stepped around him.

Zach grabbed my arm, spinning me around. "Yes. And I've had you. Several times in fact but I want more. I want all of it. All of you. Every single inch. I want to fuck your soul, Luna, but I want to make love to you at the same time."

"Prove it." My heart raced. I placed my hands on his chest. "Prove to me that you want more. Prove everyone wrong. Prove my father fucking wrong, Zach. *Show me.*"

A wicked smirk spread on his face before he crushed his mouth to mine. Pushing me up against the dresser, his hands were in my hair as he ground his hips between my legs.

Items fell off my dresser and hit the floor.

Zach shoved my dress to my hips and broke the kiss long enough to get it up and over my head.

With his hands gripping my hips, he lifted me and carried me over to my bed. Dropping me gently on it, he crawled between my legs and kept his lips fused to mine.

Zach released my mouth, staring down at me with hooded eyes. He cupped my breast, his thumb brushing over the hardened peak. "You make me lose control."

"Let me help you get it back," I murmured, running my hands through his hair.

His dark eyes snapped to mine. "I'm sorry. For everything I said. For…"

"Shhh…" I kissed his chin and started unbuttoning his shirt. When I had the final button open, I pushed it off his strong shoulders.

Zach let the shirt fall to the bed before reaching between us and unbuckling his belt. He lowered the zipper and pulled out his thick length. "This is for you, Luna," he rasped, wrapping a hand around his cock. "All of it."

"Remind me."

(Zach)

It had been three days since I had any amount of food. I wasn't sure what I did. Or how I even deserved the wrath that was placed on my shoulders. But all I could do was wait. For more. For nothing. I didn't care anymore. I was done. Finished. I was stuck in hell with no way of getting out anytime soon.

"Toy."

I shivered at the pet name.

"What are you doing?"

I cowered in the corner of my makeshift cell. The damp walls dripped, almost as if they were crying. Maybe they felt sorry for me.

"Come into the light."

I wanted to laugh. Not sure why my stepmom didn't just drag me out into the open like she usually did, I tried ignoring her.

"Toy." She came into the room which was unusual for her seeing as the room was dirty. She was always dressed in nice clothes. Her hair and makeup done. She was always well put together. While I, on the other hand, was stuck being dirty.

Her dark eyes roamed over me.

I shivered, trying to shield myself but stopped when she frowned. I had learned the hard way that she didn't like it when I hid from her.

"You hungry?"

My stomach rumbled. "Yes," I croaked.

"Good." She left the room.

I jumped, a sheen of sweat coating my skin. Breathing through the nightmare invading my mind, I pinched the bridge of my nose and inhaled.

Inhale. Exhale. Inhale. Exhale.

Breathe. Keep breathing.

The nightmares didn't come as much as they used to. I was sure my parents were thankful for that. A child's screams got old and quickly.

I covered Luna's hand that was on my chest, taking all the strength from her that I could muster.

She continued sleeping beside me when a knock sounded on the door. I kissed her cheek, slid off the bed, making sure not to disturb her, and put my pants back on.

Trudging to the door, I made sure I was at least a little decent and greeted whoever was up at this godforsaken hour.

"Hey." Gigi stared up at me with Meadow standing behind her.

Meadow yawned, running a hand up and down her face before giving me a small smile.

"What are you two doing up?" I asked, keeping my voice low so not to disturb Luna.

"Couldn't sleep and…" Gigi looked at her sister before meeting my gaze. "We heard a noise."

Meadow snorted. "Gigi heard a noise and she woke me up."

I stepped back into Luna's room and grabbed my dress shirt before joining the girls out in the hall. I slipped into the shirt when I remembered. *Fuck*. My scars.

Gigi and Meadow both stared at me with wide eyes.

"Don't," I grumbled, stomping down the hall. How the hell could I have forgotten about them? Not that they covered my front really but as soon as I turned around, they could for sure see the marks on my back. *Shit*.

"I didn't see anything." Meadow walked past us and headed into the living room.

"Zach," Gigi said gently.

"It's nothing," I murmured, running a hand through my hair.

"Maybe not now it isn't."

"Listen." I dropped my arm to my side. "If anyone is going to know anything about my past, it'll be Luna. Until then, you didn't see fuck all. Now tell me where you heard the noise."

"Fine." Gigi started walking down the hall. "It was outside. We hear shit all the time. The neighbors aren't exactly quiet. But this was different."

"How different?" It wasn't like I could do anything. I wasn't trained but I knew people who were. We all did.

"I don't know." Gigi huffed, heading to the patio door. She turned on the backyard security lights. "It just was. But we can't call our dad, or he'll lose his shit and make us move home."

"No. He would make *you* move home," Meadow pointed out. "I'd go hole up with someone else."

Gigi rolled her eyes.

"Where did you hear the sound?" I asked, ignoring their banter.

"In the backyard." Gigi rung her hands nervously in front of her.

"I'll go check it out." I held out my hand. "Give me your phone."

She placed her cell in my palm.

I turned on the flashlight and headed out into the backyard. Not really sure what I was looking for, I checked both sides of the house. Nothing was out of the ordinary. It was a rather warm night. Humidity was thick in the air, but something was off. The hairs on the back of my neck tingled. Yup. Definitely fucking off.

Once I was done checking out the rest of the yard and satisfied that everything was fine, I headed back into the house.

"Well?" Gigi asked, chewing her bottom lip.

"I…" I glanced back outside. "Nothing was out of place. I didn't see anyone, but I'll tell the twins since they're here more than I am."

"Okay." Gigi joined her sister at the kitchen table. "I hate being paranoid, but I swear I heard something."

"I believe you," I told her as Luna came into the living room.

"What are you guys doing up so early?" Luna asked, rubbing her eyes.

"They heard a noise," I told her, my body vibrating with the need to wrap her in my arms. To take her away from here and keep her safe. Fuck it. I went to her and cupped her face.

She stared up at me with wide eyes. "Zach?"

Before she could protest, I crushed my mouth to hers.

(Luna)

Voices sounded around us followed by a squeal and maybe some cheering. Either way, I wasn't sure. All I could focus on was Zach's lips pressed against mine. In front of our friends. Holy hell. Although the kiss didn't last long, and it remained PG at best, it still stirred something inside me that he laid claim on me in front of people.

He broke the kiss, leaning his forehead against mine which I had come to love. To crave. To expect. I knew that the forehead touch was calming for him in a way.

"Well it's about fucking time," I heard Meadow say.

"No kidding," Gigi responded.

"Maybe you should take a note from them."

"I…it's complicated," Gigi mumbled.

Zach chuckled, grabbed my hand, and led me to the dining room table.

"So…" Meadow waggled her eyebrows.

"Stop." Gigi smacked her.

"What?" Meadow scowled. "I'm just happy alright? It's about time and I'm just…happy." She sighed. "I'm not a romancy type girl but this gives me all the feels."

I laughed, my cheeks heating. "So you heard a noise?" I asked, changing the subject.

"Yeah." Gigi stood. "I'm going to go make coffee." She left the table and headed to the kitchen.

"What did you mean that she should take a note from us?" Rumors had gone around that Gigi had a thing for my brother, but I wasn't sure how true that was.

"It's complicated. Apparently." Meadow shrugged.

"Well, I'm good with it. If the rumors are true, I would love for Gigi to date my brother. Lord knows he needs a good girl." I grimaced. My brother dated some major bitches. I had no idea where he found them, but they were vile human beings. Especially his most recent ex who he remained friends with even though I had no idea why.

"Who's dating whose brother?" Gigi asked, coming back into the dining room and placing four mugs on the table followed by the coffee pot.

"You are," I said.

She coughed. "I'm not dating anyone's brother."

"Maybe not now but you will." I grabbed a mug and poured myself a cup of coffee then did the same for everyone else. Once I had milk in my cup, I sat back and took a sip, embracing the heavenly aroma.

"That will never happen." Gigi sat at the table across from us, resting her chin in her hand.

"It will," I said. "Give it time."

Zach placed his arm on the back of my chair, brushing his thumb back and forth over my bare arm.

I sighed. This was bliss. Zach and I were moving forward, and life just seemed almost too good to be true.

"You would be fine with that?" Gigi asked.

Before I could answer, a bang sounded from the backyard.

"See!" Gigi cried, shoving to her feet. "I wasn't losing my damn mind!"

"Stay here." Zach rushed to the patio doors and turned on the light leading into the backyard. "You have got to be fucking kidding me."

"What's going on?" I asked, my heart racing.

Zach looked back at us before opening the doors and stepping outside.

I passed a glance at Gigi and Meadow before I jumped to my feet and followed him. "Zach?"

Once I stepped a foot outside, my eyes widened.

Zach was walking toward me with…

"Aiden?" I rushed to them.

"He's drunk," Zach muttered, helping Aiden walk toward the house.

I went to his other side and hooked his arm around my shoulders, helping Zach.

"What the hell?" Meadow demanded, coming up to us. "You said you were going to stop this shit," she said, scolding Aiden.

He only grunted.

"He probably won't even remember anything you say to him," I told her.

"Fine. I'm going to go bake." Meadow spun on her heel and headed into the kitchen.

Zach and I brought Aiden into the house and laid him on the couch.

"Here." Gigi handed me a glass of water and two Tylenol.

"Take these," I said, handing them to Aiden.

"Fuck," he grumbled, doing as he was told. When he was done the water, I took it from him and placed it on the table before kneeling on the floor beside him.

"What happened?" I asked him, not wanting to judge but when this had happened more often than not, it became a bit of a concern.

"Nothing." He rested his arm across his forehead, shielding his eyes.

"Luna." Zach reached down and grabbed my hand, pulling me to my feet. "Let him sleep it off. It's all he can do right now."

"Fine." I pulled the blanket off the back of the couch and covered him.

"Thank you," Aiden muttered, his breaths soon becoming even.

I sighed.

"Well, I'm going to get ready and head to the center early," Gigi said. "Or I can stay here with him."

"No." I looked back at Aiden sleeping soundlessly on the couch. "I don't have to work today. I'll go to the center when he wakes up."

"Luna," Zach bit out. "You're going to stay here with him? By yourself?"

"On that note, I'm off." Gigi rushed down the hall to her room, the sound of the door closing a moment later.

"What are you accusing him of, Zach?" I demanded, placing my hands on my hips. "He's not Ashton. He hasn't made a move on me if that's what you're worried about. You need to trust your friends."

"I'll trust my fucking friends when they stop hitting on you."

I rolled my eyes. "He hasn't hit on me. That was his dickhead brother. Who I also love, like a brother." I raised my hand when Zach went to speak. "You need to trust me."

Zach blew out a slow breath, running a hand through his hair. "I do trust you. I just don't trust…"

"Anyone else," I finished for him.

"Exactly." Zach wrapped his hand around my upper arm and pulled me into the alcove before wrapping his arms around me. "I know I shouldn't worry but you're beautiful, Luna. You don't see what I see."

I scoffed. "Please. Ashton only made a move because you did."

"No." Zach leaned back and cupped my cheek. "He made a move because I didn't."

"That doesn't matter. I meant what I told you. My feelings for you." I placed my hands on his chest, feeling the beating of his heart beneath my palm.

"I know," he said, his voice low. He leaned his forehead against mine. "I have to head to the city, so I should get going."

"Okay." I tilted my head back, placing a soft peck on his mouth. "So…we're good?"

"Yeah, Moonbeam." He smirked. "We're good. We're very good."

(Zach)

As much as I didn't want to leave Luna, I had a long day at work ahead of me. But first, I needed coffee. And a lot of it.

Once I left the girls' house, I was checking my phone. When I looked up, I almost bumped into... "Ashton. Sorry."

"No problem." He jutted his chin. "How's my brother?"

I glanced back at the house. "Sleeping," I said, putting my phone in my pocket. "One of the girls call you?"

"Yeah, Meadow did. She also ripped me a new one." Ashton whistled. "Geeze, that girl has a mouth on her. Giving me shit for letting Aiden drink." He grunted. "As if I have any control over what my brother does."

"She's worried about him. We all are." I went to walk past him when his next words stopped me.

"I'm sorry, Zach."

I slowly turned around. "For what?"

"Shit, man." He rubbed the back of his neck. "You're going to make me say it?"

"Yes." I crossed my arms under my chest. "What are you sorry for, Ashton?"

"Fuck," he muttered. "Listen, I'm sorry for the shit I said. For causing problems and for..."

"And for kissing Luna?" I asked, raising an eyebrow.

"You know about that?" Ashton took a step back.

"I do. I won't kick your ass now, but you touch her again and I'll make my mother come out of retirement." I spun on my heel and headed down the driveway.

Once I was seated in my car, my phone rang. I frowned, wondering who the hell could be calling me so damn early.

"Porter," I said, placing my phone on speaker and setting it on the passenger seat beside me.

"Zach," came a feminine whisper.

"Mom?" I picked up the phone. "What's wrong?"

"Your father."

My heart jumped to my throat.

"Zach," her voice wavered. "He had a heart attack."

TWENTY-ONE

ZACH

"WILL YOU ALWAYS BE *my father?"*

Coby frowned. *"Of course I will, buddy. Why wouldn't I be?"*

"Well…" I chewed my bottom lip. Although I wanted to tell him what was on my mind, I didn't want to upset him. I didn't want to give him any reason to hurt me.

"Hey." Coby dried his hands and hung the towel over the edge of the sink before turning around to face me. "Talk to me."

"I don't know how," I confessed.

"Okay." Coby pushed away from the sink and sat at the table beside me. He grabbed my hands. "Listen. I'm going to tell you a story. Brogan and I wanted to have a baby. We wanted so badly to have a baby. We tried. For many months, we tried."

I didn't understand exactly how babies were made but I listened intently, interested in what he had to tell me.

"One day, we found out that we were successful. We were so happy. Your mo—Brogan was pregnant. We celebrated that night by going out for supper. But a week later, God decided to take that baby home with him."

"How come?" I asked, my eyes wide.

"Maybe he felt this world wasn't safe for a baby." Coby leaned forward. "I know you're a smart boy."

"I'm almost twelve," I told him.

"You are." Coby grinned. "I also know that you're strong and you can handle this world. Your life may have started out rough, but I know that it'll shape you into one of the strongest people I know. Maybe the strongest."

"So you think God took your baby home because they couldn't handle the world but gave me to you because I can?"

"Exactly." Coby looked down at our joined hands.

I followed his gaze.

He turned my hands over, palms up, and slid his hands beneath them with mine resting on top.

"I know we're not blood. I know Brogan didn't give birth to you. But we love you, Zach. We love you with every inch of us. You've made us stronger. You've made our love for each other grow. You've made us happy. And I promise to take care of you. To help you be the best man that you can be, and I also promise, to show you the motherfucking world."

After I got off the phone with my mom, I sped across town to the hospital my father was at. The tires screeched as I turned into the parking lot. Thankfully, I found a free space rather quickly.

I couldn't think straight.

Please be okay. Please be okay.

It was at the back of my mind that I had to call the office. That I had to call someone. Anyone.

Luna.

Once I parked the car, I quickly dialed her number and ran to the doors of the emergency room while I was waiting for her to answer.

"Zach," she greeted after a couple rings. "Sorry I was a—"

"I need you," I blurted.

"What's wrong?"

"Come to the hospital." I barged through the doors and ran to reception.

"Oh God. Are you okay?"

"It's not me." I blew out a slow breath. "It's my dad."

"I'm on my way." She hung up, the sound vibrating through every inch of me.

When I reached the receptionist, I went to demand where my father was when a gentle hand touched my arm.

"Zach." My mom stared up at me, her chin quivering.

"Oh, Mama." I threw my arms around her and crushed her to me.

She sniffed, hugging me tight. "I'm so glad you're here."

"Of course I'm here." I released her and cupped her face. "What happened?"

She shook her head. "I..." A shuddered breath left her. "I'm not even sure. We had gone to a club just as a night out. Sometimes you need to get out of the house, you know? We rented a room and were laying on the bed watching a lame romance movie. Your dad...he..."

"Hey." I grabbed her hand, leading her to a nearby room for visitors. Sitting her down, I kept her hands in mine. "Take a breath."

She inhaled, blowing it out slowly.

"Again," I demanded gently.

She did it again, a small smile creeping across her lips. "God, you may not be our blood, but you are so much like your father, it's uncanny."

"He's the best man I know." My throat became thick. "So, thank you."

Her breath hitched. "I can't lose him."

"You won't." I squeezed her hands. "Tell me what happened after you started watching that lame movie."

"He sat up, complaining that he wasn't feeling well. He's been working hard this week, helping the guys get the center expanded. I wish I could help too but I only design. I don't build." Mom shook her head. "Anyway. I offered to get him a glass of water. When I came back from the bathroom, he was on the floor." Her eyes welled. "I've done some things. Bad things. Scary things. But none of that compared to what happened tonight. If I lose him…Zach, I'm not strong enough to live without him."

"Don't say that." But it was easier said than done. I knew it too. My parents had a love that you didn't see in a lot of people anymore. I envied them and strived to have that of my own one day.

Luna.

I cleared my throat. "Listen to me." I kissed my mom's knuckles. "Dad's strong. He's the strongest man I know, in fact. And so are you."

When she went to pull away, I only held on tighter.

"I'm serious. How many times have I heard you put dad in his place because he was being a grumpy ass or how many times have I seen you put the guys in check when they weren't building what you designed." I remembered one of the times my mother called Asher out because he wasn't following her instructions.

Mom laughed, wiping the tears from under her eyes. "I remember Angel and Dale stood back and laughed while I yelled at Asher. Which would have been funny to see I'm sure, since he's so much taller than I."

"Exactly. And look what you've done for me. Hell, the shit I put you through when I was younger. And, you've stood up to Stone for me."

She frowned. "You know about that?"

I nodded. "I was in the bathroom and overheard you two talking."

She sighed, leaned back in the chair, and rested her head against my shoulder. "I understand he's protective, but I think he worries too much."

"I would never hurt his daughter," I told my mom. "She told me she loves me."

"Really?" Mom sat up. "What did you say?"

"I told her I care for her. Which I do. But I don't know if it's love. Could it be? Yes. Even I know it could definitely turn into love."

Mom smiled. "I'm—" She frowned, glancing past me.

"What is it?" I followed her gaze, finding… "Clara." I stood from the chair. "What are you doing here?"

"I came to drop lunch off for my mom. She's one of the nurses on this floor." She peered around me before looking back at me. "I'm sorry to interrupt. But I just wanted to make sure everything was okay."

Mom came up beside me. "I'm sorry, we haven't met." She stuck her hand out. "I'm Brogan. Zach's mother."

"Oh. I'm Clara." Clara returned the handshake. "It's nice to meet you. Although, I wish it could be under better circumstances."

"Right." Mom held Clara's hand a little longer than deemed necessary, her dark eyes boring into the woman the twins had tried setting me up with. "How do you know my son?"

"We…uh…" Clara's cheeks turned pink.

I placed my hands on my mother's shoulders, pulling her away from Clara. "The twins set us up on a date but that was after Luna and I started becoming closer. So I told them no."

"But Ashton never told me that it was cancelled."

"That doesn't surprise me. Ashton's an ass. Love that kid." Mom shook her head. "But definitely a shit disturber."

"We're just friends," I told her.

Mom glanced up at me then. "Good."

"Will you give me a minute?" I asked my mother. "And then I'll check with the doctors and see what we can find out on Dad."

Mom nodded. "Okay." She slowly turned away and headed back to one of the seats.

I grabbed Clara's arm, pulling her out into the hall. "Listen, now's not a good time. My dad…"

"Is he okay?" Clara asked, her brows narrowing in the center.

"He had a heart attack and we don't—"

"Oh, Zach." She threw her arms around my middle, knocking me back a step. "I'm so sorry."

"Uh…I…" I cupped her neck. "Thank—"

A gasp sounded.

I glanced up, finding Luna staring directly at us.

Oh.

Fuck.

(Luna)

Squeezing the small teddy bear that was in my hands, I stared at the display before me. I didn't know who the woman was that had her arms around Zach, and I didn't care. What I did care about was that they seemed to be close and I had no idea who she was. Not that I had to know every single woman he knew of course. God, I was losing my mind. He made me this way. He made my feelings all fucking jumbled and now he was hugging another woman when it should be me consoling him. He called *me* and yet there he was, standing with...*her*.

But whoever she was, she was well put together. She had long blonde hair that was pulled back into a ponytail. Her slender but curvy figure fit perfectly in Zach's arms. The sight of it forced bile to my throat.

Zach released her and stepped back, running a hand through his dark hair.

The woman turned around slowly, her bright blue eyes widening when they landed on me. "Luna?"

"Clara," I gasped.

Zach looked between us. "You two know each other?"

"Yeah, from the center." I shook my head, a light laugh escaping me. "Well, this is fucking great."

I swallowed hard. Clara had always been beautiful but seeing her in Zach's arms made me see her in a different light. She was stunning. Tanned skin, sapphire eyes, and a perfect complexion. Even her tits were fucking perfect. Although she was covered completely, I could still see the swell of her breasts hidden beneath the white loose dress shirt she wore.

She tilted her head to the side.

Yeah, I'm checking you out.

But much to my surprise, she ran toward me. "I'm sorry. I'm so so sorry. I didn't know. I never knew it was you. I swear I didn't know." She pulled me in for a hug. "We never went on that date. I promise we didn't. Zach said there was someone else." She held me at arm's length. "Please believe me."

"He told you about me?" was all I could say.

"Yeah." She leaned back, cupped my shoulders, and gave me a big smile. "I wish I would have known it was you. I would have kicked his ass in your direction from the moment I met him."

"You never saw him at the center?" I asked, not that Zach made an appearance there often, but I still needed to know.

"No, I didn't. I know this is fucked up, but I promise you, I am not that girl."

"What are you doing here?" I asked her, vaguely aware that Zach was watching this whole exchange between me and Clara.

"I was meeting up with my mom for breakfast. She's one of the nurses on this floor. And I saw Zach. I would love to get together with you though. Know more about you instead of just bumping into each other at The Dove Project. We could go on a double date." She shrugged. "That kind of thing." She grabbed my hand, pulled me toward Zach, and pushed me into his arms. "He needs you." She started walking away and waved over her shoulder. "I'll text you." And with that, she disappeared down the hall.

What the hell just happened?

"Luna."

The deep voice sliding into my ears, pulled me from my thoughts.

"How's your father?" I asked Zach, taking a step back and putting some distance between us.

"We haven't heard anything yet." Zach's breath hitched. "He had a heart attack."

I gasped. "I'm so sorry." I handed Zach the teddy bear. "This is for your dad. I'll go see how your mom is." I went to head into the waiting room when his next words stopped me.

"I didn't realize you two knew each other. You don't need to be jealous."

I glanced at him over my shoulder. "And you wouldn't be?" I raised a hand when he went to speak. "We are not having this conversation here."

"Did I interrupt something?" Brogan asked, stepping out of the waiting room with a coffee cup in her hand.

"No." I walked past her and sat in one of the chairs furthest away from him.

"I'm going to go check with the doctors," Zach muttered. "Maybe they have news."

I could feel his eyes burning into me, but I didn't care. I didn't care about anything.

"Hey." Brogan sat down beside me. "Did you want to talk about it?"

I snorted. "As if you don't have better things to worry about than my little crush on your son."

She smiled softly. "I know it's more than a little crush, Luna."

My cheeks burned. "But you don't really want to hear about my...issues. Not right now anyway."

"I do." Brogan cupped my hands. "It'll help distract me until I know what's going on with my husband. So please, talk to me."

I inhaled a sharp breath before blowing it out slowly. "I'm in love with Zach. And I told him this, but he never said it back. Which I never expected him to, but I was thankful that I finally had the balls to admit my feelings for him and that he never laughed at me or whatever. Also, I heard the twins set him up on a date, but he never went on it and now, knowing that it was with Clara, bothers me. And then seeing her hugging him..." I winced. "Add to the fact that I know her and she's beautiful." I snapped my mouth closed, waiting for Brogan to tell me that I was being unreasonable.

"I get it."

"Wait..." I shook my head. "You do? So I'm not being unreasonable?"

"No." She laughed lightly. "Not at all. Let me tell you a story." She released my hands and sat back in the chair, pulling her legs up onto the seat. "A month before Coby and I got married, we decided to go out one night. We don't drink but we wanted to dance and stuff our faces with a bunch of good food. We had been eating really well for months before that. We wanted to pig out."

I smiled, nodding for her to go on.

"Anyway, when we were at the club, I had to use the washroom and I came back to some broad all over Coby. And I hate using that term because I'm all about women empowering women, but this chick *was* a broad." Brogan scowled.

"Wow." My eyes widened. "What did you do?"

"I punched her, went home, and fucked my fiancé."

I coughed. "Oh…uh…"

Brogan laughed harder. "You all think your parents are innocent. But trust me. None of us are innocent. Not in the things we used to do. Not in the shit we do now. We get by. Coby and I have instilled that into Zach. He's a good man and that boy loves you."

My cheeks burned. "He hasn't said—"

"Doesn't matter." Brogan turned to me and placed her hand on mine. "He does. I've seen the way he looks at you. And yes, he has a past. We all do. But I've been around long enough. Sure, he may have been set up with Clara but remember, that date never happened. Besides, I didn't see her look at him how you look at him. And he definitely doesn't look at her the way he looks at you."

"I'm just not used to him being friends with someone outside of our group. I know that's lame but it's the truth."

Brogan sighed. "Trust me. Zach loves—" She turned her head, a deep frown settling between her brows. "Stone."

"What?" I followed her gaze, finding my father coming toward us along with Angel, Dale, and Asher following behind him. "Daddy?" I rose from the chair and walked up to him. "What are you doing here?" I asked, giving him a quick hug.

"I called them," Zach said, coming into the room. Lian and Henley, two more men who had been in their squad, joined us.

"How's he doing?" Angel asked.

Asher and Dale stood off to the side, muttering softly between them.

"I think I can answer that."

All of us turned as a young man dressed in a white lab coat entered the room. "Mrs. Porter?"

"Yes." Brogan rushed to him. "Dr. Silvaggio, tell me my husband's okay."

"He is," the doctor answered.

"Oh, thank God." She reached a hand out.

Zach caught it, wrapping his arm around her shoulders.

I moved to the other side of him, linking our fingers.

His stiff body relaxed at that.

"Do you know what happened?" Brogan asked, her voice shaking.

The doctor glanced around the room.

"You can tell me in front of them. They're his brothers. We're all family," she explained.

"Okay." The doctor nodded. "Your husband had a mild heart attack that was caused from a heart defect that we can only assume, he's had since birth."

"Really?" Brogan shook her head. "He's never said anything about that."

"He said he wasn't sure what medical conditions ran in his family." The doctor flipped through his file.

"He's awake?" Zach asked, pulling me closer.

The hairs on the back of my neck burned. I chanced a glance at my dad. His eyes were locked on us, that tick in his jaw jumping.

I quickly looked away.

"He is but right now he's resting." Doctor Silvaggio closed the file. "Bottom line is, with lots of rest, he'll be back to his old self in a matter of days. And to answer your question, anything could have caused this. Stress. An unhealthy diet. Strenuous activity."

Brogan's cheeks reddened. "Can we see him?"

"Of course. But just you and your son right now. I'll wait for you out in the hall." He turned and left the room, barking orders at staff.

"Let's go see him." Zach hugged his mother. "He'll need you."

She nodded, wiped under her eyes, and turned to the group of large men who were currently sucking the air out of the room.

"Thank you for being here," she said softly.

"Of course."

"No need to thank us, Brogan."

"We're family," that was my dad.

While Brogan talked to them, Zach pulled me out into the hall.

I stared up at him. So many questions fell between us, but it wasn't the right time, so all I could do was wait and hope for the best that we could continue moving forward.

Zach cupped my nape, leaning his forehead against mine. "Fuck, Luna."

"I know," I whispered, wrapping my fingers around his biceps. "Go see your dad. I'll be here."

"You don't have to stay," he murmured.

"Yeah." I tilted my head back. "I do. I'm not leaving you." I stood on tiptoes and placed a soft peck on his mouth. "Go to him and I'll be in the waiting room."

Before I could pull away, Zach grabbed my arm and crushed me to him. His big body shook, his hands roamed down my back, hugging me tight.

"Spend the night with me," he pleaded, pushing his face into the crook of my neck. "Please, Luna."

"You don't have to ask me," I told him, leaning back and cupping his face. "Unless this isn't as real for you as it is for me." I didn't expect him to tell me he loved me. I wasn't that kind of girl. But I needed to know that we were doing more than just sleeping together. Or else for sure my father would kick his ass.

"Yes, Moonbeam. It's real for me. It's very fucking real." He grabbed my hands and kissed my fingertips. "We have to talk but I promise you, this is very real."

He kissed my knuckles and pulled away from me just as Brogan came out of the waiting room. He hooked an arm around her shoulders, and they walked down the hall with Doctor Silvaggio.

"Luna."

I stiffened, turning slowly to greet the judgmental eyes of my father but he just looked at me with a furrowed brow instead. "What?"

"Nothing." He pulled me in for a hug. "I'm going to head home and fill your mom in on the good news."

"Okay," I said, thankful that he didn't say anything about Zach and I.

Dad squeezed me one last time before pulling away. "You'll be fine here by yourself?"

"Yup. I have my phone. I can read and play games while I wait."

He nodded. "Be safe, *Piccola*."

Knowing my father was only keeping his opinions to himself because it wasn't the right time, I had to wonder what would happen when he finally revealed exactly how he felt.

TWENTY-TWO

ZACH

WITH MY MOM'S ARM hooked in mine, we walked with Doctor Silvaggio to the room my dad was staying in. A heavy weight had lifted off of my shoulders when the doctor said that he would be fine. My mom was strong, but I knew that if she lost her husband, it would break her.

"He's in here," Doctor Silvaggio said, stopping in front of a door. "I'll give you some time alone, but he needs his rest. There's a cot beside him for you, Mrs. Porter. He already said that he wasn't spending the night if you couldn't be with him."

Mom laughed lightly. "Yeah. He won't even let me sleep on the couch when I'm sick and hacking up a lung. He said that we're married, so we sleep together even when we're sick." She sighed. "He's a stubborn man, that husband of mine."

Doctor Silvaggio only smiled and headed back down the hall we just came from.

"Ready?" I asked Mom, unlinking our arms and taking her hand instead.

"Definitely." She led the way with me following behind her but kept her hand in mine. As soon as we entered the room, Dad looked our way. He held out his arms, his eyes locking on his wife.

She released me and ran to her husband. "Don't ever do that to me again," she cried, crashing into him.

He grunted, wrapping his arms around her small frame. "I'm sorry, little one."

"You scared the shit out of me." She sobbed into the crook of his neck.

"I know." He murmured something else to her that only she could hear.

Her shaking body relaxed but she continued to softly cry. "Don't do that again." She released him and sat on the edge of the bed. "You hear me, Porter?"

Dad nodded, cupping her face. "I hear you."

I waited at the edge of his bed, not wanting to interrupt their moment.

Dad reached his hand out, meeting my gaze.

I joined them, sitting on the opposite side of him and taking his hand. I placed my palms up in his, like we had done when I was a boy.

"Son," he said, his voice gruff.

I swallowed hard, the lump thick in my throat.

"Look at me," he demanded softly.

Mom sniffed.

"If I lost you," I finally said. "If *we* lost you." I looked up then. My dad blurred in my vision.

"Hey, I'm not going anywhere." He looked between us. "Are you trying to get rid of me already?"

"No," Mom cried, punching his arm.

He winced, grabbing her hand and bringing it up to his mouth.

"Sorry. I'm sorry." She took a breath. "It brought me back to…" She shook her head.

"Zach." Dad looked at me then. "Will you give us a moment?"

"Of course." I stood from the bed and leaned over, giving him a hug. "I'm glad you're fine. I'm really fucking glad."

"Me too, Son." He swallowed noisily. "Me too."

"The teddy bear is from Luna." I released him and placed the toy on the shelf by the window.

"Tell her thank you." Dad gave me a small smile.

"I will." I gave Mom a quick hug and left the room. Closing the door behind me, I breathed out a sigh of relief. As much as I knew that I should go to Luna, I leaned against the wall instead and slid to the floor. Dropping my head in my hands, I rubbed the back of my neck, trying to massage out some of the tension resting on my shoulders. But it didn't work. It didn't do shit in fact.

"Zach?"

My head popped up, finding Luna coming toward me.

"Can I sit?"

I nodded.

She slid to the floor beside me, wrapping her hand around my forearm. "How's he doing?"

"Good. My mom's pissed that he scared us." I shrugged. "But she's happy. We both are."

"I bet."

Bringing my knees up to my chest, I rested my arms on top of them. "I'm just glad—" My phone rang at that point. Pulling it out of my pocket, I muttered a curse when I saw that it was my secretary calling. "Dennis," I answered. "I'm so sorry."

"Why are you apologizing? You are the boss and all."

"Yeah." I sighed. "Listen, I should have called earlier but I wasn't thinking straight. I need you to cancel all of my meetings today. I won't be in the office due to a family emergency."

"Oh God. Is everything okay?"

I smiled at his concern. "Yes. It is now."

"Oh good. But I'm on it. You take care of yourself, Mr. Porter."

"What did I tell you?" I chided.

"Zach." He laughed nervously. "Right."

"I'll be in on Monday," I told him and disconnected the call. It was Thursday but having an extra day wouldn't hurt. Or that would be what my parents would say.

"Dennis?" Luna asked a moment later. "You have a male secretary?"

"I do." I leaned my head against the wall. "He's actually Clara's brother. That's why we kept in touch. He was looking for an internship because he wants to run his own business one day. He's a freshman in college and also needed some extra cash. I needed the help anyway and gave him a job instead. He's a good kid."

"That's good."

I glanced at Luna. She was chewing her bottom lip.

"Hey." I pulled her lip from the onslaught of her teeth. "You have nothing to worry about. I'm yours, Luna."

She searched my face. "Are you really?"

I frowned, opening my mouth to argue with her when my mom took that moment to come out of the room.

"What are you two doing on the floor?"

Luna pulled away from me, a flush hitting her cheeks.

My brows narrowed.

"We were just talking," Luna told my mom.

"Oh okay. Well…" Mom glanced down at me. "You can go home, Zach."

"I should stay," I said, rising to my feet.

"No." Mom placed her hand gently on my arm. "He's fine. I promise. And if anything changes, I'll call you but that's not going to happen. Your father is stubborn remember?"

"But what if something happens and I'm not here," I said, not liking the desperation in my voice.

"He'll be fine." Mom wrapped her arms around my middle. "Go. Go home. Rent a hotel if you want to stay close. Go to Luna's. I don't care. But I don't want you having to spend the night here."

"But I—"

"Go," Mom pressed. "Please. I love you and I appreciate you being here, but you need to rest. You look like you didn't get much sleep last night anyway."

Luna coughed.

My dick stirred but other than that, I didn't say anything.

Mom laughed. "Right. Go. Please."

"Alright." I gave her another hug. "Call me if anything changes."

"I will." Mom gave Luna a quick hug as well and headed back into the room.

"So…" Luna stared up at me.

"I can't go home. I need to be close just in case something changes but I don't want to go to my parents' place either." It would be weird being there without them and knowing what they were going through currently, I just needed away.

"I'd say we can go to my place, but it's always overrun with people. And Aiden's probably still passed out." Luna paused. "We can rent a hotel for the weekend."

Every inch of me came alive at the thought of having Luna all to myself for three days. No distractions. No questioning stares. Just her. And I.

I leaned down and placed a hard peck on her mouth. "That's perfect."

TWENTY-THREE

Luna

SPENDING THE WEEKEND ALONE with Zach would be a step in a different direction for us. We wouldn't have my father breathing down our necks. We wouldn't have our friends questioning us. I loved them, and I knew Zach did too but sometimes, they could be a little overbearing.

When I left my place earlier, Aiden was still passed out. I felt guilty for leaving him, but Zach needed me.

Zach and I drove to a hotel on the outskirts of town. It had been one that I saw quite frequently whenever we went into the city a few hours away, but I had never actually stayed there. It was only a few stories high but one of the nicer ones I had seen in the area.

"This isn't much but honestly, I just need you tonight. No fancy shit."

I nodded, grabbing Zach's hand and holding it tight between mine. "Just us."

"I know our parents are getting older. We're all getting older but today..."

"It scared you." I linked our fingers. "I get that, Zach. No one wants anything to happen to their parents. Ours aren't getting any younger but they are still pretty young."

"They are."

"And your dad is healthy. Besides the heart defect of course."

"True." Zach brought our joined hands up to his mouth, placing a soft peck on my knuckles. "Thank you for being so fucking amazing."

I laughed, my cheeks heating. "I'm really not but you're welcome."

"You are." Zach put the car into park. "Ready?"

To spend the night with you and help you feel better? Oh yeah. "I am."

He winked. "Good."

We slipped from the vehicle.

Zach came around to my side of the car and wrapped an arm around my shoulders. "Hey, I think that's my uncle's crew."

I followed his gaze, finding several motorcycles parked by one of the bottom floor rooms. "Is Jaron still the vice-president?"

"He is," Zach answered. "He'll be president when his dad retires."

We had grown up with Jaron Mercer but with him being from another town a few hours from us, we didn't see him often. Especially not now that we were older.

"Did you want to go say hi?" I asked Zach, linking my arm in his.

"Let's get a room first and then we will."

We headed to reception and Zach got us a room rather quickly. Thankfully the rooms weren't booked completely. Apparently once people found out that there were bikers staying at the hotel, they decided to go elsewhere. But personally, I would rather be by bikers. It was safer that way.

"Now we can go say hi." Zach stuffed the key cards in his pocket and held out his hand.

I slid my fingers in his, letting him lead the way.

We headed back outside to where the bikes were parked when a younger man left a room, followed by several other guys. They all wore leather cuts with the Hell's Harlem logo on the backs. The skull with black eyes looked almost like it was grinning every time they moved.

The younger man who left the room first, lit up a smoke and leaned against the wall. He looked our way, recognition dawning on his face.

"Zach Porter. Motherfucker." He pushed off the wall and came toward us. "How are you?"

"Good, Sammy. You?" Zach gave the guy a one-armed hug, keeping his other hand still locked in mine.

"Not too bad. Your uncle has us doing a ride. Apparently, we've been on edge lately." The man, Sammy, shrugged. "I don't know. I just follow orders."

Zach chuckled. "Right." He glanced down at me. "Luna, this is Sammy Butcher. Sammy, Luna."

Sammy stuck out his hand. "Nice to meet you."

"It's nice to meet you too," I said, returning the handshake.

"Jaron's here." Sammy nodded to the door he had come out of. "Wanna come say hi and have a beer?"

Zach looked down at me.

I shrugged. "I could always use a beer."

"I could use something harder," he mumbled.

"Something hard sounds delicious," I blurted.

Sammy laughed.

My cheeks heated.

Zach only grinned.

I couldn't believe those words slipped from my mouth. Meadow was the flirty one of us girls. She said anything that was on her mind. Me? Not so much. Until now that is.

"Well, kids. Let's go have some beers then." Sammy led the way to the room.

"You want something harder, do you?" Zach murmured, placing a soft peck on my cheek.

"I want it whenever you're ready to give it to me." He had a stressful day. There was no way that I was going to hint at sex just because I had become addicted since having it for the first time the other day.

"I'll give you something hard later, Moonbeam. It'll be so fucking hard, you won't know what to do with it."

"I think I can handle it," I said, patting his chest.

He chuckled, the sound dark and sinister. "Sure. Keep telling yourself that, Luna. Remember who's had way more experience than you."

I shrugged. "Semantics."

A laugh boomed through him.

I grinned, giving him a wink.

"I'll give you that, Moonbeam. You know how to make me laugh. Even when I've had a shitty day."

"I aim to please." I stood on tiptoes and kissed his cheek.

A throat cleared, forcing us a part.

"Zach."

I turned, finding Jaron Mercer coming toward us. He was Zach's cousin, being the son of Greyson Mercer, the current president of the Hell's Harlem motorcycle club.

"Jaron, how are you?" Zach gave him a quick hug. "It's been awhile."

"Too long." Jaron smiled down at me. "How are you, Luna?"

"Not too bad." My heart stuttered. Although I had never been attracted to Jaron, his gray eyes were mesmerizing.

"Come. We have beer. And pussy. But I'm sure you don't need the latter." Jaron turned, heading back in the direction of his hotel room. "Isn't that right?"

"No. I'm good." Zach grabbed my hand and kissed my knuckles. "Very good."

I cupped his face. "You better be." I was already jealous over Clara. I didn't need more women added into this.

Zach smirked, pulling me along beside him. We entered the hotel room which was much larger than I would have thought. People milled about. The men were dressed in leather cuts while women wore scantily clad clothing. They hung off the men but much to my surprise, they left Jaron alone. He headed to a couch across the room and sat.

Jaron grabbed two bottles out of a mini-fridge on the floor beside him. He handed them to me and Zach before picking a bottle of beer off the table in front of him. "So how is everyone?" he asked, taking a swig.

"Good," I said. "We're working on expanding the center."

"Oh yes." Jaron sat back, placing his ankle on the opposite knee. "I heard about that." He paused. "How's Piper?"

"She just got back from Europe but she's good," I told him.

"Interesting. I was just in Paris."

I thought a moment. My eyes widened. "Wait, she said…"

Jaron only winked.

I laughed.

"What?" Zach frowned.

"Piper said she met someone in Paris," I told him.

Zach looked between Jaron and I, a chuckle escaping him. "Interesting," he repeated.

Jaron grinned. "Let's just say, Paris is my new favorite city."

"I bet it is." I liked that it was him she had met up with. Even though he never outright said it. But something told me that it was hard for them. Especially when Piper had been doing her own thing with the twins. Also, as much as I liked Jaron, I had a feeling he wasn't the type to settle down.

"How are your parents, Zach?" Jaron asked, taking the subject off of him.

"Well...they were doing okay but my dad had a heart attack."

"Holy shit." Jaron sat forward. "Is he okay?"

"He is." Zach reached for me. "Thank God for that."

I squeezed his hand.

Jaron shook his head. "You know, no matter how old I get, I always forget that our parents are getting older as well."

My stomach twisted.

"Yup." Zach looked down at me. "We should get going."

I nodded.

"Well, it was good seeing you both." Jaron stood at the same time we did. "Tell Piper I said hi."

(Zach)

As much as I loved my cousin and wanted to continue visiting with him, I needed to wrap myself up in Luna more. Since finding out my father had a heart attack, I was on edge and on the verge of snapping and losing the very control I had spent years fighting for.

"Zach?" Luna turned toward me as soon as we entered our hotel room.

I leaned against the door, shutting it behind me and clicking the lock into place. "I need you, Luna. I need you in ways that I'm not going to apologize for. I won't be gentle. In fact, I might even get fucking mean. But right now, it's all I can give you." I took a step forward, forcing her back. "But I promise you, I respect the hell out of you. You're my best friend. The only woman who knows more about me than my own mother does. But right now, this has nothing to do with that. So say the word and this stops. Right now."

She swallowed, backing up another step. "What do you want to do?" she asked, her voice coming out shaky and unsure.

"Everything, Luna." A sly grin pulled at my lips. "I want to do everything."

TWENTY-FOUR

Luna

ALTHOUGH ZACH AND I had sex already, several times in fact, I had a feeling that I was about to get the real him. The part of him that he's been holding back since the first time he kissed me. Or the beast within that he's kept in check from the moment he made me come apart in his arms.

"Luna," Zach barked. "Stop thinking and answer me. Yes or no."

My heart started racing, my skin became clammy. I could take him. I could handle him and push back just as good as him, if not better but this…this was something else on a whole other level.

Instead of answering like he demanded, I dropped my bag on the floor. Pulling off my sweater, I threw it on the chair by the large patio window.

Zach's eyes burned into me the whole time as I undressed for him. His hands clenched into fists at his sides, the electric energy snapping between us.

Hooking my fingers into my white tank top, I lifted it up and over my head before tossing it aside. Pushing down my leggings, I kicked them off my feet, which left me standing in just a black lace bra and panty set.

"Turn around," Zach demanded, his voice rough.

I did as he said, turning away from him.

"Kneel," he instructed.

Lowering to the floor on shaky legs, I did as I was told and placed my hands on my thighs. My blood rushed through me, every inch of my skin alive and tingly from the mere demands leaving Zach's mouth.

I felt him before he touched me.

I was attuned to him before he laid his fingers on my skin.

When he knelt behind me, a shiver rippled down my spine.

"You're fucking perfect," Zach murmured, his hot breath fanning over the side of my face. His fingers brushed along my upper back, pushing the bra strap off my shoulder and down my arm. "So perfect." When his mouth touched the soft spot beneath my ear, all breath left me on a whoosh.

"Zach," I whispered.

Suddenly, my head was ripped back.

A gasp escaped me, my heart hammering inside the walls of my ribcage.

He chuckled, the sound dark and inviting. Like a predator offering candy and God, did I ever want that sweet sweet candy.

"More," I heard myself say.

Zach shoved me forward, pushing my face against the floor. "How much more do you want, Luna?"

"All of it," I pleaded. "Whatever you want to do. I want it all." I dug my fingers into the carpet, the abrasiveness rubbing against my cheek.

With a firm hand, he held the back of my neck and pushed his waist into my rear. "Hmm…I'm not sure you can handle more. Maybe I should stop. Or I could tie you up and jerk off. Make you watch. What would you like, Luna?"

"No. I want…" But the idea of him pleasuring himself when I couldn't touch him, was exhilarating all on its own.

"Tell me what you want," he demanded, his voice dark and deadly, dripping with the promise of seduction and power. With a finger, he hooked it into the crotch of my panties and ran his knuckle over my slick skin. "You're wet. You're fucking drenched, baby. You like this."

"I do." My cheeks burned. There was no point denying it when he could feel how much I was enjoying this new side of him.

Zach removed his finger from between my legs. "Last chance, Luna."

I pushed against his hand, rising on all fours. Looking at him over my shoulder, I licked my lips. "Do it. Whatever you want. Use me to make yourself feel better."

A wicked grin spread on his face.

He hooked his fingers into my panties, pulling them down and below my ass. "I'm going to use your body to make us both feel good. Turn around and take off your panties."

I did as I was told and took off my bra as well. I knelt there. Naked before him. Completely bare. Utterly vulnerable. And just waited.

(Zach)

She was absolutely breathtaking. It took everything I was made of to rein in on the control that was seeping from my very fingertips.

Luna stared up at me through her dark lashes. A rosy hue hit her milky skin. Her dark nipples hardened the longer I stared. She had told me a few days ago that she wasn't like the previous women I had been with. She was right about that. She was better. So much better.

"Get on the bed," I bit out, my voice gruff.

She did as she was told, spreading out before me on the mattress.

I rose on shaky legs, paced back and forth, and just stared at her. How could this woman, someone so damn innocent and precious, want me? After everything I had been through, even though it was never my fault, I still used women to get what I wanted. And Luna was offering herself up to me like I was being served a meal on a platter.

"Zach." She leaned on her elbows, staring at me. "Is everything okay?"

"Why do you want me?" I blurted, stopping directly in front of her. My hands reached out, wrapping around her ankles.

"I think you already know why," she said breathlessly. Her knees separated, falling to the sides and showing me her perfect, pure, little pussy. But no, it was no longer pure. Not since I took her virginity. Not since I wanted to destroy her innocence and make her crave the dark, dirty part of sex as much as I did. I wanted to fucking ruin her.

I gripped her ankles, pulling her to the edge of the bed. Lowering to the floor, I ran my hands up her calves to her knees, and spread them in a rough move.

Her breath caught, her dark eyes watching me.

"I still can't believe you gave your sweet cherry to me." I hooked my arms around her waist, pulling her toward my face and taking a deep inhale. The scent of her desire wafted into my nose, forcing pre-cum from the tip of my dick. "It makes me so motherfucking hard knowing that I'm the only one who's been inside you. That I'm the only one who's made you come." I pulled off my shirt and threw it to the floor beside me. "That I'm the only one who knows what you look like when you truly let yourself go."

I unbuckled my belt and reached a hand into my pants. When my palm connected with my throbbing cock, a groan escaped me.

"Zach," Luna breathed, watching me.

Pulling my pants lower, I kicked them off and went back to stroking my dick. "Move to the edge of the bed, Luna."

She moved her ass closer, the scent of her becoming more pronounced the longer time went on.

"Fuck, your smell is driving me insane," I said, my voice raspy. My hand tugged on my cock, pinched the tip, and went back to the base.

Up. Down. Squeeze. Repeat.

My balls ached. My dick swelled. I was torturing myself by not fucking her, but I needed this. To give her some control. For the first time in my life, I needed to submit.

"Tell me what you want, Luna," I said through clenched teeth.

"Whatever you want," she whispered.

"No," I barked, my dick swelling even more at her willingness to give me whatever I wanted. "What do *you* want?"

"I'm not sure," she said, sitting up.

"Luna," I growled, resting my forehead on her knee. "Tell me."

"I don't know, Zach. You've never asked me before." Her fingers traced over my nape.

"Please," I said, my voice desperate.

"I want everything," she finally said. "You inside me. To touch me. Fuck me. L-lick me."

I shivered.

"But I want to give you what you want more." She gently tugged my head back. "I like giving you what you want. I like when you take control. I want you to make good on your promise and ruin me. Make me hurt. Make me beg. Make me plead for more."

"Fuck." I shoved to my feet, forced her onto her back, and slammed my mouth down hard on hers. I swallowed her gasp of surprise and shoved my tongue deep between her lips.

Her hands roamed down my back, cupped my ass, and pulled me farther between her legs. She reached between us, wrapping her fingers around me and guiding me to where both of us wanted my cock most.

Without even hesitating, I thrust forward.

She arched beneath me, taking me even deeper.

Her hot pussy squeezed me, sucking me in. She took everything I had to give her and more.

(Luna)

"Are you good?" I asked Zach later that night. I was lying on my stomach, naked, and kicking my feet back and forth behind me.

"I am." But he wouldn't meet my gaze.

I slid off the bed and crawled back beneath the covers and straddled his waist.

"Luna." His hands gripped my hips, stopping me from taking it any further.

"What? You're still on edge." I leaned over, placing a soft peck on his mouth. "Let me help you feel better." As soon as the words left my mouth, his cock grew beneath me. I wasn't sure how I was good to go again. Or even him for that matter. I was sore. Used up. But I also felt so damn good at the same time, that I wanted more. I was an addict. A druggie needing their fix.

"You want more," Zach murmured against my mouth, cupping the back of my nape.

"Yes." I rocked against him, sliding my body up and down the rigid length sporting between his thighs. Even though he wasn't inside me, the pleasure from my clit running along the veins of his cock, sparked a need I had never felt before.

"You're a greedy little thing." He licked along my bottom lip, giving it a gentle nip.

I whimpered, moving my hips faster and faster.

"Fuck." His eyes rolled into the back of his head. "So fucking good."

"God." I threw my head back, a hard moan leaving the back of my throat.

Zach suddenly sat up, wrapping an arm around my waist. He reached between us, circling his fingers around his cock.

I covered his hand, helping him ride out that delicious high. That ultimate pleasure that neither of us could deny. No matter what came of this, this was what I would always want. Him. Me. Moving. Breathing. Just being together.

"Luna," my name left his lips on a breathless whisper.

Rising to my knees, I slid my body down his length.

"Fuck." He kissed my chin, his mouth brushing down the length of my jaw to my ear. "I'm in love with you, Luna. I'm so fucking in love with you."

My heart jumped, my body burning as his confession slid over me. "God, Zach." I cupped his face, crushing my mouth to his. "I'm in love with you too."

"I know," he said against my lips.

I grinned, pushed him back onto the bed, and started moving my hips up and down.

"That's it, Luna. Take from me what you want. What you've always wanted."

"Zach," I cried out.

In a quick move, he flipped me over, so I was lying beneath him. "Say it again."

"I love you," I said, staring up at him as he took us both past the brink of madness.

TWENTY-FIVE

ZACH

MY PHONE RANG SOMETIME during the night. Or maybe it was morning already. I rolled over, my body stiff but relaxed. So damn relaxed.

Reaching for my pants, I picked them up off the floor and fished out my cell. "Yeah," I said, slumping back down onto the bed.

"Zach."

My eyes widened. I sat up. "Mom? Is everything okay?"

"Oh yes." She sighed. "Everything's fine. So damn fine. Your dad is coming home today. I just wanted to let you know that. He was giving the nurses a hard time, saying that he would get more rest if he was at home with me."

"Oh, thank God." I moved to the edge of the bed, dropping my head in my hands. "I'm glad."

"You and me both. Are you home?"

"No." I glanced back at Luna's sleeping form. "I didn't want to go home or to the city, just in case something happened, so Luna and I rented a motel room." And I spent the night making love to her. Love. I told her I was in love with her. A grin broke out on my face.

"Oh okay." Mom hesitated.

"What is it?" I dropped my hand to my lap. "Mom?"

"It's nothing really. Or maybe it is. I don't know anymore. But just…be careful. I love Luna. And I love her for you. But I worry. Stone is overbearing and with good reason. It has to do with what happened to her real mom. I just don't want you to get hurt. That's all."

"I…" I glanced back at Luna again. Her back rose and fell but she didn't stir. Rising from the bed, I went into the bathroom and shut the door behind me. "I feel like you're warning me about something."

"I don't want to step in where I shouldn't, but I feel like…Stone is a good guy. I love him like a brother. He's family. But you are my son. And Luna is his daughter. Just like him, I will gut a bitch who hurts you."

"Somehow, I'm not surprised there," I mumbled, leaning against the counter. "Are you telling me to step aside?" I didn't want to. Hell, I told Luna how I felt last night. There was no way either of us could go back to the way things were after that.

"No. God no. Just be prepared that if Stone butts his nose in, it could cause more problems. Luna might…she might have to make a choice."

"Fuck," I muttered. "I mean…sorry."

"Don't apologize for swearing, Zach. Not this time. Listen, I know you've been pushing people away whenever they get too close. You did it to me and your father as a boy."

I rubbed the back of my neck. "I'm sorry."

"Don't be. Zach, I get it. I really do. When your father and I first got together, something happened that forced him to push me away as well. He needed time to heal and I could only do so much. But honestly, even though what he went through was fucking hell for him, I think it made us stronger in the end."

I didn't know the full extent as to what had happened to him, but I knew it involved another woman. "Stone scares the fuck out of me," I confessed.

"Honestly, I'd be more worried about Creena." Mom laughed lightly. "But I understand that. He wouldn't be doing his job as a father if he didn't scare you."

"True."

"The only thing you can do is let Luna in. Prove to her and her father, that you are worth it. That you are enough for her. But you also have to believe that yourself."

"You know me way too fucking well," I mumbled.

"I have to go and help your dad get ready so I can take him home but please take heed in what I said."

"I will. I'll head to the city tonight so you two can have some time alone."

"I love you, Zach. I think you need to talk to Luna."

Great. "Love you too, Mama."

We said our goodbyes and as much as I didn't want to admit it, my mother was right. Luna loved me. I knew she loved me. But she also loved her dad. I just wasn't sure if our relationship was strong enough to withstand whatever came next.

Deciding to take a shower, I stepped beneath the hot spray just as the door to the bathroom opened.

"Zach?" Luna stepped into the room. "Is everything okay?"

"Yeah. I just got off the phone with my mom. I didn't want to disturb you, so I came in here. My dad's going home today."

"Oh, that's wonderful news." Luna came into the shower, pressing her body up against me. "I'm happy that he's doing better."

My dick lengthened when her chest pushed against my back. Turning around, I cupped her face. Moving my hand to the back of her head, I fisted her hair and crushed my mouth to hers.

She gasped, arching against me. "Zach," she whispered against my lips.

I broke the kiss, leaning my forehead against hers. "Sorry. I just…" A thought came to me. "I have to head to the city tonight. I'm going to give my parents some time alone. Come with me."

"Really?" Luna asked, leaning back. "I don't think I've ever been to your apartment."

"It's a condo but that doesn't matter." I pushed my hips into her, pressing her up against the wall. "I want to take you out for dinner. I want to go dancing with you. I want you. All of you. With me."

"I would love that," she breathed. "I would love all of that."

"Good." As much as I knew we needed to talk about…everything, we didn't. Instead, I used her body to please us both for the next hour. The shower turned cold before I was done with her.

"God, Zach." Luna shivered, her teeth chattering.

I chuckled, wrapping a large terrycloth towel around her. "I got a little carried away."

"That's fine." She stared up at me with those big beautiful eyes of hers. "But I need to know, is everything okay? I know you said your dad's fine, but I feel like something else is going on that you're not telling me."

"No." I kissed her softly on the mouth. "Everything's fine." I didn't want to ruin this moment. So, I lied. Fucking hell, I lied to her.

(Luna)

As much as I wanted to press for more answers, I didn't. But Zach closed up completely after that. Something was eating at him. Every so often that muscle in his jaw would tick. Or his hands would clench on the steering wheel.

We left the motel shortly after our shower. We had said goodbye to Jaron and the guys, and they even asked Zach if everything was okay. I wanted to know what was going on but a part of me didn't want to all at the same time.

"Zach?" I said once we pulled onto my street. I needed to grab some clothes and also tell the girls that I wasn't going to be home for the night.

"Yeah," he said, tightening his grip on my inner thigh.

"Are we good? I hate being a nag or whatever, but I just want to make sure that I didn't do anything."

"Fuck, no." He grabbed my hand and brought it up to his mouth. "You haven't done anything at all. I'm sorry. I'm good. We're good. I promise." He gave me a small smile in reassurance, but I still felt like he was lying.

"Okay, well, if you want to talk about it, I'm here."

"I know, Moonbeam." Zach pulled into my driveway and put the car in park.

"Are you coming in?" I asked, opening the door.

"I will but I'll stay out of your bedroom or else we won't be going anywhere." He winked.

I laughed, the heaviness billowing around us, simmering some. "Alright then, Zachary. Let's go so I can get my clothes and you can take me to your condo."

He grinned. "I think I'm going to enjoy having you in my space."

I smiled, shaking my head.

When we entered the house, it seemed like all of our friends were over, even though it was just pushing two in the afternoon..

Meadow and Piper were setting the dining room table when Gigi came into the house from the backyard.

"Hey guys," Meadow said. "How's your dad, Zach?"

"Good. He's going home today. I'm sure the doctors were hoping he would stay longer but you know him," Zach said as we walked farther into the house.

"Yeah." Gigi laughed. "I think all of our dads would be the same way."

"Definitely." Meadow sat at the head of the table. "I decided to make lunch. Trying to practice my cooking skills outside of baking. You're welcome to join us."

"I'm always up for a home-cooked meal," I said. "I'll get ready after," I told Zach.

"Of course." He brushed his fingers down the length of my arm before linking our hands. Leading me to the table, he pulled a chair out for me.

"Awww, so sweet," Meadow swooned.

I laughed, my cheeks burning. I sat, pulling the chair forward. "Thank you."

Zach only nodded and sat beside me.

"This looks amazing," Piper said as Ashton and Aiden came into the house from the backyard.

Meadow's smile widened. "Thank you."

"It really does." Aiden moved beside Piper, standing close.

"I'm going to eat outside." Piper grabbed her plate and headed out into the backyard.

Ashton went to follow her when I shot up from the table. I acted first before I could think about it. I stepped in front of him.

His brows narrowed.

"Leave her alone," I said gently.

"I was going to keep her company," he said.

"Right." I could see Zach moving beside me out of the corner of my eye. He didn't say anything. He didn't need to. Ashton needed to back off. "I don't know what's going on between you three." I looked at Aiden before meeting Ashton's gaze once again. "But give her some space."

"I think you should mind your own business," Ashton muttered, grabbing a bun out of the bowl on the table.

"I think you should think before you make a stupid decision." I turned and headed to the patio door. "I'm going to keep her company." I passed a glance at Zach.

He only nodded, giving me all the encouragement I needed.

Once I was outside, Piper's head shot up.

"It's just me," I told her.

She sighed, her shoulders slumping. "I broke things off with them. Although I did that after Paris, they never got the hint. So I did it again."

"They're still not getting the hint," I said, sitting beside her on the patio couch.

"They aren't. After Ashton realized that he never had a chance with you, he came back to me." She shook her head. "God, it's all confusing. So damn confusing. I never wanted to hurt them but…things weren't official. I just want to be left alone."

I wanted to tell her that I knew it was Jaron she had met up with in Paris but thought better of it. I knew that she had spent years having a crush on him but never acted on her feelings. I wasn't overly sure why. Jaron was a good guy. Maybe she didn't like the fact that he was a biker.

"He kissed me," I blurted.

Piper's head whipped around. "Who did?"

"Ashton." I wrung my hands in my lap. "I'm not sure why. I don't know if he was just trying to make Zach jealous. But it was weird. Really weird."

"I'm not surprised. Aiden is the levelheaded one, but Ashton always reacts first before thinking." She let out a huff. "I just want things to be back to normal. But I know that'll never happen. Anyway." She clapped her hands together. "Tell me about you and Zach. Please."

"Oh gosh, that's boring."

She laughed. "As if. Have you seen him? He's beautiful in a broken, dark kind of way."

"He is." I sighed. "He told me he loves me."

"Oh, Luna." Piper turned her body toward me. "That's wonderful. You guys are going to have pretty babies before you know it and make us aunties. God, I want to be an auntie."

I laughed. "Let's not get carried away."

"Why? You two would make beautiful kids. I can't wait."

I shook my head, but I couldn't help but smile. The idea of Zach getting me pregnant…I cleared my throat, not needing to think about that right at the moment. As much as I wanted kids, Zach and I had some other stuff to work through first. Not that either of us wanted to discuss it.

At that moment, the patio door opened, revealing Zach.

My breath caught.

"We should head out soon," he said, looking squarely at me.

I nodded, rising from the couch. "I'll see you soon," I told Piper.

"Have fun," she sang.

I laughed, heading into the house.

Zach peered down at me.

"You good?" I asked, placing my hand on his chest.

He nodded but he wouldn't look my way.

My heart skipped a beat. "What's wrong?"

"Nothing," he finally said, brushing his fingers down the length of my arm. A path of goosebumps followed.

"Alright, lovebirds." Meadow came up to us, holding a plate of cookies. "Try these. They're healthy. I made them for Gigi so she could still get her treats in while she's training."

"But it doesn't help when they're so damn good that I want to eat them all." Gigi slumped onto the couch and patted her stomach.

"I don't think you could ever get fat, if that's what you're implying." Ashton sat beside her and stole a cookie off her plate before stuffing it into his mouth. "I don't give a shit if these are healthy. Meadow, you're a fucking queen."

Gigi coughed, her cheeks reddening.

I laughed.

Meadow giggled.

And the guys looked at us like we were sporting appendages out of our foreheads.

"What was that about?" Zach asked, snatching another cookie off the plate Meadow was holding.

"I'll tell you later," I told him.

"So, I'm going to take these and head to the studio." Gigi shot up off the couch before anyone could argue. She grabbed her purse off the chair and quickly left the house.

I laughed again, shaking my head.

"I have no idea what's going on right now." Ashton popped another cookie into his mouth. "But I do know that these are so motherfucking good."

"Thanks, guys." Meadow grinned. "You're the best. But you know, eating a dozen cookies defeats the purpose of them actually being healthy."

Ashton patted his stomach. "That's what all the sex is for." His eyes flicked my way.

I opened my mouth to say something when I felt Zach's hard body press up behind mine. He placed his hands on my shoulders, giving them a light squeeze.

Leaning down to my ear, he brushed his lips along the shell of it. "I don't give a fuck who he is. Whether he's your friend, my friend, a fucking stranger. If he so much as even thinks of kissing you again, I'll gut him where he sleeps, leaving him to bleed out."

My heart hammered. "Possessive much?" I whispered.

Zach chuckled, the sound dark. "Baby, you have no fucking idea." He released me and joined Meadow in the kitchen. "Need any help?" I heard him ask.

I shook myself and headed to my bedroom but not before I caught a look from Ashton. I wasn't sure what that look meant, but I had a feeling that it wouldn't be long before any of us found out.

TWENTY-SIX

ZACH

WHILE LUNA WAS GETTING ready for our weekend at my condo, I helped Meadow prepare some more cookies. Or I pretended to help. She would slap my hands away every so often and scowl. Someone clearly liked being in control in the kitchen.

"Have you thought of opening your own bakery? Or…" A thought came to me. "I could put your desserts in the restaurants at my dad's hotels."

Meadow stopped what she was doing and turned around. Her dark brows narrowed. Blowing a loose curl out of her eyes, she opened her mouth and then snapped it shut.

"What?" I frowned.

"You would do that?" she asked. "No. I can't," she said before I could respond. "It would ruin them."

"How would it ruin them? Your desserts would be in half the hotels in the city. And more. It would take some time, but I can help you—"

"I appreciate that, Zach. I really do but I think right now, I just want to keep things local and make desserts for people I know." She took a step back. "Although, I could use a bigger kitchen," she said more to herself. She tapped her chin, her dark eyes moving around the area in front of her. "I would give my left arm for one of those industrial ovens where I can stock them with dozens of cookies and pastries." She sighed. "One day."

I knew when not to press. Meadow was different than the other girls. She was younger, but it didn't mean she wasn't headstrong and determined. She wanted something. But she never told us what that was. Hell, I wasn't even sure if *she* knew.

"Stop staring at my pretty face and go to your girl, Zach."

I chuckled. "You are something else, Meadow."

She blew me a kiss. "I know." Her gaze flicked behind me. "Hey…uh…I heard Ashton's been causing some problems."

"It is what it is," I mumbled, leaning against the counter. Luna really needed to hurry up.

"Listen, I know he can be an ass. Hell, we've all seen how he goes through women. But I think he's doing it just to get a rise out of you. Shock value and shit."

I passed a glance at her. "Why though? He's never shown interest in her. Why now?"

"Why does he do anything?" Meadow shrugged. "But if you need me to distract him, I can."

I hesitated. "And how are you going to distract him?"

She laughed. "You're a guy, Zach. How else do us women distract you? It's either with beer, food, or sex. I've given him food plenty of times. And beer." She scoffed. "He can get that whenever he wants. We always have beer. But sex...no one else here will have sex with him and I know Piper isn't riding that anymore."

"I..." I rubbed the back of my neck. "I don't—"

"Holy shit balls," Ashton yelled.

Meadow and I glanced at each other before we left the kitchen.

"When did you get back?" Ashton was standing with a man by the front door.

"Holy fucking hell," Meadow whispered.

The man's gaze flicked our way.

My eyes widened.

"I got back last night." He came toward us. "I went to see Mom and Dad and now I'm here." He stopped in front of Meadow. "Hey, sis."

Meadow's eyes shone. She shook her head, holding her arms out.

He chuckled, scooping her up into his arms. "Fuck, I missed you. I missed all of you. Being home. This. Where's Gigi?"

A sob left Meadow, but she didn't answer.

"She went to the studio," I said.

He nodded toward me. "How's it going, Zach?"

"Good." It was like seeing a ghost. Even though we had known Ryder was alive and well, Gigi and Meadow's brother was a hard guy to get a hold of. He had joined the military fresh out of high school, shot up the ranks and who the hell knew what he was doing anymore. It was all hush-hush and highly classified. He made their dad proud. Hell, all of our dads were proud.

We would get random postcards and phone calls every now and again, basically just letting us know that he was alive. But we hadn't seen him in almost a year.

"You guys act like you haven't seen me in a long time," Ryder joked, poking his little sister in the ribs.

"It's been a while, asshole." She wiped under her eyes. "God, way too fucking long."

Ryder only grinned. "Well I'm home now."

He was but for how long. That was the question.

While Ryder and Meadow talked amongst themselves, I realized that Ashton was nowhere to be found.

My stomach twisted. I loved the fucker, but he was starting to get under my skin, and I didn't like that. I didn't like that one fucking bit.

"So, anything new?" Ryder asked, sitting at the dining room table.

Meadow went into the kitchen and came back a moment later with a plate of cookies. "Luna and Zach are fucking."

"Yeah, because I'm sure that's what he wants to know after being gone for months on end," I pointed out, sitting at the head of the table.

"Oh, I do." Ryder nodded. "Tell me all the news. So, Piper still banging the twins?"

Meadow laughed. "See? And you all thought I was weird for the shit I want to know."

"You are weird," I reminded her.

She shrugged. "True. Normal is boring." She sat beside her brother, pushing the plate toward him. "I tried a new recipe. Luna and Zach are humping like rabbits. Piper wants nothing to do with the twins anymore and they're sad. Gigi is still lusting after Vincent Jr. Who knows what's going on there? And me?" She sat back. "I'm going to distract Ashton, so he leaves Zach and Luna alone. I think that's it. Oh. And Luna's dad is a protective dick." She tapped her chin. "I don't think I missed anything."

"Interesting." Ryder sat back, stretching his thick arms up and over his head. He had filled out since the last time we saw him. He was the middle child, but you would think he was the oldest. He definitely took after his dad in the size department. "So, Gigi likes a younger guy, does she?"

"Yeah." Meadow shrugged. "But like I said, I don't know what's going on there."

"Hey, Zach." Luna came down the hall and into the living room. "I'm ready but I feel like I grabbed too much." She held two bags in her hands. "Do I need more or less clothing?"

Less. Definitely less.

I stood from the table and went to her, helping her with the bags. "Look who's home," I said, ignoring her questions.

She looked around me, a soft gasp leaving her. "Ryder."

Ryder rose from his chair and held his arms out.

She rushed into them. "God, it's good to see you. I'm so glad you're home safely."

As much as I knew we were all friends and grew up together, it still didn't mean I liked seeing her in another man's arms. I didn't give a shit who he was.

Ryder caught my gaze. He gave me a knowing smirk, tightening his hold on Luna.

A growl rumbled from somewhere deep inside me.

He laughed, releasing her. "Well this is new." He came toward me, clapping my shoulder. "I missed you."

"I missed you too, fucker." I pulled him into an embrace, thankful he was no longer touching my girl.

(Luna)

I couldn't believe Ryder was home. After all this time. I was sure his parents were happy about that as well.

While Ryder and Zach stood off to the side, Ashton came back into the living room.

"Where did you go?" I asked him while rummaging through my bags. I was sure I had way too much.

"I had to take a piss and then my brother called, saying something was going on with the center." Ashton slumped beside me. "I'm glad Ryder's home though."

"Me too." I couldn't help but watch Ryder and Zach together. They could almost pass for brothers. Or at least cousins. Both had black hair and dark scruff on their strong jaws. And both of them had those chocolate brown eyes that made it feel like they were looking into your soul. While Zach was big, Ryder was bigger and taller.

Ryder caught me staring and gave me a wink.

My cheeks burned.

Zach's head whipped around. He raised an eyebrow.

I couldn't help but laugh, which in turn, made Ryder chuckle.

"Dude, trust me, your dick is the only one she wants," Ryder told him.

Zach scowled, something flashing behind his dark eyes.

I blew him a kiss. There was no point in denying it. Everyone knew I had a crush on the guy since I was a kid. And now that we were together, it was just...right.

"He better not—Meadow, what are you doing?"

I turned back around, finding Meadow standing in front of Ashton with her hand out.

"Distracting you," she said.

"I don't know what that means," Ashton mumbled.

"Use your head." She let out a huff. "Fine." She grabbed his hand, trying to pull him to his feet but she was tiny, so she didn't get very far. "Stand, Ashton. God.

Do you want me to spell it out for you with neon lights and glitter?"

Ashton stood, looking at each of us. "I don't know what's going on, but I also don't need your brother kicking my ass when he just got home."

Ryder chuckled. "Have fun, kids. I know when not to step in where Meadow's concerned."

"Come." Meadow grabbed Ashton's hand and led him down the hall to her room.

I shook my head, unsure as to what just happened there but happy that Ashton wouldn't be a problem for at least a little while.

"Well...I guess I should get going. Seeing as my sister is preoccupied and you two have plans."

"We're going out for dinner," Zach explained. "But we're going to hit up a bar after if you wanted to join us for drinks."

"That sounds perfect." Ryder clapped his shoulder. "Have fun. I'm going to head to my parents' place and catch a nap. My mom's going to lose her shit that her son's home and all he wants to do is sleep." He laughed to himself, heading to the door. "See you later."

When Zach and I were alone, I couldn't help but wonder if maybe Meadow was making a mistake. Not that I judged. She was a big girl and all. Even though she was the youngest of our group, she was definitely the most determined to get what she wanted out of life.

"Sorry I made plans for us without asking you," Zach said, pulling me from my thoughts.

"Oh, that's fine," I told him, rising from the couch. "It would be nice to have drinks with Ryder anyway. Maybe we can get everyone else to join us too." I looked down at my two bags sitting on the couch. "Should I get ready now then?"

"Sure." He sat down beside me, brushing a finger down my arm. "I can also help you get ready."

My breath caught at the heat in his dark eyes. "I think we both know that it wouldn't be much help."

"Maybe not. So if you don't want to end up hearing Ashton and Meadow, I suggest getting ready quickly."

"I'm sure we've all heard each other." Although it would be weird hearing them. I couldn't imagine having sex with someone just for the sake of having sex.

"Does it bother you?"

I frowned. "What?"

Zach leaned forward. "Does it bother you? Knowing that Ashton hinted for more with you not too long ago and now he's probably balls deep inside another woman."

My heart jumped. "Way to be graphic, Zach."

"Hmm…" He tilted his head, searching my face. "Yeah, I think I like their idea."

"What are—" Zach shot up from the couch and before I could get my question out, he had me over his shoulder. "Zach, what are you doing?"

"Shut up." He landed a hard swat against the seat of my ass. "Let me take care of you, Luna."

(Zach)

An hour later and I was lying on Luna's bed, watching her flutter around the room. She was getting ready for our date, but I rather enjoyed this instead. Although, I should feed her.

"God, my muscles hurt," she muttered, stretching her arms up and over her head. "I should really start training with Gigi or something."

I chuckled, leaning against my arm behind my head.

"You're proud of yourself, aren't you?" she asked, pulling a pair of red panties up her long legs.

"I am actually." Even though the words came out of my mouth, my body hurt as well. I wasn't sure what sparked the need to completely consume Luna but after catching her checking out Ryder and then her acting different about Meadow and Ashton fucking, I felt a force within me. I needed to distract her much like Meadow was distracting Ashton. "Does it bother you?"

"What?" Luna didn't meet my gaze.

"Luna." I sat forward, curling my knee on the bed. "Tell me."

She huffed. "Fine. It does bother me alright? I don't want Meadow to get hurt. I don't understand casual sex. I just don't get it. I know it happens. I know it can happen where people have sex and move on, but I personally don't get it. And Ashton is a player. You've seen the countless women he's been through."

"Come here." I reached out for her.

"I have to finish getting ready," she mumbled.

"Luna," I demanded. "Come here."

She huffed again, slid into her bra, did up the back, and made her way toward me. "What?"

Moving to the edge of the bed, I circled my arms around her waist. Placing a soft peck between her breasts, I inhaled the faint scent of sex on her skin.

"Zach," she whispered, running her fingers through my hair.

"Casual sex is sometimes easier. Maybe Meadow's been hurt in the past and can't handle anything more right now. Maybe Piper broke Ashton's heart, even though I know he would never admit to it." I leaned back, looking up at Luna. "Maybe they both just want to feel something other than loneliness."

Luna chewed her bottom lip. "You think they're lonely?"

I shrugged. "I know before you, casual sex was all that I could handle. I know you don't want to hear it and

I know your heart is too damn big for casual. That's what I love about you. You told me that you were in love with me long before I manned up and admitted that I was in love with you too. And, Luna, you didn't care that I never said it back. So, while our sex wasn't casual, you're not like most women out there either. Because most would have demanded to hear it in return."

"I'm really...I just...I didn't want to put pressure on you. I also didn't want you to say it when you didn't mean it because what's the point in that?"

"You're fucking incredible." I pulled her onto my lap. "You know that right?"

She laughed lightly. "I'm really not." She squirmed in my arms. "I need to get ready."

"You will." I kissed her throat. "But this outfit is doing something funny to me."

"It's not an outfit," she said breathlessly.

"Hmm..." I inched a finger beneath the thin strap on her shoulder and pulled it down her arm. "You're so fucking perfect." I licked along her throat, fisted a hand in her hair, and just held her. Touched her. Kissed her. Enjoyed her. There were so many things we had to talk about still, but I didn't want to.

"Zach," Luna whispered, pushing her fingers through my hair.

"Yeah?" I kissed her chin.

"I love you." Her dark eyes met mine. They were wild, filled with lust, and took my breath away.

"I love you too, Moonbeam." But as much as I wanted to continue this, she was right. She did need to get ready. I needed her all to myself for dinner but after, we could hang out with our friends at the bar. Until then, she was mine.

Luna placed a soft peck on my lips. "I should get ready."

"You should." Although I said the words, I couldn't find it in myself to release her.

She laughed lightly. "Zach, I really should."

I tightened my hold on her and sunk my teeth into the top of her breast.

She gasped, her head falling back.

A hard knock suddenly sounded on the door. "What the *fuck* are you doing to my daughter?"

TWENTY-SEVEN

Luna

"*I* HATE YOU!"
I remembered those words like I had only screamed them yesterday. I didn't remember what caused me to say them. But as I stared my father down, with his face red and his hands gripping the door frame like he was the Hulk, I had a feeling those words would be screamed. Again. And soon.

"Stone, what are you doing?" Mom came up to him, glanced into my bedroom and found me wrapped in Zach's arms. "Shit," she muttered. "Stone, let's go." She grabbed his arm, trying to pull him away.

He shoved her off of him. "I asked you a question," he said, the venom in his voice sending a nervous flutter racing through me.

I pulled the bra strap back up my arm and cowered against Zach.

"Let's go, Stone, so she can get dressed." Mom tugged on his arm again. "Stone, *now*."

He finally looked at her, back at us. "You have one minute," he barked, slamming the door closed, sucking all the air from my lungs.

"Luna."

I ignored Zach and slid off his lap. Quickly slipping into a black dress, I turned away from him. "Zip me up?"

"Of course," he murmured, stepping up behind me. His fingers grazed up my spine as he did up the zipper. "Luna, we need to talk about this."

"I—" The door opened again, revealing— "Okay, I've had enough of this shit." I spun on my father. Thankfully Mom was standing behind him. She mouthed a *sorry* but seeing her gave me all the courage I needed to continue. "Daddy, I love you but you're being unreasonable. I'm not a child."

"I come in here and find you naked with him," he bit out through clenched teeth.

"I wasn't naked, and haven't you ever heard of knocking?" I threw back at him. "I'm also a damn adult. Do you remember the conversation we had when I was a little girl? How you told me that you wanted me to be happy? How you couldn't wait for the day to see your little girl grow up into the woman you hoped I could be. You also told me that you wished mom could see me because you were so damn proud of me."

Dad looked away.

"Do you remember that?" I demanded. "I asked you a question," I cried, stomping my foot.

"Yes." His eyes shot to mine. "Yes, I remember that."

"Well I *am* happy. *He* makes me happy," I said thrusting my arm out in Zach's direction.

"*Piccola*," my father said gently.

"No." I raised a hand. "I'm done. Either you support us or you don't, but I'm sick of you invading my space." I stepped up to Zach and stood in front of him. "I don't know what you're thinking but Zach won't hurt me. You're not going to lose me like you lost Mom."

He flinched.

"She's right, Stone," my stepmom said gently. "You know she's right."

He looked back at her before glancing our way.

"I want to ask you a question," Zach finally said amidst all of this chaos. "If I was anyone else, would you approve of this?"

"Yes," my dad blurted.

I gasped.

Zach stood there, stock-still but no emotion displayed on his face.

"Stone." Mom shook her head, her eyes wide.

I swallowed hard. "So you will never approve of this," I said, even though I already knew the answer.

"No." Dad turned around and left my room.

"Luna. I had no idea. I'll talk to him. This isn't right." Mom gave me a quick hug. "I like you for her," she told Zach. "And I know Stone can be difficult. I don't know what his deal is, but I'll get it out of him." She touched his arm, giving it a gentle squeeze then rushed out of my room.

Once Zach and I were alone, I made my way to the door and quietly closed it. Turning around, I leaned against it and let out a slow breath.

Zach's eyes met mine from across the room.

I looked away. I couldn't handle seeing the pain etched on his face. Or the questions hidden behind his eyes. I didn't know what to do.

Warm, strong arms wrapped around me.

A soft sob escaped me. I latched on to Zach, pulling him hard against me. "I…"

"Shhh…" He held me, rubbing his hand in circles on my upper back. "I love you, Luna," he said.

I braced myself for the *but.*

He leaned back and cupped my face. "I hope you know that."

I nodded, swallowing hard. "I do."

"But as much as I love you, I won't make you choose between me and your father," he said, his voice rough.

"No. I'm not…that won't happen." I shook my head, covering his hand that was still on my cheek.

"Baby," he said gently. "I'll step aside."

"No," I cried, circling my hands in his jacket. "Don't say that shit to me. My dad will get over this…whatever it is. He has to. I can't…I refuse to lose you when I only just found you."

"You've never had to find me, Luna." Zach placed a soft peck on my forehead. "I've always been here. I'm sorry for pushing you away."

"You've stopped," I reminded him.

"I have but I refuse to sneak around. And I can't go around worrying that he's going to gut me like a pig because I touch the woman that I'm in love with."

I leaned my forehead against his chest. "I feel like this is it. That we're breaking up all because my dad is an asshole. You finally let me in and now this. I don't know what his problem is."

"He has his reasons, Moonbeam." Zach cupped my nape. "I don't know what they are but…"

"We can ask him." I looked up at him.

"I think you already know." Zach paused. "You're the one who said that you wouldn't leave him like your real mom did."

I looked away. "He doesn't like talking about her." A revelation dawned on me. Could that be why my dad had an issue with me dating? "That doesn't make sense though. It has nothing to do with you."

"I know, Luna." He kissed the top of my head. "I'll go so you can—"

"No, please, Zach." I snaked my arms around his neck. "Don't leave."

"I'm not." He cupped my forearms, running his hands up and down them. "I'm just going to leave your room, so you can finish getting ready."

"Oh…" I breathed out a sigh of relief. "You know, I don't even know why my parents are here in the first place."

"Did you have something planned tonight with them that you forgot about?" Zach asked, releasing me.

"No." I let out a hard sigh. I stood on tiptoes and placed a soft peck on his cheek. "I love you."

(Zach)

When I left Luna's room, I closed the door gently behind me, and blew out a slow breath.

"Hey."

I turned, finding Meadow and Ashton coming toward me.

"What's going on?" Meadow asked, frowning. "We heard yelling."

"I think you should go in there and talk to Luna," I told her.

"Oh, shit. Okay." She placed her hand on the doorknob before turning back to us. "I'll see you guys later for drinks?"

"Oh yeah," I mumbled, heading down the hallway to the living room. When I stepped into the open space, I saw Creena and Stone outside talking to Aiden and Asher, the twins' dad. Why were they even here?

"Zach."

I turned, finding Ashton coming toward me. "Not now." I couldn't deal with his shit. Not tonight. Because I knew that if he said something, my fist would land against his face before I could stop myself.

"No, listen. I'm sorry."

I stopped. "Why?"

He chuckled, running a hand over his head. "I get it now. I'm a dick. Alright? I know that. But I get it. You and Luna. You're meant to be. There's a spark there that even I can see, and I've sworn off love completely. Anyway." He shook his head. "What I'm saying is, fight for her."

"What do you think I'm fucking doing?" But was I really? I ignored that thought and headed into the kitchen with Ashton hot on my trails.

"Zach, I know I've given you shit over Luna, but I love you both. You're fucking family. And if you don't end up together, how do the rest of us have any hope?" Instead of waiting for me to answer, he left the kitchen and headed out into the backyard.

It made me feel like a child. That same boy that spent weeks on end locked up in that small dark room. For years, I was told I was worthless. That I wouldn't amount to anything. That I couldn't be the man a wife needed. For Luna, I could be that man. I *was* that man. But then why, after everything, after all that we had been through, why did I still feel so damn worthless. That I wasn't good enough for her. She was close. Too close. And I didn't know how to take it. I loved her. I loved her with every inch of me but that same love, scared the shit out of me. I didn't want to get hurt. And if anyone could destroy me, it would be her.

Stone caught my gaze. He continued talking but his eyes never left mine.

I had dealt with a lot. Could bring businessmen more powerful than me to their knees, but one look from the father of the woman that I was in love with and it sent a tremor of fear down my spine.

I didn't know what Stone had done for a living while he was in the navy. All I knew was that he was into some hard shit before he met Creena and Luna's mom lost her life because of it. Could that be why? Could that be the reason he didn't want me with his daughter?

I didn't know and a part of me was even scared to ask.

My phone vibrated suddenly.

I reached into my pocket and fished it out, thankful for the distraction from the man currently plotting my death.

Clara: Hey! I hope your dad is well. Also, would you and Luna like to go out for dinner with me?

Me: That sounds like a wonderful plan. Double date?

Clara: No. That ship has sailed. Do people even say that anymore? Lol! Anyway, it would just be me.

I softly chuckled.

Me: That—

"My daughter has been the only one to ever put that smile on your face. Who are you texting, Zach?"

My body twitched, my blood pounding in my ears. I looked up and put my phone away, meeting the eyes of my maker.

"What are you accusing me of?" I asked Stone. I respected the hell out of the guy but this shit with Luna was getting old. Real fast.

"I'm not sure yet." He crossed his thick tattooed arms over his chest.

"Why are you even here?" I blurted before I could stop myself. "You guys never come over unannounced."

Stone took a step toward me. "Prove to me that you're good enough for my daughter," he said, ignoring me.

My eyes widened. "What? How the hell can I do that when you keep barging into our business?"

"Stop being a fucking pussy, Zach," Stone bit out through clenched teeth. "Prove it."

"Daddy."

He stopped, glancing over his shoulder.

I looked past him and found Luna standing there, along with everyone else.

"I think you should leave," she said softly.

"*Piccola*, I just want what's best for you." He reached out for her, but she stepped back.

"How can you know what's best for me when you won't even let me figure that out on my own?" She shook her head. "Why are you here?" she asked. "Were you hoping to catch us?"

"What?" Stone looked between us both. "No."

"Then tell me, why are you here?" Luna demanded.

"He's here because I was hoping he would apologize," Creena said. "He actually told me he would. But apparently my husband lied to me." Her face hardened.

Stone looked away. "I—"

Luna's shoulders slumped. "Leave. Just leave. Please."

"Come, Stone." Creena held out her hand.

Stone hesitated but like any good man, he listened to the woman in his life and did as he was told. He took his wife's hand, letting her lead him away but not before I caught a look in his dark eyes. Sadness? Guilt? Who fucking knew anymore? But what I did know was that I had to make a decision.

Even if Luna ended up hating me for it, this would be for her. Always for her. There could be no other way.

"Prove to me that you're good enough for my daughter."

How the hell could I do that when I didn't even believe it myself?

(Luna)

Once my parents were finally gone, I stepped up to Zach. Placing my hands on his chest, I stood on tiptoes to kiss his cheek when he grabbed my wrists and pushed me back.

My eyes widened. "Zach."

"I need some time. I think we're going to have to postpone our date." Although the words left his mouth, he never looked me square in the eye.

"No," I gasped. "Please. You can't do this. You can't listen to my father."

Zach grabbed my arm and pulled me against him in a rough move. "He's right, Luna," he murmured into my hair. "He's always been right. I'm not good enough for you. I never have been, and I never will be. I think you...I...fuck..." His body shook. "I can't do this. Not with you. I can't lose you but I..."

"You can't have me either. Why?"

"It'll break me if you hurt me."

I leaned back, staring up at him. "You think I'll hurt you?"

"You can find someone else," he murmured, ignoring my question.

"No." I cupped his nape. "I don't want anyone else."

"You need to move on," he said, his voice flat.

"I…I can't believe this. After everything." I was vaguely aware that we weren't alone. That our friends were in the living room, but I didn't care. "Please, Zach. We can work through this."

He looked at me then, his eyes cold. "No."

That one word ripped my heart in half, and I knew right then that because of my father, because Zach was terrified to let me into his heart, this was it. I had lost him, and I had no idea if I would ever get him back.

TWENTY-EIGHT

ZACH

"**L**UNA.**" I GRABBED HER** hands and pushed her back gently. "I'll never love anyone else." I cupped her face.

Tears streamed down her cheeks. "God, I can't…this hurts."

Seeing her cry tore at my heart. It shredded into a million little pieces. And I knew it right then. If we never came out of this, if we never found our way back to each other, she would be my greatest accomplishment.

"I love you," I whispered.

"Don't." She pushed me. "You can't say that shit to me."

"Luna." Before she could pull away, I wrapped my arms around her.

Her body shook with silent sobs. "I hate him. I hate him for what he's done to us."

I couldn't say I blamed her, but she would get over this and her relationship with her father would be mended. She would move on.

"Is this it?" she asked, her voice small. "Are we done when we've hardly even started?"

I swallowed hard, a lump lodging its way into my throat. "We…" I didn't even know how to answer that. Leaning my forehead against hers, I breathed her in. The sweet scent of her lavender perfume. The faint scent of sex I put there. And when I kissed her, I tasted the saltiness of her tears on my tongue.

"I love you, Luna," I whispered. "I love you so fucking much."

(Luna)

Never in my whole life, did I think the first man I loved could break my heart the way he did. And the second man broke it just as much. Two heartbreaks. By two different men for nearly the same reason.

When Zach pulled away, my tears quickly dried up and the sadness that was there, turned into anger.

When I reached out for him, he only picked up his pace, I knew. This was it. We were done. Zach and Luna were no more.

But I ran after him anyway. As pissed as I was, I still needed him. That rage was the driving force behind my feet rushing toward him.

He was crossing the front lawn when I caught up with him. I latched onto his back, forcing him to spin around.

Just when I thought he was going to push me away, he cupped my face instead and kissed me. I breathed him in, taking everything that had come to light and unleashing it onto him. I didn't want this to end. No matter how difficult my father was being, no matter how scared Zach was, he and I were meant to be. We just were.

"Luna." Zach leaned back, keeping his hands on my face and staring at me.

"Please, Zach. We can get through this. I won't hurt you. I promise you I won't."

"You don't know that."

"Do you not trust me? I love you. I've only ever loved you. You stopped being with other women because of me. Because you love me. Why can't you see that? We're meant to be."

"You need to move on," he said gently, his voice thick.

"How can I do that, Zach?" I grabbed onto the collar of his shirt. "How can I when I see you all the time?"

"I'll stay away then." He leaned his forehead against mine. "You will get over me."

"I don't want to." The tears fell, rolling down my cheeks and dripping off my chin. "I can't."

"Baby, you can. You'll find some guy, make him happy and he'll make you happy in return. You'll have kids, a big house somewhere. Maybe a dog. Or a cat. Or even a fucking fish. But you'll get over me. I promise you, you will."

"This is it? All because I'm getting too close?"

He looked away.

I smacked his arm. "You didn't think I was too close when I let you fuck me."

His gaze snapped to mine, his jaw clenching. "Careful."

"What? Got nothing to say now? Go, Zach. Run away like you always do." Before I could say anymore, I turned and headed back to the house when a warm body crashed into me.

Zach wrapped his arms around me, placing a soft peck on my head. "You are the best thing that's ever happened to me, Moonbeam." When he pulled away, I didn't stop him. When he muttered an *I love you,* I didn't say it back. And when he drove away, I didn't move.

Bodies came toward me, but I couldn't look up. I couldn't face the pity in their eyes. This was a mistake. A big fucking mistake.

Gentle arms enveloped me and that was when I broke.

Sobs wracked through me, forcing me immobile. My lungs burned with lack of air.

I hated him. For giving up on us. For not fighting for me. For making me fucking cry.

The girls whispered to me, offering their sweet words and gentle touches. These girls were my life. My sisters even though we weren't blood related. They were a piece of me. And so was Zach but now that he was gone, it felt like that piece of me had died.

I had spent years loving him, probably since I was a little girl but I wasn't sure what was worse.

Knowing what it felt like to be loved by him or not knowing at all.

(Zach)

A tiny finger poked my arm.

I frowned, looking down at Luna. "What do you want?"

Her big eyes shone. She looked out on the dance floor, watching everyone.

"Zach," Brogan said gently. "I think she wants you to dance with her."

"Really?" I raised an eyebrow. "But…" I didn't know how to dance, and I didn't know these people. I was getting to know them, but it was still…weird.

"I think she does." Brogan's smile grew, giving me a nod of encouragement.

"Oh…" I stood from the chair, holding out my hand. "Okay."

Luna grinned.

I laughed. "Thank you," I told Brogan. "Mom."

"Fuck." I slammed a fist against the steering wheel. "Fuck. Fuck. Fuck." What the hell was I doing? How could I let her father get to me? How could I let him fucking win? And how the hell could I push her away? It always happened. Every time someone got too close, I shoved them aside like they were a piece of shit on the bottom of my shoe.

"Whatever you do, come to us. Don't act out. Think first before you do something stupid, Zach."

My dad's words pounded inside my head but instead of listening to him, I continued driving.

"I will make it so you all you do is push people away. You will never trust anyone. Ever."

I was a pussy for letting my stepmother control me this way. I was a pansy ass motherfucking pussy for letting her win and live inside my head all this time. And now because Luna got close, the voice was almost louder. Meaner. Colder.

Luna got into my heart.

"She's going to hurt you."

I shook my head. No. She wouldn't. She would never hurt me.

"You can't trust her. She'll hurt you. You aren't good enough."

I landed a fist against the side of my head, trying so damn hard to silence the incessant noise.

I loved Luna. But that love went further than just some feelings. I could feel her all throughout me. It had been why I stopped sleeping with the random women. But I still never made a move. Not until recently. Not until she got under my skin and burrowed herself there. It was where she belonged.

What the hell was wrong with me? I couldn't do this. I couldn't be what she needed. I couldn't prove that we were meant to be together and that I was good enough for her. I couldn't because I wasn't.

Gripping the steering wheel, I pressed my foot harder against the gas. I needed a drink. And lots of them. And pussy. But I couldn't have pussy because the one I did have, I shoved away.

Years ago, I would have called up an old fling, fucked them, and been on my way. But this wasn't years ago. This was now. And I fucked up. I used the excuse that it was Stone who started all of this shit, but I realized then that he was only a part of the problem. I pushed away the one good thing in my life all because I was scared. To open up. To let Luna in. Even though we were close, I still hadn't let her into my heart completely.

"Fuck," I bellowed, slamming my fist against the steering wheel again.

Driving to the city, I didn't stop until I pulled down a street. I shouldn't be here. I should be with Luna. In her arms. Touching her. Holding her. Giving her everything I could and taking from her what I needed, just the same. But I wasn't. Instead, I parked in front of a house. I was given this address when I thought Luna and I would go on a double date with a friend. A friend. Fucking please. I couldn't be friends with a woman and not fuck them.

Luna was proof of that. But I never fucked the other girls. I raked a hand through my hair, scrubbing it down my face. Inner turmoil rushed through me. I was confused, my mind all over the damn place. I should go home. I should drive past this house and be on my merry way. But I didn't.

My phone rang but I ignored it. I didn't give a shit who it was. Maybe it was Luna. Maybe it was my parents. Maybe she had called them and told them what happened. They could be checking on me. Making sure I didn't react first and do something stupid.

"Promise me, you'll come to us first. Promise, Zach."

I made that promise but I never intended to keep it.

I never deserved Luna. She could do so much better. Her father said it himself. Well now it was my chance to prove him right.

Stepping out of the car, I took a breath and then another before I made my way up the narrow driveway.

Once I stood on the front step, I lifted my hand to knock when the door opened.

"Hey." Bright blue eyes met mine. "I saw you pull up. Is everything okay?"

I shouldn't be here. I knew that but yet, I didn't listen to myself.

When the reason I had come over in the first place, stared up at me, I forced everything to the side. I ignored the feelings rushing through me.

Guilt. Pain. Regret.

So much damn regret and I hadn't even done anything yet.

"Zach?" Clara frowned. "What's going on?"

Before she had a chance to ask any more questions, I pushed her inside, kicked the door closed, and crushed my mouth to hers.

TWENTY-NINE

ZACH

I **SWALLOWED CLARA'S GASP** and ignored the fact that it wasn't Luna I was kissing. That it wasn't her dark hair I had my hands wrapped in. That it wasn't her slender but curvy body I was pressed up against. That it wasn't her mouth I was diving deep inside.

As much as I wanted to fuck away my feelings, as much as I needed to get Luna out of my head, my body didn't react. My cock was limp as it pressed between me and Clara. A growl escaped me. Tightening my hold on her hair, I tugged her head farther back, forcing my body to do something. Anything. But I got nothing.

"Zach," Clara said against my mouth. She tried shoving me but my hold on her was too tight.

I pushed her up against the wall, grinding into her but again, my cock did nothing.

Clara broke the kiss, shoving me back. "What the hell?" Her cheeks weren't flushed like I had just kissed the hell out of her. No lust hid in her dark eyes. Her chest didn't rise and fall with ragged breaths like Luna's always did. Her lips were swollen from my greedy kiss but that was it. "Zach, tell me."

"I think you know." I took a step toward her, my stomach churning.

She lifted her hand, stopping me. "Enough," she said, her voice firm. "You don't want this. Hell, neither do I."

"Clara," I bit out through clenched teeth. Bile rose to my throat, my stomach lurching. Hightailing it to the kitchen, I threw up in the sink. My stomach heaved.

"Here." A cloth came into my field of vision.

I muttered a thanks and grabbed it, wiping my mouth.

"Tell me what's going on. You've never hinted for more. And neither have I. I know I can come on a little strong. I get that. But I've never led you to believe that I wanted you to fuck me. You're with Luna for Christ's sake and I've always considered her a friend."

"Not anymore," I mumbled. Once my stomach calmed down, I leaned against the counter, and pinched the bridge of my nose.

She frowned. "What?"

"I'm not with Luna anymore," I repeated, taking several deep breaths. "We broke up." My stomach threatened to roll again but I shook it off.

"When did that happen?"

"Tonight." And didn't that make me sound like a fucking asshole.

"And now you're here?" Clara barked a laugh. "Tell me what really happened."

"I just did." I turned away. "I don't give a shit if you don't believe me. I'll just find someone else—"

"No." Clara grabbed my arm and pulled me to the kitchen table. "Sit." She pointed at a chair.

As much as I didn't want to, I listened and did as I was told.

Clara reached into the fridge, pulled out a bottle of water and a beer, kicked the door closed and handed me the water.

I twisted off the cap and took a long swig.

"Better?" she asked, sitting down beside me.

"No." I rubbed the back of my neck. "I'm sorry." I blew out a slow breath. "Fuck, I don't know what I'm doing. I don't even know why I'm here." But I did. I was desperate to make the voice in my head stop and I would do anything to silence it. I realized then that I was finally at my breaking point. Bottom line, I needed Luna.

"Well…"

My gaze popped up, landing on Clara.

She gave me a small smile.

"I'm sorry," I repeated. "I'm not like this. I used to be but not anymore."

She twisted off the cap of her beer and clinked the bottle against mine. "Tell me what happened."

"Luna's father thinks I'm not good enough for her. He caught us…he walked in and…" I cleared my throat. "Anyway. It went downhill from there."

"Do *you* believe you're good enough for her?"

I took a swig of the water. "Why does it matter what I believe?"

Clara laughed. "Wow, Zach. For a smart guy, you really aren't so bright. Are you?"

I scowled.

She sighed. "What I'm saying is that if you don't believe you're good enough for her, her father sure as hell isn't going to believe that either. You need to prove to him that you *are* good enough for her. That you can make her happy. That you can be the best man. For her. And fucking me or anyone else for that matter isn't going to help. At all."

"Fuck." I rubbed the back of my neck, massaging out some of the kinks that had laced around my muscles from the moment all this shit started. "I'm such a dumbass."

"It happens. Fathers can be a little much sometimes." Clara sat back. "I remember the first guy I dated in high school. My father wanted to kick his ass just for breathing the same air as me. He was the sweetest boy too. I probably could have spent my life with him. But unfortunately, life happened, and his parents ended up moving, taking him far away from me."

My chest tightened. "That's sad."

"It is but you know what?" Clara sat forward. "That same boy found me years later. While what we had in high school will never happen again, we're friends and honestly, that's enough for me." She shrugged. "I like Luna. I know she was shocked to find out that it was me you were supposed to go on that date with, but I also know that if you told her that date never happened, she'd believe you. Because she loves you."

"I did tell her that it never happened." I pulled back the rest of the water, wishing it was something stronger. "I can't believe I let it get this far."

"Listen." Clara placed her hand gently on my arm. "Luna will forgive you."

"I doubt that," I mumbled. I wasn't even sure if I could forgive myself.

"She will. I saw the way she looks at you." Clara shrugged. "It would have happened if I wouldn't have stopped it. Wouldn't it?"

"Probably. But…" I looked down at my lap. "I think it would have been a lot of convincing my body to go along with it."

"Yeah. Sorry, Zach. I like you and I consider you a friend, but I'm not attracted to you. Sure, you're hot but that's about it. And I don't fuck guys I'm not attracted to."

"Now I feel like an even bigger asshole because I'm not attracted to you either, but I wanted…"

"You wanted to fuck Luna out of your system," Clara finished for me.

I nodded.

"I get it." Clara took another swig of her beer. "What are you going to do?"

"I need to talk to her, but I already pushed her away. I don't think I can handle it if she does the same to me," I admitted. It was the first honest thing I had said all night.

"That's understandable." Clara threw back the rest of her beer and stood from the table. "I think you should either take some time to cool off, go work out or something, or go talk to Luna. But I would probably give her some time."

I stood from the table. "Thank you. And again, I'm sorry."

"Don't worry about it, Zach." She went to turn away when she paused. "Oh. I should ask though. Are you going to tell her about this?"

"Yeah." Fuck, that was a conversation I was not looking forward to. "I am."

"Good." Clara went to the fridge. "Now leave so I can get drunk by myself."

I chuckled. "Have a good one, Clara."

I left her house, feeling lighter. The razor-sharp edge of the previous rage rushing through me had turned into a dull roar. I needed to see Luna. I just wasn't sure if she would want to see me. If ever again.

(Luna)

It had been several hours since Zach left. Since he tore out my heart and stomped on it, leaving me a shattered mess. The girls and I got drunk off cheap wine, stuffed our faces with Meadow's delicious desserts, and now I was lying in bed, wallowing in my own self-pity.

My head pounded but with as much wine as I had, it didn't mask the feelings of hurt and anger I had toward Zach. How could he listen to my father after everything we had been through? How could he love me and push me away at the same time? I should have fought harder. I should have gone after him. I should have done something. Anything. But instead, I let him leave and got drunk instead.

I groaned, rolling over onto my stomach. The room spun. Looked like the buzz was wearing off and quickly. Turning onto my back, I let out a hard sigh.

The scent of musk invaded my nose, another smell following right along with it.

Sex.

My stomach twisted.

Sliding out of bed, I pulled the covers off of the mattress and tossed them on the floor. I was still wearing my black dress; the dress Zach had helped zip up. The dress that he loved every time he saw me in it.

Hooking my fingers in the hem, I ripped it up and over my head, tossing it to the floor. Pulling off my bra, I threw it aside and did the same with my panties. I stood in front of the bed, naked and alone.

My chest ached, my head throbbed, and I was tired. So damn tired.

Heading to the blood red chair in the corner of my room, I pulled off the crocheted blanket I had since I was a kid, wrapped it around myself, and sat. I curled into a ball, hugging the blanket to my chest and let the tears fall.

A hard crash sounded throughout the room. I startled awake, finding Zach standing at the doorway. His nostrils flared, his eyes were dark, and his body was stiff like he was ready to pounce.

"Zach?" I sat up, holding the blanket around me. "What's wrong?"

"What's wrong?" He laughed, the sound dark and evil. It was laced with venom and directed right at me.

I swallowed hard. Was I dreaming? Was I still drunk? "What's going on?" I asked, rubbing the sleep out of my eyes.

"Why don't you ask him?" Zach said, jutting his chin.

"What?" My head whipped around. I was no longer in the red chair. Ashton was sitting up. On my bed. Looking like he just got caught with his hand in the cookie jar.

I swallowed hard, my heart racing. Was I that drunk last night? No. It wasn't possible. Ashton was a player but even he wouldn't stoop that low.

"Listen." Ashton slid off the bed, still in clothes. Thank God for that.

But I was naked. Very naked. And I only had a blanket wrapped around me. "Zach, this isn't what it looks like." Not that I knew what happened because I couldn't remember but it wasn't possible. Ashton would never take advantage of me like that.

"What do you think it looks like, Luna?" Zach demanded, stepping farther into the room. "Do you think it looks like my girl fucked another guy? Do you think it looks like you're fucking naked and the evidence is clear?" His brows narrowed. "Did you enjoy her after I broke her in for you?"

"Zach." I gasped.

"What?" Ashton scowled. "You have no idea what you're fucking talking about."

"No?" Zach laughed. "You know." His gaze met mine. "I went to Clara's tonight."

My heart jumped. "Y-You did?"

"Yes, but nothing happened because I couldn't get you out of my head. As much as I wanted to."

I looked away. He went to Clara's to fuck her. Bile rose to my throat. "I don't even know what to say."

"No? Well it looks like we're even," Zach said, his voice flat.

"Are you fucking kidding me right now?" I snapped, jumping off the bed. "I didn't fuck Ashton. I had no intention of fucking him either, but you did. You went to Clara's to fuck her. So what happened, Zach? Did she not want you? For once in your life, is there a woman out there who's not attracted to you? God, I'm so stupid." I headed to my dresser to grab some pajamas. Being naked, even though I was covered, it left me too vulnerable. I didn't like it. I didn't like it at all.

"Tell me what happened," Zach demanded.

"You don't fucking deserve her," Ashton said.

My head whipped around.

Before I knew what was happening, Zach charged for him.

(Zach)

The rational part of me knew there had to be a reasonable explanation why Ashton was sleeping in Luna's bed. But when I walked in and found her wrapped in a blanket with him beneath the same covers I had been under, all of that rationale disappeared. It turned into cold blooded rage. Rage for the fact that it wasn't me sleeping beside her. Rage over me pushing her away. Rage over that her father was right.

When I had broken things off with Luna, I never meant for us to be broken up forever. Both of us needed time. But like the asshole that I was, I ended up at Clara's house.

The pain etched on Luna's face over my confession, tore at my heart. I had a lot of work to do if I ever wanted her back in my life.

And now I was staring down at my friend as my fist repeatedly landed against his jaw.

My name was screamed over and over. Hands grabbed me. Arms tried wrapping around me, but I shoved them off. Instead, I continued to pummel Ashton into the ground beneath us.

"Fuck." He grunted, pushed me back, and swung a fist into my jaw.

My head rang, pain slicing up the side of my face, but it never stopped me.

"Zach, stop!" Someone screamed, swore, and tried again to pull me away from Ashton.

Gearing my arm back to try and shove them away, my elbow connected with something hard.

A sharp cry sounded.

With my hands still clutching Ashton's shirt, I turned, my eyes widening when they landed on Luna.

"You…" Her eyes welled. Her hand was pressed against her bloody nose. "You hit me."

THIRTY

Luna

AGONY BURST BEHIND MY eyes. I touched my upper lip just under my nose and pulled my hand back. My fingers were coated with a dark crimson liquid.

"Luna." Zach released Ashton and took a step toward me, his face pale.

I held up my hand stopping him from coming any closer. "You should leave," I whispered.

"Please." He swallowed hard. "I'm sorry."

"You're sorry," I repeated. "You're sorry?" I reached into the laundry hamper and pulled out a dirty towel before pressing it up against my nose. "Just leave, Zach," I said, turning away. My shoulders slumped. A heavy weight came crashing down on me. This was it. We were officially over.

My eyes welled but not from the pain shooting behind them.

The door quietly closed a moment later, taking all of the air in my lungs along with it. "Will you get the girls for me please?" I asked Ashton, grabbed my pile of clothes off the dresser then went into the bathroom without waiting for him to answer.

Quickly getting dressed, I glanced in the mirror. My heart jumped. My hair was a mess. My eyes were bloodshot and my nose looked like hell. Keeping the towel under my nose, I went to leave the bathroom when voices sounded on the other side.

Slowly opening the door, I found Gigi, Meadow, and Piper sitting on the edge of my bed. Ashton leaned against the wall with his hands shoved into the pockets of his jeans.

"What happened?" Gigi asked, rising from the bed and coming toward me.

"Zach came in and found Ashton sleeping on my bed and lost his shit." I understood. I got it. I wouldn't have reacted nicely either if I found another woman in his bed. But he still shouldn't have accused me of sleeping with Ashton.

"You kicked him out," Meadow said, almost like she was impressed.

"I…" I turned to Ashton. "Why were you here?"

"Uh…" He hesitated, his cheeks turning a bright shade of pink.

"Ashton." Meadow looked between us. "Were you trying to piss him off?"

"What?" Ashton scowled, shaking his head. "No. Of course not. You girls drank a lot of wine. I went to the center, helped my brother with fixing up some shit and came back here after. I needed to make sure that you were fine. So, I actually checked on all of you. I came in here and saw Luna's bed torn apart and she was sleeping in her chair. Which couldn't be comfortable. I picked her up and brought her to her bed." His gaze flicked to mine. "I know I shouldn't have slept in your bed. I was worried about you. But I promise that I didn't see anything, and I swear to God, I didn't try anything either."

"That's actually kind of sweet," Meadow muttered.

"I would never think that of you." I rubbed the back of my neck, trying to ease some of the kinks resting on my muscles. "This...I don't even know what to do now," I told them.

"I think you and Zach need some time apart," Piper said. "And I could really use another drink."

"It's only ten," Meadow pointed out. "Wow we drank early."

"Hmm..." Piper tapped her chin. "I'm down if you are."

"What about Luna?" Gigi asked.

"I'll be fine," I told them but there was no way I was even remotely close to being in the mood for socializing.

"I'll take you to the hospital," Ashton said. "You should get your nose looked at anyway. It could be broken."

"God, I can't believe he elbowed you in the face." Gigi shook her head.

"I know." As much as I was pissed at Zach for accusing me of having sex with Ashton, add to the fact that he almost fucked Clara, I wasn't mad that he elbowed me. Yeah, it hurt, but it was my own fault for stepping in when I shouldn't have.

"You sure you're good if we head out?" Piper asked. "We can stay."

"Yeah, I'm fine." I went back to the bathroom and checked myself out in the mirror. "I don't want to go to the hospital."

"We should go so they can make sure you're fine," Ashton insisted. "And I don't need your father kicking my ass for not bringing his daughter to the hospital."

"Fine." I threw the towel in the laundry hamper. "My dad is going to have a field day with this one."

(Zach)

Once Luna kicked me out of her room, I didn't know where else to go. I knew my dad had finally come home from the hospital, much to the doctor's dismay of course. I wanted to give my parents time alone but right now, I needed my dad.

When I stepped into the house, all was quiet. They usually didn't go to bed early.

Closing the door silently behind me, I locked it up tight and kicked off my shoes before unbuttoning the top three buttons of my dress shirt.

"Zach?" Dad came around the corner. "I wasn't expecting you home."

"I know," I mumbled. "How are you feeling?"

"I'm fine." His brows narrowed. "What's wrong?"

"Can we talk?" I asked, feeling like a little boy again.

He nodded. "Of course. Does this call for a drink?"

I grunted. "I wish."

"You're in luck." He went into the kitchen and came back a moment later with a bottle of liquor and two tumblers.

"You have alcohol?" My parents weren't drinkers. "Since when?"

"Since a client gave this to me as a present a few months ago." He shrugged. "Let's go to my office."

I followed him. "Where's mom?"

"She's sleeping. My heart attack stressed her out." He muttered a curse as we walked by their bedroom door. "I'll never forgive myself for causing her that kind of pain."

"It wasn't your fault," I reminded him.

"Well…" He didn't continue until we stepped into his office and he shut the door. "Truth is, I've been feeling off. Stressed maybe. And it's nothing big that I've been stressed about either. Your typical shit which is even more frustrating."

I sat on the leather couch by the far wall, crossing my ankle over the opposite knee. "You didn't know about the defect?"

"Nope." He sighed. "That's frustrating too."

"I get it. It's like the older you get, the more stressed you become."

Dad grunted. He poured some of the amber liquid into the tumblers and handed me a glass before sitting down beside me. "Now, tell me what happened."

(Luna)

"Are you sure this is where you want to be?"

I gave Ashton a small smile. "Yeah."

"Your dad's going to say something you know." He nodded once. "You know, about your nose."

I let out a soft sigh. Ashton had taken me to the hospital. My nose wasn't broken but hurt like a bitch. It had slight bruising but when the doctor moved it to check to see if it was in fact broken or not, I almost threw up. I had never felt pain like that before and I didn't want to experience it ever again.

"I *am* sorry," Ashton said, pulling me from my thoughts.

"I know." I glanced out the window, my gaze landing on my parents' house. It was almost six in the morning. The emergency room had been busy, so it took a while to be seen but Ashton never left my side.

"Luna." Ashton cursed. "This shit needs to end. You and Zach need each other. I'm sorry. I'm so fucking sorry for everything. I never meant for this to happen. And I get it now."

I looked at him then. "What do you get?"

"That love you both have for each other. That all of our parents have. I want that." He rubbed his nape. "I really do."

"So, I take it you're going to leave Piper alone then?" I asked gently.

"What Piper...it was fun but I'm not stupid. There's nothing there. And then Meadow." He chuckled. "I never thought that would happen. Ever."

I laughed. "Meadow likes her one-night stands but you're actually one of the first guys she's had in her bedroom."

Ashton straightened. "Really?"

"Don't get your hopes up." I patted his arm. "Remember, you're too young for her. Our friend likes the older guys."

"I don't get it, but I know there's nothing there with her either." He reached across my lap and opened the door. "Go talk to your parents. I know this situation with Zach will get resolved. I promise it will. If I have to drag him to you myself, I will."

I laughed. "Thank you. And thank you for bringing me to the hospital."

"You're welcome."

Before I could leave the car, Ashton hooked an arm around my shoulders and pulled me in for a hug.

"Stop worrying about it," I mumbled, returning the embrace. Giving him a small smile, I thanked him again and left his car. Taking a deep breath, I made my way up the sidewalk to my parents' place. It had felt like a lifetime since I had been there. Moving in with Piper, Gigi, and Meadow a few years ago, it seemed like such a long time since we all lived at home.

My dad was going to kick Zach's ass once he saw my face. I let out a hard sigh. Pulling my key from my purse, I unlocked the front door and stepped into my home. Even though I hadn't lived there in quite a few years, nothing had changed, and it would always be home to me.

The house was quiet. My dad had it built just after Vincent Junior was born. It had a large backyard with an open concept for the living and dining rooms. The kitchen was large, and I knew that it would make Meadow happy just to step foot in it.

I laughed softly to myself.

Dropping my bag on the couch, I trudged into the kitchen and started making coffee. It had been a few weeks since I had been home, but everything looked the same. It even smelled the same. Mom had started baking recently after Meadow gave her some tips.

Although the house was over fifteen years old, my dad had it revamped a few years back. Everything was modern, but most of all, the kitchen was stunning. My dad, all of our fathers actually, did a great job. With the help of Zach's mom designing the house after discussing it with my mom and dad, it was perfect.

The kitchen had gray cupboards, with a slate flooring that matched the dark countertop. The appliances were stainless steel and against the dark gray of the walls, they really popped.

"Luna?"

I jumped, spun around, and found Mom coming toward me.

Her dark brows narrowed. Her normally olive skin looked darker.

"Have you been tanning?" I asked her.

She laughed, shaking her head. "No. I was outside a lot yesterday." She came up to me and poured herself a cup of coffee. "What are you doing here so early? Not that I'm complaining of course."

I poured myself a cup as well and took a sip before meeting my mother's gaze. "I needed to come home."

"Okay." She took a sip from her own mug and leaned a hip against the counter. "Are you going to tell me how you got that bruise on your nose or am I going to have to ask?"

I swallowed hard. "I…" I sighed, placing my mug on the island behind me. "Zach and Ashton got in a fight. I got in the way and Zach accidentally elbowed me."

"What did you do after that?" Mom asked, staring at me over the rim of her mug.

"Uh…I kicked him out after."

"Good girl." She placed her mug on the counter beside her. "Listen, I know there is a lot of history between you two. You've been best friends since you were kids."

"We have and I've had a crush on him for that long too. I've watched him go through countless women, but I've never said anything. And then he stopped sleeping with random women and we…" I let out a shaky breath. "I love him but he…he left me. Last night. Or broke things off first I should say." God, I wasn't making sense.

My mom's face softened. "How come?"

"He believes Dad," I muttered. "But it's what he does. He pushes people away and I don't know how to show him that I'm not going to hurt him. He let his parents in. Why can't he let me in too?"

"Oh, Luna." Mom wrapped her arms around my shoulders. "I know it's hard. I know it hurts. I don't know what happened to him as a boy, but he went through a lot. Didn't his real dad die?"

I nodded, swiping my hands across my cheeks to wipe away the tears.

Mom held me at arm's length. "What you have with Zach, is different than what he has with Coby and Brogan. I remember when they first adopted him. It took quite a few years for that boy to smile. For him to laugh. For him not to jump at every small sound because he was terrified that he would get into trouble. Or worse."

"I remember that," I murmured.

"You see." She hooked her arm in mine and led me out to the dining room table. "Our men are one in the same. Even though your dad doesn't like to admit it. But when I first met him, I was actually the one who pushed him away."

"Really?" I asked, my eyes widening. "Why?"

"Because he got too close. You are so much like him, it's unreal. You inch your way into someone's heart, and we can't do anything about it until we have to give in."

"But Zach left. He went to another woman's place." I looked away, not wanting to see the look of pity on my mother's face.

She sighed. "Did anything happen?"

"No." I looked at her then. "What do I do?"

"Give him time." She paused. "Listen, I've tried talking to your dad, but something is...I know it's not right. You're a grown woman but he has his reasons for his issue with you being with Zach. But honestly, I think it's mostly Zach doing the pushing and your dad's issues with the whole thing is just added pressure. But Zach isn't the only one who feels like he's not good enough."

"What do you mean?"

"Your dad. Me. All of us. We all felt like we weren't good enough for each other." She shrugged.

"What's going on?"

Both of us turned to my dad coming toward us. His dark eyes met mine. "I'll give you one second to tell me why you have a bruise on your face before I drive over and kill him myself."

"See?" I said to Mom. "This is what I have to deal with."

"Luna," Dad grumbled. "Explain."

I let all the words spill from my lips. Although I had reassured my dad that it wasn't Zach's fault, his face only became redder and redder. I also left out the part that I was naked even though I had been wrapped in a blanket.

"I…" Dad blew out a slow breath and pinched the bridge of his nose. Much to my surprise, he closed the distance between us and gently cupped my face. Tilting my head back, he examined my nose. "Does it hurt still?"

"Only if I touch it or walk into a wall," I told him.

He grunted. "You're not funny."

"I don't know what you want me to say," I pulled my head from his grasp. "I'm fine and it was an accident." Guilt rested heavily on my shoulders that I had kicked Zach out. I needed to talk to him. If he ever wanted to talk to me again that is.

"*Piccola*," Dad said gently.

"No." I stomped around him. "This wouldn't have even happened if you wouldn't have butt your nose in to my business, in the first place."

"Luna," he said, his voice firm. "I went over to apologize."

"Well that obviously never happened, now did it?"

"I told him to prove to me that he's good enough for you." Dad crossed his arms under his broad chest. "I was going to say that it hasn't happened yet, but I've been watching him. He thinks I'm not watching but I always am. I see the way he looks at you. But the problem no longer lies with me."

"What do you mean?" I asked, wishing this whole mess would end and we could go back to the way things were.

"I mean that Zach needs to prove to himself that he's good enough for you."

I opened my mouth to argue but nothing came out. "I know he believes that but hearing you say it…"

Dad's face softened. "He loves you."

I nodded, looking down at my feet. "I love him too."

"I lost your mom when you were six months old."

I looked up then, meeting eyes that matched my own.

"We had stopped dating long before that. We were better off as friends. But I loved her. Not the way I love…" He glanced at my stepmom. "Not the way I love you."

"I know," she said softly.

"Your mom got caught up with the wrong people. That's why she died. It fucked me up, Luna. It fucked me up bad." Dad rubbed a hand over his nape, looking everywhere but at me. "Zach reminds me of me," he finally confessed. "At first, I didn't like it. Hell, I wouldn't like it if any man laid their hands on you. You're my first. My *Piccola*."

"I'm not going anywhere," I whispered.

"I know you aren't. I know that now. And I'm sorry for everything. But after last night…after seeing the hurt in your eyes over me butting into your business, I decided to back off. But Zach needs to know that you're there for him and that you're not going anywhere."

I shook my head. "I'm not."

Dad reached out for my stepmom, the only mother I had ever known, and pulled her into his side. "When I met you, if your father would have been alive, I'm sure he would have said the same thing. I didn't deserve you then. Hell, I still don't deserve you, but I will live the rest of my life until I do."

Mom's eyes welled. She cupped his face. "I love you, Stone, and Luna loves Zach. He looks at her how you look at me."

"I know." Dad kissed her forehead before looking my way. "I'll make this right, but this is no longer on me."

"Do you think Zach could ever let me in?" I asked, hope twisting throughout my body.

"Yeah." Dad smiled. "I do." He came toward me. "I *am* sorry, *Piccola*. I didn't realize that I was causing more damage."

"I know what you went through was hard and losing Mom was even harder. But I love Creena like she's my real mom. She's the best mother I could ever ask for and Zach is the best man for me." I just needed him to realize that too.

Dad leaned his forehead against mine. "I don't want to lose you."

"You..." My breath hitched. "You haven't lost me," I whispered. "I'll always be your little girl, but I need him."

"I know." He paused. "I love you, *Piccola*."

"I love you too, Daddy."

He released me and headed back into the kitchen.

"It is way too early for this shit," Vince Junior grumbled, rubbing his eyes.

"What are you doing here?" I asked him.

"My apartment was being fumigated. And I'd rather stay here than at a friend's place." He grimaced. "I think I'm getting old. My friends are fucking pigs."

I laughed.

Vince's brows narrowed. He reached out, brushing a hand over the bridge of my nose.

Pain shot out behind my eyes. I gasped, pulling away from him.

"Who do I need to kill?" he demanded, his voice rough.

"God, no one." I punched him in the shoulder. "That hurt."

"What happened? Is that why Dad's stewing?" Vince asked, nodding toward the kitchen.

I followed his gaze. Dad was leaning against the counter while Mom cooked breakfast. She would push him out of the way every so often.

"Zach accidently elbowed me in the face," I told my brother.

"Wow. And he's still alive? I'm surprised you didn't kill him yourself."

I spun on my brother. "What's with all the killing jokes? No one is dying. Just once I would like a normal fucking family."

"Luna," Mom gasped.

"Sorry." My cheeks burned. Our parents were good about us swearing but even I had to admit, that was a little much.

Vince chuckled.

"Why don't you go back to the hole you crawled out of," I mumbled, shoving past him and stomping down the hall to my old bedroom.

"Love you too, Sis," he called out.

"Yeah, yeah." I waved at him over my shoulder. Once I reached my bedroom, I opened the door and breathed in the familiar scent. It was a bit of rose mixed with vanilla and chai. It was incense that I found years ago and would light them only on special occasions. But no matter how long time went by where they weren't lit, I could still smell my favorite scent.

"Luna."

"I'm going to lay down," I told my dad. "It's been a long night."

"I know." He shifted from foot to foot, ran a hand through his black hair and cleared his throat.

"What is it?" I asked, my stomach twisting over the nervousness rolling off of him in waves.

"I promise you. I'll make this right again," he said, turning on his heel and heading back the way he had come.

I closed the door to my room and leaned against it. I wasn't sure how my dad was going to make this right, but I hoped that it worked.

Before it was too late.

THIRTY-ONE

ZACH

IT HAD FELT LIKE just yesterday that I ended things with Luna when really, it had been three weeks. After telling my dad what had happened and how I accidentally hit Luna, we had a few more shots between us and I passed out on the couch in his office. I woke hours later, feeling somewhat lighter. Even though nothing was resolved between me and Luna, just telling my dad everything and getting it all off of my chest helped. It helped a lot.

Bottom line. I needed to talk to Luna, but I also needed to give her space. I knew that. Even though I didn't like it. I also needed to own up to the fact that I was scared and that was why I pushed her away.

But like the pussy that I was, I sat at the bar across from her work and watched her through the big pane window instead. It wasn't like I could do anything anyway. There was no way I could make this shit up to her. I hit one of our friends. In fact, I almost beat him senseless because I was too damn jealous. Over other men. Over anyone who even breathed the same air as her.

My phone dinged, indicating an incoming text.

Clara: Did you sort things out with Luna?

I sighed. I hadn't heard from Clara since I went to her place to fuck her. My stomach twisted. I still couldn't believe I did that.

Me: Not yet.

I didn't want to talk about what happened. Not with anyone besides my dad, before I could fix things with Luna. My Moonbeam.

As cliché as it sounded, she was the damn light in my darkness. The very air I breathed. It had been almost a month, but it felt like a damn lifetime.

I was losing my mind and I didn't know how to get it back. I didn't know how to approach Luna and make things right again. Could things ever go back to normal?

Clara: You'll work it out.

I sure as hell hoped so.

I pinched the bridge of my nose, remembering Stone's words that he had only ever seen Luna put a smile on my face. Sure. Clara made me laugh but not the way his daughter did.

The fact that he accused me of more, didn't sit well with me.

I put my phone away, ignored the ding of the incoming text, and signaled the bartender for another beer. I preferred something stronger, but this would have to do. For now.

Watching Luna was like watching a majestic animal through the bars of their cage. They were so close, but you still couldn't touch them.

I was on the verge of losing control. It took everything in me not to stomp over to the tattoo shop she worked at and pull her into my arms.

"Give her time."

My dad's words bounced around in my head. He was right. As much as I didn't want him to be, I knew I had to give Luna space.

But I still craved her touch. Her hands running over my body. Her nails scratching into my skin. My name leaving her lips on a breathless moan. I needed more. I was so damn greedy for her, my cock pushed against the fly of my dress pants. No matter what I did, I couldn't get her out of my head. Or out of my damn system. She was the perfect drug and I never wanted to be rid of my addiction to her.

After I spent last weekend with my parents, I drove to the city and spent most of my time there. I drowned myself in work and drove myself into the ground at the gym. Every night since, I would limp back up to my condo, take a shower and go to bed.

Job. Work out. Sleep. Repeat.

Scrubbing a hand down my face, I lifted the glass to my lips to take a long swig when a large shadow loomed over me.

"Zachary Porter."

My stomach dropped to the ground beneath me.

Oh fuck.

I took a breath as Stone sat beside me on my left and Asher sat on my right.

"You're a hard man to get a hold of," Stone pointed out.

"I've been busy," I mumbled.

"Having a good time?" Asher asked, taking my beer from my hand and drinking it down in one gulp.

"I was," I muttered.

They laughed.

I had never been nervous around Asher. Even though as he got older, he became the largest of our fathers. But I also wasn't fucking his kid.

"You're a funny guy."

I bristled at the new voice.

Angel stepped up behind me, cupping my shoulders.

I was caged in by the three of them. Three men I had known since I was a boy. Men my father worked with. Men I looked up to but right now they scared the absolute shit out of me. I was man enough to admit my fear of them.

I passed a glance at the door.

"Waiting for someone?" Angel asked.

"I'm waiting to see if Dale is going to show up," I mumbled, expecting to see Piper's dad join our little party.

"Nah." Angel gave my shoulder a squeeze. "Dale's busy. He sends his love."

I scoffed.

"Luna works across the street," Stone stated, ignoring our banter and signaling the bartender over.

I didn't say anything. He already knew that I was aware of that. I had been coming to the bar every day and watching her since we had our fight.

"You're in love with my daughter." Stone handed me a new beer. "And she's in love with you."

He already knew that as well. What the hell was he getting at?

"My daughter was pure before you. Innocent. I know she's an adult and can make her own decisions of course, but I'm not stupid." Stone cupped my nape. "Isn't that right, Zach?"

There was no point in denying it. These men may be retired but they would always have the SEAL in them. And Stone was a father. That made him even more lethal. "How do you know that?"

"Because my *daughter*," he stressed that word. "Talks to my wife and my wife tells me everything. But I won't betray her trust and tell Luna that I know."

"That's why we're here." Angels grip on my shoulders tightened.

"What would you do if it was Angelica or Meadow we were talking about?" Stone asked Angel.

Angel chuckled, the sound deep and threatening. "I would kill the fucker who popped their cherries."

Little did he know; Meadow's cherry was already popped.

"You see," Stone continued, cracking his knuckles. "I woke up the other morning to her and Creena talking. Luna had a bruise on her nose. Care to tell me what that was about?"

"Not really," I muttered.

Asher chuckled. "We have an honest one. I'm so fucking glad I have boys. I only have to worry about their dicks and not the whole damn world. But I love these girls like my own. You hurt Luna. That doesn't sit well with me."

I swallowed hard.

"Does your dad know what you did?" Asher asked. "You punched my kid in the face."

"Thanks for the reminder. And yes, he does. Trust me, I feel like a shithead over it. I never meant for it to go that far." I hoped my explanation would give me some leeway with them but if it were me, I would still kick my ass no matter how much I apologized.

"Ashton does have a nice shiner though. I also heard he hit you back." Asher sat back, crossing his arms under his broad chest.

"He tried to." As soon as the words left my mouth, I regretted them. I never meant to sound cocky. But Ashton wasn't a fighter. That was his brother. Although they were both big like their father, I'd rather scrap with Ashton because then I at least had a chance at winning.

"Now is not the time to be cocky." Angel squeezed my shoulders, digging his fingers into the muscle.

I winced.

"Tell me why you've been here every day for the past three weeks," Stone demanded.

"I'm trying to figure out how to apologize to your daughter. And also, not get killed in the process." Luna may have been tiny, but she was raised by Creena, who was as ruthless as they came. Rumors went around about her past, but she never confirmed them. Hit man, contract killer. The list went on.

"Give me a moment alone with Zach." Stone clapped my shoulder. "We need to have a chat."

"I thought that's what we were already doing," I mumbled.

"Now is not the time to be funny." He squeezed my shoulder, digging his fingers in hard.

A sharp pain shot throughout the muscle, but I refused to let him see that it hurt.

He smirked.

Asher and Angel moved to the other end of the bar, keeping watch. Probably making sure I didn't bolt.

"Zach."

My gaze snapped back to Stone's.

"I don't like that you took my daughter's virginity. Hell, I wouldn't like it if any fucker took it. But you were raised by two of my best friends. I see a lot of Coby in you even though you're not technically blood related.

He's a good man and he loves Brogan. Before I met Creena, I'd never seen a love like that before. It was what I strived for. Why am I saying this instead of killing you right now?"

"The question crossed my mind," I mumbled.

"Because my *piccola* loves you. But we are men and we fuck up. So, you have to go to her instead of sitting here like a pussy. Man up. And you have a good role model, so I know she's in good hands."

My jaw dropped a bit.

"Don't think this is me giving you my approval. Because I'm not. You need to prove to me that you would do anything for her. Her happiness comes first."

"That's all I care about," I told him. "I never meant to hit Ashton. But I couldn't stop myself."

"It's funny because I know exactly how that feels. We all do. We've also all fucked up before too, but we were able to get our women back."

"Why now?" I asked, unsure if I wanted the answer or not.

Stone looked everywhere but at me. "Because I realized that I hurt her by butting my nose in. I never wanted that. I have my reasons why I acted the way I did. Will I ever tell you? I'm not sure. Hell, my wife didn't even know at first. But I now understand that it's not just me. It's you."

I swallowed past the bile that had suddenly risen to my throat.

"When people get too close, you push them away. I get it. Creena did the same to me in the beginning, but if you love Luna like I think you do, you won't let your past stop you." Stone paused. "But I promise you, if you can't make Luna happy and I see my baby crying again because of you, I will hunt you down and scatter your bones across this fucking earth. You got me?"

I nodded. "I got you."

"Now." Stone clapped my shoulder. "The real question is, what are you willing to do to get Luna back?"

Everything.

(Luna)

After getting off work late, I made my way home and crawled into bed. Gigi was throwing another party, but I just wanted to be alone. I wasn't in the mood to be social. Not that I ever socialized really before. The parties were her thing.

I hadn't seen Zach in almost a month, and I needed to talk to him. About us, about our future and what the hell we were doing. I refused to believe that it was over between us because no matter what happened, we would always be in each other's lives.

My thoughts were scattered, all over the place as I tried pushing Zach out of my head. Maybe I should have joined the girls for a drink and tried to socialize but not hearing from Zach, threw me off.

I had asked my mom and Jay if I could work as much as possible at the tattoo shop and I also spent a lot of time at the center. Between both places, I was able to distract myself from thoughts of him. But now that I was home and curled up in bed, my thoughts traveled back to him. His touch. His kisses. His sweet and sometimes dirty words. The way he looked at me like I was the most beautiful woman in the world. Like I was all that mattered. Like I was *his*.

So many times, during the past few days, I had picked up the phone to call him or even send him a text, but I couldn't.

Meadow told me to wait for him to come to me.

Gigi said she had crappy experience with guys, so her advice wouldn't help.

Piper had fallen into herself and we didn't know why.

No one said whether they heard from Zach or not. If they did, they never told me. The only time I heard anything was when Ashton told me they had talked, and Zach had apologized for hitting him.

My heart felt lighter then, but it still didn't help the fact that I never saw him or talked to him myself.

A commotion sounded outside my door, but I couldn't be bothered to go see what was going on. I just didn't care anymore.

Opening my eyes, I glanced at the clock and saw that it was only midnight. The party was in full swing outside. Muffled voices could be heard while the low beat of the music thrummed in the background.

I could usually ignore the parties and sleep through them but tonight was not one of those times. Rolling over onto my back, I caught a shadow move out of the corner of my eye. I jumped, shooting up in bed.

The shadow came closer, revealing…

"Zach?" I placed my hand on my chest, easing my racing heart. "You scared the shit out of me."

"Sorry." He gave me a small smile.

"What are you doing here?" I asked, my body coming alive at the mere intensity rolling off of him.

"I…" He started pacing. "I know I shouldn't be here. But I can't wait anymore. I'm sorry for everything. I can't work. I can't sleep. I can't even fucking think straight." He stopped and turned toward me. "I need you."

"You hurt me, Zach. You broke my heart."

He looked away. "I know. I'll never forgive myself for what I put you through."

I moved to the edge of the bed, swinging my legs over the side. "Come here," I said, holding my arms out.

He rushed toward me but much to my surprise, he dropped to his knees and wrapped his arms around my waist.

My chest tightened.

Zach placed his head on my lap, squeezing me with everything in him. Everything that made up us. "I'm so sorry. I tried staying away. I know you need space, but I can't do it anymore. I can't go on and not have you by my side. And I'm sorry for pushing you away. I know you won't hurt me. I know that but I'm scared, Luna."

"You thought I needed space?" I asked, running my fingers over the back of his head.

He looked up at me. "I was giving you time. So I threw myself into my work and the gym. The next thing I knew, three weeks had come and gone."

"Oh, Zach, I actually thought…I just…" I shook my head. "I don't know what I thought. But I've tried calling you and stopped myself. Because I was giving you time too. I thought it was over for good. And you have nothing to be scared of. I won't hurt you. Ever."

"I know that now, but I hurt you instead." Zach grabbed my hands and pulled me off the bed and onto his lap. "I'm sorry. I don't expect you to forgive me right away, but I am truly sorry. I'll spend the rest of my life making up for it. For what I did. For pushing you away and running to Clara. I shouldn't have done that. I'm…"

I cupped his nape, pulling him against me. "I know nothing happened and I'm sorry you felt the need to push me away."

"Don't." He leaned his forehead against mine. "Don't ever apologize to me. You did nothing wrong. At all. It's all me.

"I was giving you time," I whispered, reveling in the fact that he was finally back in my arms.

"I never need time when it comes to you, Luna." He inhaled a shaky breath. "I wanted to come by sooner but in all honesty, I was scared. I pushed you away and I thought you would do the same to me. I knew I wouldn't be able to handle it if that happened. So that's why I stayed away."

"You ever feel like running again, you come to me. Do you hear me?"

He looked away.

"No." I cupped his jaw, forcing him to look at me. "I asked you a question."

"Yeah, I hear you, Moonbeam," he said, his voice low.

"Good. I'm glad. But what do we do now? Where do we go from here, Zach? You broke my heart. Things got bad and you shoved me away and went to the arms of another woman."

His body stiffened. "I'm sorry. I know I keep saying that but it's the truth. I will make this up to you. I promise I will."

"You can't go to another woman if we have a fight." I leaned down, making eye contact with him. "You know that right?"

He nodded. "I know, baby. I know. I don't deserve your forgiveness but I'm on my knees, begging for it anyway."

My chest tightened. "What made you come by? What else gave you that push?"

"Your father."

I leaned back. "Really?"

Zach nodded. "I talked to him. He's still not one-hundred percent on board but he's better."

A breath I didn't realize I had been holding, left me. "So, what do we do now? Where do we go from here?"

"I want you, Luna." He ran his hand up and down my arm. "But I understand...I get it if I'm too much for you."

"No." I cupped his face with both hands. "I love you. That never went away just because you're jealous and possessive. But I am concerned that your anger is going to control you." I ran my fingers through his hair, itching to kiss him. To taste his breath on my tongue but I knew I needed to control myself. I released his face and leaned against the edge of my bed.

"That's one reason why I started working out more," he told me. "It helps with my moods. I'm going to start seeing a psychologist that my parents recommended. But I never should have assumed you fucked Ashton. I'm sorry for that. And I'm sorry for elbowing you." He brushed his thumb along the bridge of my nose. "Does it hurt anymore?"

"It's better," I whispered, my skin tingling from the soft touch.

"Good." He placed a soft peck on the tip of my nose. "I love you, Luna. I love you so fucking much."

My breath hitched. "I'm glad you're going to be getting the help you need but can we move on from this?"

"I'm hoping we can." His eyes searched my face.

"Good." I swallowed hard. "Because there's something I need to tell you."

Zach stiffened.

"It's nothing bad. Or I don't think it is. Honestly, I'm not really sure but…" I inhaled a sharp breath. "I'm pregnant."

(Zach)

Before Luna, I never actually wanted kids. I thought I wasn't good enough for a woman, let alone raising children as well. But as soon as Luna said those two words, everything that had happened in my life, came crashing down around me. It was like all the shit I had been through as a kid, the fights I had with my parents growing up, the stresses of work, none of it mattered anymore. All because Luna was carrying my child.

"You're pregnant," I repeated slowly. "You have my baby in your belly, Moonbeam?"

She nodded, giving me a soft smile. She grabbed my hand, placing it on her lower stomach. "Not too far along yet though. I missed my period and thought it was stress related, so I thought nothing of it. But then I started doing the math, took a pregnancy test and it came back positive."

"Holy shit." I stared in awe at my hand splayed on Luna's stomach. "I...How far along?"

"Just over a month. I didn't think symptoms could happen so quickly, but I Googled, and they can. Everyone is different." She shrugged. "I haven't told anyone though. Just you."

That confession stirred something feral inside of me. Clearing my throat, I lifted the hem of her tank top and rested my hand against her bare stomach. "Did you go to the doctor's by yourself?"

She nodded, covering my hand. "Yeah. They had me do a blood test to confirm. I didn't want to make a big deal of it. We need to tell our parents but right now, I just want to keep this between us. At least for a little bit."

I pushed out from under her and stood. Holding out my hand, I waited.

Luna placed her fingers in mine, letting me help her to her feet.

Dropping to my knees, I wrapped my arms around her, lifted her shirt, and placed soft pecks on her stomach. "I love you. I don't even know you yet and already I am so in love with you."

Luna's breath hitched but I only continued.

"I broke your mommy's heart and I will spend the rest of my life making it up to her. You will realize that being in this world is hard. You will probably want to stay in your mommy's belly forever, but you can't, okay? I need to meet you. I need to show you that even though life is difficult, you will own it. You will also make mistakes but that's okay. Just make up for them and learn from them. Own them, little one." God, I never thought I would love something as much as Luna. And I hadn't even met our baby yet.

I looked up, finding Luna wiping under her eyes.

"I didn't mean to make you cry," I said, rising to my feet.

She shook her head, her chin wobbling. Turning away from me, she crawled onto the bed.

Before I had a chance to ask her what was wrong, she turned back around and pulled me against her. Crushing her mouth to mine, she ran her hands through my hair to the back of my head.

I sighed, breathing her in and taking everything she had to offer me. But before we could take it any further, I released her. "As much as I would love to continue this, you need rest."

She nodded, a yawn trembling through her. "Spend the night with me?"

"You don't even have to ask." I kissed her once again and waited for her to lay down before sliding onto the bed beside her.

"You don't have to stay dressed," she said, her eyes fluttering closed.

I chuckled, kissing the side of her neck. "Sleep, Moonbeam. Everything else can wait."

"Okay," she whispered, her breathing evening out.

I pulled the blankets up and over us, holding her in my arms.

The heavy weight that had been put on my shoulders as a small boy, was suddenly lifted.

I made a promise to myself that night. I would be the best man Luna could ever hope for and I would be the best damn father our baby could ever have. They would want for nothing.

The love Stone had for his daughter almost cost us our relationship but even someone like him could admit when he was wrong. I earned more respect for him that night and I had meant what I told him.

I would do *everything* I could to keep Luna.

I finally realized that I was worthy of her. Of having a good career. Of being happy. With life. With our family. With friends. And most of all, with Luna.

The voices weren't always silent but now with Luna and our child, they merely whispered instead of shouting.

With my family and doctor, I was confident I could overcome them.

EPILOGUE

Luna

STARING AT OUR PARENTS, I had to bite back a laugh. Four pairs of eyes. Four sets of grim expressions. Four minds probably wondering what the hell was going on.

"Did you threaten my son again?" Brogan asked.

Stone grunted but didn't respond.

"Did he?" she asked Zach.

"No, Mama," he said, shaking his head.

"Good." She sat forward. "Not that I'm not happy to see the both of you…well…I need to know what's going on."

I laughed then, unable to hold it in anymore.

I glanced up at Zach and nodded. Both of us turned to our parents and said…

"We're pregnant."

"Do you think they're happy?" I asked Zach later that night in bed.

"I do." He ran a finger down the side of my body. "I think they're happy that we're back together. That we're giving them their first grandchild and that we're…"

"What?" I asked, resting my head on my arms.

"Happy." He rolled over onto his stomach, watching me.

"What?" My cheeks burned under the scrutiny.

"You're beautiful." He lifted his head and bent his elbow, resting his head on his hand.

I cupped his cheek, placing a soft peck on his mouth. "I love you."

He gently pushed me onto my back. "Let me show you again how much I love you."

Zach made good on his promise for the next hour, showing me over and over again how much he did in fact love me.

When he had passed out beside me, I slipped out of bed and threw on a robe. After we told our parents that I was pregnant, Zach had taken me to his condo in the city. It was the first time I was ever there, but I could understand why just the same. The place was modern but cold. Even though Zach lived there, it didn't feel like home to me. Not yet. It needed some flowers and a pop of color here and there.

But first, it needed a little something on the fridge.

Rummaging through the drawers, I finally found Scotch Tape. Ripping off a piece, I taped the picture in my hand against the freezer door.

Warm arms enveloped me suddenly, pulling me back against a hard body.

I grinned. "What do you think?"

Zach kissed my neck. "It's perfect," he mumbled against my throat.

I laughed, pushing away from him. "I mean about the picture."

"It's…" He went to the fridge, running his thumb over the black and white picture. "It's perfect too."

My eyes welled. "It's ours."

He looked down at me, his eyes shining. "He or she, is definitely ours."

We stood like that for a while. Looking at the ultrasound picture of our baby and just dreaming and hoping that we could give them the life that they deserved.

And more.

THE END

BONUS SCENE

THE MOMENT I STEPPED inside the house, I was hit with a scent that smelled absolutely delicious. My mouth watered. My stomach rumbled, reminding me that I hadn't eaten anything since breakfast that morning.

Throwing my keys into the dish sitting on top of the small table that stood by the wall, I loosened the tie around my neck.

The farther I went into the house, the more intense the scent became. It smelled of steak, mashed potatoes, and other types of food I couldn't quite make out.

"Zach?" Luna called from the kitchen. "I'm in here."

Everything inside of me stirred the closer I got to my wife.

Once I stood outside the entrance to the kitchen, I stared at her.

She was humming to herself, holding our son in her arms and flipping through a magazine. Her hair was a mess on top of her head. My gray sweatpants sat low on her hips with a black tank top tucked into them.

Women said that gray sweat pants were like an aphrodisiac and I never understood why. But seeing my wife wearing mine? Yup. I got it now.

Leaning against the wall, I crossed my arms under my chest and just watched her.

"I can feel you staring," she said, looking over her shoulder and giving me one of those wide smiles of hers. A smile that was meant for only me. A smile that had taken quite awhile for me to put on her face.

"I was enjoying watching you," I told her, letting my eyes roam down the length of her.

She laughed, the sound low and husky. She came toward me, hugging our son, Benjamin, against her chest. "How was your day?"

"Better now." I pinched her chin, brushing my lips along hers before giving her soft peck.

"You say that every day," she whispered.

I took Benjamin from her, hugging him against me. "Because it's true." I kissed our son's head. "Isn't it?" I asked him.

He cooed, slapping his chubby little hand against my cheek.

I chuckled, my heart swelling as I stared into our baby boy's dark eyes; eyes that mirrored my own. The only difference was his didn't hold years of pain, and I was thankful for that.

He was named after my uncle who passed away years ago. I remembered when we told my mother what we were naming him. She cried, hugged both of us and cried some more, but said that he would have been honored.

"You good?"

I met Luna's eyes then. Wrapping an arm around her shoulders, I pulled her against me. "I am now, baby. I promise."

"Okay." She kissed my cheek and pulled away from me. "Supper is almost done. Oh, and I know we haven't had any time alone really since he was born. So my parents have offered to take him this weekend. If you wanted."

"I...not yet." I placed him in his bassinet that Luna had moved into the kitchen while she cooked and cleaned.

She nodded, kissed my cheek again, and went back to preparing supper.

"I can't believe he's almost six months," I said, staring at our son in awe.

Luna laughed lightly. "Time flies when you're having fun."

I grinned, continuing to stare at something we made. A human. We made a human being. It shocked the hell out of me every time I saw him. And the way Luna was with him? She was my hero. She cleaned, cooked, took care of our son, all while I worked. She was the strongest woman I knew. Hell, she kicked my ass every damn day just by giving me one of her smiles.

We hadn't been married for long but I had been hers forever.

"You good?" Luna asked later that night.

Benjamin was in her arms, laying against her chest, sleeping peacefully.

I pulled her against me, careful not to disturb him. "I am, Luna. You have no idea just how good I really am."

"I love you," she murmured, her eyes fluttering closed.

"I love you too, Moonbeam." I kissed the top of her head.

As both her and our son slept against me, I still couldn't believe that this was my life. After having years of pain, I never imagined that things would turn out this way.

While I saw a psychiatrist to help me with my thoughts and the rage coursing through me, Luna was the one who truly healed me. Her love gave me the strength I needed to get by, and I could never thank her enough for that.

For not giving up.

On our friendship.

On our love.

On us.

THE END

Add With Us (Next Generation Novel, #2) to your TBR list:

Goodreads -

https://www.goodreads.com/book/show/49232974-with-us

ACKNOWLEDGEMENTS

I am so excited for this next generation and I couldn't have done it without my girls.

Angie, Jen and Christina. Thank you as always for your help in making my books better.

Joanne Thompson, my editor and friend. Girl, thank you really isn't enough. Just know that I appreciate everything you do for me and my words.

J.M.'s Jems! You all are my rocks. Your support means everything to me.

Bloggers: I can't thank you enough for everything you do. Your sharing of my posts, reading my books and more. Because of you, we get to do what we love.

Readers, you are amazing. Your excitement for books. Your fan-girling. Thank you for reading. Thank you for loving our books. Just, thank you for being you.

ABOUT

J.M. Walker is an Amazon bestselling author who also hit USA Today with Wanted: An Outlaw Anthology. She loves all things books, pigs and lip gloss. She is happily married to the man who inspires all of her Heroes and continues to make her weak in the knees every single day.

"Above all, be the HEROINE of your own life..." ~ Nora Ephron

Website: http://www.aboutjmwalker.com/
Facebook: https://www.facebook.com/jm.walker.author
Reader Group: https://www.facebook.com/groups/JMsJems/
Twitter: https://twitter.com/jmwlkr
Instagram: https://www.instagram.com/jmwlkr/
Goodreads: https://www.goodreads.com/author/show/5132169.J_M_Walker
BookBub: https://www.bookbub.com/authors/j-m-walker
Amazon: https://tinyurl.com/y7dpjkud
Newsletter: https://tinyurl.com/ya9hycak

Want more? Head on over to my website for my complete backlist!
https://www.aboutjmwalker.com/books

CPSIA information can be obtained
at www.ICGtesting.com
Printed in the USA
BVHW042347230321
602865BV00002B/2

9 781989 782019